The Blue House on the Corner

by

Joan E Histon

Also : by Joan E Histon

<u>The Senator Series:</u>

The Senator's Assignment

    ISBN 978 1 78535 855 5

    978 1 78535 856 2 (eBook)

The Senator's Darkest Days

    ISBN 978 1 78904 222 1

    978 1 78904 223 8 (eBook)

The Senator's Sons

    ISBN 979 8 35997 412 7

    ASIN : BOBKTMBTW 6

Thy Will Be Done … Eventually!

    By Alex Annand and Joan E Histon

    ISBN 1 85852 140 8

The Shop on Pilgrim Street

    ISBN 0 9519 6264 7

Tears in the Dark

    By Mark Edwards and Joan E Histon

    ISBN 1 85078 545

The Blue House on the Corner

    ISBN 9798877055315

For Colin, Julie, Tom, Sue
and my brother Bill

Contents

Chater One	5
Chapter Two	12
Chapter Three	22
Chapter Four	29
Chapter Five	39
Chapter Six	50
Chapter Seven	63
Chapter Eight	71
Chapter Nine	79
Chapter Ten	92
Chapter Eleven	102
Chapter Twelve	113
Chapter Thirteen	122
Chapter Fourteen	130
Chapter Fifteen	137

Chapter 1

She flinched as the double decker bus whooshed past throwing sheets of rainwater in her direction. As it landed on her BMW it sounded like bullets from an armoured tank. Not that she'd ever been in an armoured tank, she brooded, but right now, in the middle of the rush hour one wouldn't come amiss. Her eyes flickered up to her rear-view mirror as the dazzling headlights of a black Land Rover bore down on her. Nervously, she moved into the inside lane.

'You're not the only one wanting to get home, *mate,*' she muttered, but then came that awful sinking feeling. She didn't really want to get home at all, did she?

The brake lights on the silver Honda in front blurred red in the curtain of rain as it approached the roundabout. Braking gently, she wondered if she dared visit Freddy and Susan again, but then just as quickly dismissed the idea. Even spending another night in an empty house was preferable to listening to her brother trying to fix her life for her. And what did he know, she thought crossly? The funeral was less than three months ago, so wasn't it natural to feel you'd had all the life drained out of you? And with the ongoing investigation, wasn't it natural to try to make sense of everything that had gone wrong? The trouble was, she couldn't seem to make sense of anything lately, not with this awful fog of confusion swirling around in her head. She bit her lip. Perhaps Freddy was right. Perhaps she had gone back to work too soon? Extracting rotten teeth from foul smelling mouths, drilling cavities and fixing root canals was never what she had envisaged herself doing in the first place.

'I hope you're not suggesting I pushed you into dentistry?' Freddy had huffed defensively when she had tried explaining how she was feeling. 'If you ask me …'

'I'm not asking you anything, Freddy, so just shut up,' she had snapped and then she had felt guilty for snapping. After all, Donald's death wasn't her brother's fault. None of it was … She pressed her foot lightly on the accelerator as the Honda in front smoothly negotiated the stream of traffic on the roundabout, but then braked sharply as the black Land Rover bull-dozed her even closer to the curb. She glared at him. Not that he could see her through the driving rain but it made her feel better. Drumming her fingers impatiently on the steering wheel she waited for a break in the traffic. That was when the headlights of a heavy goods lorry roaring around the roundabout lit up the 'for sale' board to her left. She only caught a glimpse of it through the wind-blown trees, but she wondered why she had never noticed there was a house behind those ivy-covered walls before.

What madness possessed her to indicate sharply left into Grange Avenue, she had no idea. It might have been the bullying tactics of the heavy black Land Rover, or the need to get off the dual carriageway and away from the rush hour traffic. It might even have been a delaying tactic to avoid returning to an empty house again. Whatever the reason, she left the stream of traffic, manoeuvred her BMW between two narrow eight-foot stone columns, and drove slowly up an overgrown driveway littered with fallen branches, a discarded shopping trolley, an old pram, and crates of bottles. Her tyres crunched on the gravel as she braked in front of the house. It was only when she switched off the engine that the silence came crashing down on her. She sat for a moment, slightly stunned by the quietness before turning off the lights. And then she realised there was something rather pleasant about being hidden away behind these tall walls, away from the noise and clamour of solicitors, police and investigators, away from well-meaning friends, relatives and colleagues who were more than ready to offer condolences, sympathy and advice. She took a deep breath, blew softly through her lips, and stayed in the moment, not thinking, just soaking in the inner peace; listening to the wind whistling through the trees, the drum of rain on the BMW, and the distant hum of traffic on the dual carriageway. How long she sat there she had no idea. She was lost in the silence; she felt safe in the silence, and for the first time in weeks, content in the solitude behind these walls. Even the swirling fog in her head didn't seem so bad. Leaning on the steering wheel, she turned on her headlights and peered curiously through the streaming windows at the house.

It was Victorian, she guessed, not like the other houses on the quiet tree lined avenue. From what she remembered of those they were Edwardian, and most of them had been renovated into smart offices or apartments by speculative builders. But this house on the corner, was larger and appeared to have extensive grounds. The only down-side was that a massive oak tree had fallen on one of the tall chimneys leaving a gaping hole in the roof; the decorative red brickwork and stone quoins were badly in need of repair, and most of the windows were either smashed or boarded up. Her gaze drifted up the wide steps to the front door where vandals had torn down the boards so they could gain entry. The door itself was hanging off its hinges.

'You poor old thing,' she murmured. 'All the life has gone out of you, hasn't it? Her voice sounded loud in the confines of the car. Resting her chin on the back of her hands, Abigail Hunter stared contemplatively up at the derelict building, listening to the wipers swish across her windscreen, the rain hammering down on the roof, and the gusts of wind lash at the trees.

It was the thin grey spiral of smoke wending its way from under the arches that drew Tom's attention to the bridge. Smoke meant fire, and fire meant warmth in his reckoning. Glancing up at the heavy black clouds tumbling across the night sky he guessed that it wouldn't be long before they opened up and he got another drenching. That decided him. Carefully side-stepping the pot-holes, he made his way across the derelict piece of land towards the grey film of smoke, hoping he wouldn't be walking into trouble; he'd had enough of that to last him a life-time, he brooded. But as he stepped warily under the archers, he was relieved to see that the only other occupant was a grey-bearded old man in a shabby overcoat tied in the middle with rope; a battered trilby sat on thin strands of uncut hair, and a faded scarf was wrapped around his neck. He was warming his hands over a half dead fire in a dustbin lid. Tom edged towards the fire. There was an overpowering stench of petrol and urine under the arches, but he reckoned he could put up with that if there was warmth. The old man squinted up at him, gave an indifferent sniff, then dropped his gaze back into the failing embers.

Keeping his eye on the old man, Tom squatted down with his back to the wall and stretched out his frozen fingers to the dustbin lid. That was when he noticed that a large cardboard box was providing shelter for a gigantic hump in a dark anorak. A black woollen hat was pulled down over his eyes and he was clutching a small haversack.

As the old man was ignoring him, and the hump appeared to be asleep, Tom pulled the zip of his hoodie up to his chin and wondered whether there was any danger of him being mugged and his few precious coins stolen if he dared fall asleep. But as the warmth from the fire drifted his way, his exhausted body made up its' mind for him, and he drifted into an uneasy sleep which was only disturbed when the old man threw more wood on the fire, or the hump cried out in the night.

It was the sound of the rush hour traffic thundering over the bridge that woke him. His eyes flashed open and landed on brilliant sunshine and a white covering of snow outside. Grey ash was all that was left of the fire in the dustbin lid.

'Breakfast!' The old man was rolling up his blanket. Whether he was speaking to him, the hump or to himself, Tom had no idea but it was a sharp reminder that he was hungry.

The cardboard box shook as the hump yawned and stretched, his gigantic body demolishing his cardboard shelter in the process. It didn't seem to bother him, nor did he appear surprised at finding another occupant under the arches. He gave Tom a lopsided grin; a simple, trusting, childish grin. Still, it was friendly. Tom smiled weakly back. He took the lad to be in his early twenties, a year or so older than himself. Grabbing his haversack, the hump lurched after the old man.

Breakfast! That's what the old man had said, wasn't it? Tom scrambled to his feet, flinching, as stabbing pains shot through his frozen legs. After running his chilblained hands briskly up and down his jeans to restore his circulation, he thrust them into the pockets of his hoodie and curled his fingers around the few precious coins he had left. There wasn't enough for a fix, he knew that, but with a bit of luck there might be enough for breakfast.

Leaving the arches, he followed the old man and the hump along the riverside with its ancient stone law courts, expensive apartments and fancy restaurants. It was an uncomfortable walk as the snow had turned to slush and was seeping through the holes in his trainers, so that it wasn't long before his feet were wet and he was squelching with every step. Eventually, they reached the cobbled back streets of the city with its odd array of shops. That's when Tom got his first whiff of food. His stomach gnawed at his insides hopefully and wasn't disappointed. As he rounded the corner, he saw a mobile van serving food, and judging by the sleeping bags and well wrapped occupants gathered around it, the vehicle was there to feed the homeless of the city.

Gratefully he took a steaming mug of vegetable soup and bread bun offered him by a cheerful, fat-faced woman in a bright red hat, scarf and fingerless gloves. The soup was pleasantly hot against his frozen fingers. Burying his nose over the steam he slurped the hot liquid. It burnt his chapped lips but he could feel it warming his insides. He lingered over his breakfast, not quite knowing what to do when he'd finished it. He wouldn't dare go home, that's for sure, and if nights on the streets had taught him anything, it was that his next objective should be to find shelter.

'Where are you off to now, Joe?' the cheerful woman in the mobile van called.

Joe, the old man from the arches, jerked his head towards the traffic lights. 'Blue House,' he answered spewing a mouthful of crumbs over the hump.

The Blue House? Tom tuned into their conversation. Perhaps the Blue House was a shelter for the homeless? Perhaps it was a place that served free food? Coming to the conclusion that as Joe seemed to know his way around living on the street, his best bet might be to stick with him, he waited until Joe and the hump moved on. Keeping his head down, Tom followed at a distance.

It seemed an interminably long walk to get to the place Joe had called the Blue House. In fact, it was almost mid-morning before they came to a neat row of shops on the outskirts of the city. There was a hairdressing salon, newsagents and butchers, and sandwiched between a fish and chip shop and greengrocers was blackened stone church making a bold statement on a large notice board that said, '*Your Heavenly Father loves YOU*'.

Leaving the shops, Joe led them alongside a tall ivy-covered wall, through two concrete pillars and up an overgrown driveway with leafless trees and shrubs. A rusty shopping trolley, an old pram, bottles, and newspapers littered the gravel path but it was only when they came up to a faded blue door hanging off its hinges that Tom's heart sank. The Blue House was nothing more than a derelict old house. Moving the board half covering the door, Joe and the hump scrambled through the opening. Tom debated briefly whether he ought to return to the city, but coming to the conclusion that he was too cold, wet and exhausted to tramp all the way back, he squeezed through the blue door after them.

\he unexpectedly found his eyes drawn up a wide winding staircase to a long window halfway up the stairs. The sunlight was streaming through the broken panes of coloured glass making a delightful rainbow effect in the spacious hallway below; the rays catching speckles of drifting dust on their way down. Too afraid to move, in case his shadow disturbed the rainbow or his movement dispersed the colourful speckles of dust drifting in the air above him, Tom stood watching this phenomenon in silence, hardly daring to breathe. After living in squalor for so long, seeing such beauty was a rare occurrence.

It was Joe's boots crunching over broken glass that broke his special moment. 'Y' coming lad, or what?' he growled.

Relieved to have been acknowledged, Tom took one final look at his rainbow before joining his travelling companions in a high-ceilinged kitchen dominated by a heavy black kitchen range, and a tall green dresser. A long wooden table stood in the centre of the room; discarded sleeping bags, stained mattresses, two clapped out settees, broken chairs and stools took over the rest of the dirty shabby kitchen.

Joe shuffled over to the kitchen range. 'See if you can find a wooden crate or summat to get a fire started, Big Ben. It's perishing in here.' Turning to Tom, he jerked his head towards the mattresses. 'If you wanna bed lad, grab one those. What's y' name?'

Tom grabbed the end of a mattress. 'Tom,' he said dragging it towards the kitchen range. 'Where did all this stuff come from?'

'Squatters,' Joe informed him. 'They'll have raided skips for it.' He threw him a sleeping bag with the stuffing hanging out. 'See if you can find newspapers to start a fire.'

As Tom explored the rest of the house, he discovered the kitchen wasn't the only room to have been inhabited by squatters. Most of the downstairs rooms were littered with empty tin cans, food wrappers, cardboard cups or abandoned sleeping bags. There was even a foul-smelling toilet – used but not flushed as there was no water. Finding a pile of 1970's medical journals tucked away in an old desk, he returned to the kitchen.

'Twist them papers into tight balls and put 'em in the grate,' Joe instructed.

Ripping up the medical journals, Tom placed the paper in the grate and Big Ben strategically placed wooden slats on top, as if he were building a castle. The old man produced a box of matches from his pocket and struck one. At first the wood smoked and crackled, but eventually the flames began to take hold. Tom backed away as it spat shards in his direction, but it wasn't long before the fire settled down to a steady flicker. Taking off his wet shoes and socks he placed them close to the range, then dragged his mattress closer to the heat and lay down. As he watched the flames disappear up the chimney, it occurred to him that he actually felt safe here, in this derelict old house with the beautiful window. Warm, safe and relaxed. It was a while since he had felt like that. Yes, quite a while. Now if Joe could tell him how to find food, then ... then he could perhaps stay – for a while at any rate. At least it was better than the streets.

It was the blow to his guts that knocked all the air out of him. He doubled up.

'Give it over!' The voice was harsh, demanding, but he clutched on to the few precious coins in his hand.

The second blow caught him squarely on the jaw. He tottered back. He saw his assailant approaching fast, a raised iron bar in his hand. He knew what was coming, but he wasn't quick enough to lift his arm to defend himself. The bar smashed across the side of his head narrowly missing his eyes. Lights flashed, the buildings around him swam. He clung fiercely on to consciousness before his whole body slumped to the ground. He felt fingers trying to prise the coins out of his hand, but instinct made him cling on to them.

'Too fancy coat for a bloke like him, eh?'

He heard their heavy breathing as they tried pulling off his coat. He did what he could to resist but all that got him was a kick in the jaw. He heard it crack before he felt the pain; then his mouth filled with blood. He lashed out wildly with his fists, but one of his assailants grabbed him around the neck, his fingers digging into his flesh. He tried to pull the hands away but he was weak from lack of food. He couldn't breathe. He was choking ... he felt himself losing consciousness ...

'Hoy!'

There was the sound of boots running in his direction. The fingers chocking the life out of him slackened. He gasped air into his lungs.

'Let's go!' There was a shuffling of feet, and one last vengeful kick; this time to his groin. He doubled up in agony. And then, blessed relief, he heard his attackers splashing away through the puddles. He rolled over gasping, still holding his groin.

'Cowards! Bloody cowards!' his rescuer bellowed after them. Big black boots came to a standstill beside his face. He tried to look up but his bloodied eyes blurred everything, in fact, one of them wouldn't open at all. He felt a hand on his shoulder. 'Can you move, mate?'

He couldn't.

'Well, we can't leave you lying here. You'll freeze to death.'

One of his arms was lifted and dragged around a broad shoulder. Then he was dragged to his feet. He opened his mouth to cry out in pain but no sound came out.

'You were the bloke curled up in the doorway of the tobacconists, weren't you?'

Then he remembered; a big chap in a denim jacket had stopped when he'd seen him. 'You look like you need a decent meal, mate,' he'd said and had dropped a few coins into his hand. 'And I wouldn't hang around here; bad neighbourhood this is.'

His rescuer half-dragged, half-carried him across the road. Every movement was agony. Fortunately, the bloke was tall, even taller than him, and clearly more heavily built as he was able to drag him towards a row of old terraced houses, haul him through an open door and up a flight of stairs. His boots clunked on the floorboards.

'I'm gonna have to hang you over the banisters like a piece of washing mate while I get my keys out,' the bloke panted. 'Don't pass out on me, will you?'

His mouth was too clogged up with blood to answer. A moment later his one reasonably good eye was staring blurrily down into a shadowy hall lit by a single light bulb; no shade. A pushchair sat in the lobby and an old bike rested up against the wall. He heard a key in a lock, a door open, and a light switched on, then he was dragged inside and deposited like a sack of coal on to a settee. There was a 'plop' as a gas fire was lit, the sound of a tap running, a kettle being filled, and then another 'plop' which he guessed was a gas ring being lit.

'I'm Charlie,' his rescuer said.

He squinted at him through his bloodshot eye. Mid-thirties, built like a bruiser, hole in his jeans, snake tattoos peering from under the sleeves of his baggy jumper, and a blonde pony-tail dangling through a baseball cap.

'Lie still, fella. That was quite a beating you took.'

Mugs were placed on a table then Charlie said, 'That's an expensive coat you've got there, mate. Pick it up at one of the charity shops, eh? Should've got yourself a waterproof for sleeping rough. Now stay still. Tea won't be long.'

He did as he was told. He had no option. Besides, the little room was warming up nicely and he needed warmth. He heard tea being poured into a pot, then the clatter of pans.

'Here's your cuppa mate. It'll warm you up. You look half starved. I'll open a can of soup. It'll be easier to get down.'

Charlie hauled him into a sitting position and thrust a large steaming mug of tea into his hands. He tried to say thank you but nothing came out. Gingerly he touched his throat.

'Don't try to talk. Just drink that then I'll bandage that gash on your skull. Your face is gonna look a pretty picture, I can tell you. Ruin your good looks for a while, that's for sure. Hope there's no lady waiting to be swept off her feet 'cos she's gonna be mighty disappointed.' And then he laughed as though being beaten up, homeless, cold and starving were all part of life. And perhaps it was in Charlie's world, he thought. But not in his. Never in his – until now.

At what point he fell asleep he had no idea; after tea, after soup? He wasn't sure. But he did remember that for the first time in weeks he felt safe enough to do so.

He was woken with Charlie shaking his shoulder. 'Come on, wake up mate.'

His one good eye struggled to open. The other refused to budge.

'Aye, just as I thought.' Charlie was leaning over him. 'You're a pretty picture this morning. Sit up. I'll make breakfast.'

It took only seconds to discover that sitting up wasn't that easy. Not only was his neck badly swollen from having been half strangled to death, but he could barely see, his head pounded, and he guessed from the severe pain in his chest that he'd broken a few ribs. But once upright, he let his one good eye travel around Charlie's accommodation. It was surprisingly tidy, but then it only consisted of a bed, a table, two chairs, a settee and a cooker. His eye fell on his whisky bottle; the one he'd been carrying around in his coat pocket.

'Went through your pockets while you were asleep mate,' Charlie explained when he saw the direction of his gaze. 'Thought I better find out who you were in case you snuffed it in the night.' He shrugged. 'No phone, no keys, no papers. So why would someone with an expensive overcoat be on the streets?' Charlie peered at him closely. 'You've not lost your mind or nothing, have you?'

He shook his head, carefully.

'That's okay then. So, you're a whisky drinker, eh?'

He wasn't; or at least he hadn't been until ...

'In that case I'll call you JD. You know, Jack Daniels, after the whisky? Got to start calling you something; can't keep calling you 'mate'.

JD? Yes, JD would do nicely. It gave him a sense of anonymity - he liked that.

'As for breakfast, JD, cupboards almost bare. I haven't had a chance to do much shopping since I got out.' Charlie poured two mugs of tea from a brown teapot and handed him one. 'I've had enough of being inside I can tell you.'

Inside? Charlie had been in jail? He forced the steaming mug through his swollen lips. The teat was hot, sweet, and stung his throat when he swallowed.

'Good, eh?' Charlie said buttering a slice of bread. He hesitated. 'I'm gonna have to level with you, JD. There's this chap I know. He reckons I owe him money. I reckon I don't. So, we've got ourselves a … situation shall we say.' He licked a dollop of marmalade off his finger. 'The bloke I was inside with says I can shack up at his place till the heat dies down, but his place is the other end of town.' Charlie examined him apprehensively. 'Trouble is, if they come looking for me and find you here, you're likely to get another beating.'

Was that a hint for him to leave?

Charlie handed him a slice of bread and marmalade. 'But you can come with me, if you can handle a long walk.'

Go with him? Go with Charlie? But … he dropped his head. What option did he have? JD simply took the bread and nodded.

Chapter 2

'Oh, my …!' Abigail Hunter stepped back in alarm at the sight of the hulk in a black woollen hat, and the skinny teenager hunched over a blazing fire. 'What on earth are you doing in my kitchen?'

Startled by her sudden appearance, both stared at her apprehensively, then turned instinctively to the old man slumped across the couch. The old man sat up slowly, gawping at her in a manner that suggested she was the intruder, not him. '*Your* kitchen missus? I've been coming here for years.'

'Oh, you have, have you?' she asked tartly. 'Well, I'm sorry, but as of today, this property belongs to me, so you're trespassing. You'll have to find shelter elsewhere.' Her arm shot out towards the back door. 'Now!'

The old man followed her finger, before his eyes strayed towards the kitchen window and the thick layer of snow which had left morning traffic disrupted and the city smothered in an icy hug. 'Go? Where do 'y expect us to go to?'

'What?' Her hand dropped awkwardly to her side.

'Always the same over Christmas, missus. The shelters 'll be full. I blame government cut-backs myself.'

'You blame … what?'

'Government cutbacks. Never used to be as bad as this.' The old man wiped the drip on his nose on the sleeve of his shabby overcoat.

'Government …?' Abbie couldn't think of a thing to say. Having a political discussion with a vagrant over the state of the country's housing was the last thing on her agenda at that hour of the morning. 'Yes, well, government cutbacks or not, I'm about to turn this house into a hotel and I don't need anyone taking up early occupancy.'

'Hotel?' The old man sucked sharply through his teeth. 'That'll cost you a pretty penny.'

'Believe me, it is.'

'When do 'y start?'

Abigail Hunter scowled at him. 'That's none of your business.'

He chewed thoughtfully on his gums for a moment. 'I dare say you'll be getting a firm in to clear that rubble from when the chimney fell through the roof.' He shook his head. 'Big job that. Then there's them old beds and desks left by the last residents; then there's the mess the squatters have left. Disgusting! And the cellar? Dunno if a clearance firm 'll touch down there with all them rats. And that's just the inside, missus. Have 'y looked outside?' He gave a faint whistle. 'It'll cost you a pretty penny to deal with that lot, I can tell 'y that.'

'Yes, it will. But as I said before, that's none of your business.'

The old man scratched his whiskers. 'On the other hand, me and the lads could get rid of it all for 'y for next to nothin.'

Abbie stared at him in horror. 'You're not suggesting I employ you; I hope?'

The old man looked quite affronted. 'Why not?'

'Well …' Taken aback she found herself asking, yes, why not? Because they were homeless? Because they were dirty, smelly and God alone knew where they had come from, or whether they were even honest? She played uncertainly with the doorknob. Although, the old man was certainly right about the costs. The house clearance estimates had come in considerably higher than she had anticipated, as had the builders' estimates and, annoyingly, both were reluctant to give her a starting date. Could be March or April they had said noncommittally. She couldn't afford to wait that long. It was all a bit of a worry really. She bit her lip. But hiring three *vagrants* to clear her house just to save money, wasn't that a bit extreme? Her eyes drifted to the snow outside. 'If you could do it in two weeks ...?' she found herself saying.

'Two weeks?' The old man sucked sharply through his teeth again. 'Never get all those rooms cleared in two weeks, missus. Not if you want the boards off the windows, the cellar emptied and the chimney rubble dragged all the way downstairs. It 'd take five, six weeks.'

She played indecisively with the doorknob. 'And you're suggesting ... what?'

The old man adjusted the rope around his coat as if he was well used to negotiating multi-million-pound business deals. 'Three meals a day, coal for the fire, blankets, cash in hand and ...' he regarded her warily. 'Whisky to keep out the cold.'

Abbie pursed her lips thoughtfully. 'Coal for the fire, blankets, three meals a day, forget the whisky, cash in hand and I want it done by mid-January.'

The skinny teenager's face lit up, the giant looked bemused, and the old man continued chewing on his gums. But then, spitting on the palm of his filthy hand he offered it to her to cement their deal.

She backed away in disgust. 'Right! So, my car is parked out back. You can start by storing my luggage in those cupboards, then help yourself to soup and bread out of the box of food.' She looked around the kitchen. 'How exactly do you cook …?'

The old man pointed to the fire and the burnt pan on the hearth.

'Ah! Yes, I see.' And then her ears tuned in to the hum of a familiar engine pulling up at her front door. She stifled a groan. 'Right! I'll leave you to it then.' Slamming the kitchen door behind her, she swept across the hallway trying not to ponder too deeply on the wisdom of her latest action. But at the sight of the silver Audi on her driveway and her sour faced brother storming through the snow towards her she braced herself.

'Can you imagine how humiliating it was for me to ring your B&B this morning only to discover that you'd checked out, Abigail?' he snapped.

'Good morning to you too, Freddy.' She gave him a hug. His immaculate overcoat was damp, his black hair flecked with flakes of snow, and his body stiff and unyielding. 'I didn't tell you because I knew you'd try to stop me.'

Dark brown eyes glinted angrily behind his steel framed spectacles. 'You are darn right I would. So, where are you staying?'

'You're not going to like it.'

'Really? Why not?'

'Because …' She took a deep breath. 'I suppose I better show you.' Reluctantly making her way back into the house, she led him across the hallway and into a corridor strewn with empty cans, bottles, and boxes. He swore when he tripped over a rusty bath tub then clicked his tongue impatiently when she couldn't get the swollen back door to open, although he didn't bother to help her. Eventually, it relented, shuddering on the stone step and letting in a blast of cold air. Following her out into a winter wonderland of virgin white trees and bushes she watched anxiously as his eye landed on the dilapidated two-tone green caravan.

'Are you serious?'

'I'm only living there until my apartment is habitable,' she assured him. 'It sleeps four and has a gas cooker so I shall be quite cosy. What do you think?' She bit her lip, wishing she hadn't asked that.

Freddy flared his nostrils. 'What do I think? You don't want to know what I think, Abigail,' he said grimly but it was obvious he couldn't resist telling her. 'Firstly, you'll freeze to death in that thing. And secondly, the last time you went camping you cried all night and had to be brought home.'

'I was six, it was raining, and we were in the back garden,' she snapped. 'Why do you always have to criticize everything I do, Frederick? Anyway, my reason for buying that 'thing' as you call it, was that it was costing me a fortune staying at the B&B, and I do need to watch what I spend until Donald's business concerns and this complicated business of the accident insurance are … well, until my finances are sorted.'

'Which is all the more reason why you shouldn't have sold your house and given up a well-paid job for …this!' He flung his arm in the general direction of the house. 'It'll have taken every penny you possess – I assume. Not that you bothered consulting me.' He gave a sniff of disapproval. 'It would make more sense to let me find you a reputable builder to take this on, then sell up. Meanwhile, you can stay with me and Susan.'

'I don't want to sell up, Freddy. I've been trying to tell you that for weeks, but you don't listen; you never listen. I'm thirty-two years old and what do I have to show for it? Nothing! I want a change of lifestyle; a new challenge.'

'Challenge?' Freddy's voice rose an octave. 'You've found yourself a challenge all right. Even if, by some miracle you got this ... this ... *hovel* habitable, what do you know about running a hotel? You're in the middle of grieving Abigail, and now is not the time to be looking for new challenges.'

'And when is the right time, Freddy?' she asked steadily. Turning her back on him she stared across the snowy wilderness of overgrown trees, shrubs and weeds from summers long gone. 'I had to do something,' she said softly. 'You've no idea how lonely I was rattling around in that big empty house. It has too many painful memories. I needed to move away from ...' and she couldn't stop her voice from shaking when she added, '... the shame of it all.' She heard broken glass crunch under his feet as he came to stand behind her.

'You meet people at the dental hospital.'

'You can hardly have a stimulating conversation when you're drilling teeth!'

'You have me.'

She turned, touched his arm and gave him a wan smile. 'I know I have, Freddy, and don't think I'm not grateful for all you and Susan have done for me. But ... every time I look at this old house, I have a vision of what it could become; of what *I* could make it. I actually find having a new project exciting. I need this. Can't you be pleased for me?'

Judging from Freddy's sour expression, obviously not. 'I doubt we're ever going to agree on ...' He trailed off, frowning up at the thin spiral of smoke wending its way lazily into the sky from her kitchen chimney. 'What's that?'

'Ah!' She ran her tongue nervously across her teeth. 'That's the ... workers I've hired to clear the house for me.'

'They're here already? I hope you've hired a reputable company and not some cowboys.' And before she could stop him, he had stormed back along the corridor and flung open the kitchen door. When he saw her three new workers slurping soup at the table his jaw dropped open in undisguised revulsion. *'Tramps? You've hired tramps?'*

'I think you'll find the politically correct term is 'homeless', Freddy.'

'And they think they're going to make this their home?'

'Let me explain.'

'Please! Do!'

'Hoy Missus!' the old man bellowed. 'Shut the door, while 'y doing 'y explaining. You're letting the heat out.'

Grabbing Freddy roughly by the arm she dragged him into the hall and slammed the door behind them. 'I found them here this morning. The shelters are all full, and I hadn't the heart to throw them out so near Christmas.'

'Then I'll do it!' Freddy made to open the door again but Abbie hauled him back.

'No, you won't! I've decided to give them food and shelter over Christmas and in return they'll clear the house for me. It'll save me money.'

Removing his glasses, Freddy pinched between his eyes. 'You have no idea, have you Abigail?' he said wearily. 'Those ... *creatures* in there could be criminals, thieves, drug addicts, alcoholics or even rapists.'

'Why are you being so objectionable, Freddy?'

'I'm not. I'm being realistic. You should have consulted me before starting all ... this.'

'I've always consulted you. Even when Donald was ….' Her lip quivered. 'But now I want … I *need* to make my own decisions.'

Returning his glasses to his nose he blew softly through his lips before making his way slowly across the hallway, down the steps and on to the drive. She followed his footprints in the snow and they stood in silence examining the outside of the house. Tired of arguing but unsure how to move on, she pulled the fur collar of her leather coat firmly around her ears and watched the old man with the battered trilby shuffle down the steps towards them. She was vaguely aware there was a shaggy off-white mongrel at his heels.

'Please Freddy. Don't let's argue. I am grateful to you for drawing up the plans for this place. I hope you know that?'

Freddy shrugged the thanks away. 'I'm an architect. It's my job,' he said flatly. And almost as though he couldn't help himself pointed to the fallen chimney and hole in the roof. 'That'll need to be your top priority.'

'I know. I thought fifty roof tiles might do the job. What do you think?'

'Now you're asking my opinion?'

The old man stopped and joined in their viewing session. 'Fifty tiles? Nah! More like a hundred for a job that size.'

'And you would know, would you?' Freddy glared at him before consulting his watch. 'Look; I'm sorry, Abs. I hate to leave you with er.,' he glanced apprehensively at the old man. 'But I've a meeting in twenty minutes.' He opened his car door. 'There's a builder's merchant on the other side of the dual carriageway. Ask the manager about roofing tiles. Tell him I sent you.' Sliding into his car he slammed the door. The window hummed as it slid down. 'And if you're cold in that tin box, ring me and I'll come and get you.' Turning the key his engine roared into life. 'I'm not trying to be awkward, Abs.' He rested his gloved hand over hers. 'But I know the amount of work involved in a project like this, and I simply don't think you realise what you've let yourself in for.' He paused a beat. 'And I certainly don't think you've got what it takes to turn it into a hotel.'

Pulling her gloved hand sharply away she said, 'See you over Christmas, Freddy. Love to Susan and the boys.'

She watched the Audi slithering down her drive ruminating that as usual, twenty minutes with Freddy and she was left feeling like a wrung-out dishcloth. Rolling her shoulders, she rubbed the nodules on the back of her neck and hoped she hadn't been too hard on him. She'd been fourteen, Freddy nineteen when their parents had drowned in a boating accident. Various Aunts and Uncles had promised to look out for them, but it hadn't taken them long to realise that Freddy was doing a far better job of caring for his sister than they ever could. The trouble was, he was still doing it, and she was still letting him.

'Aye, more like a hundred.'

Startled, she turned to find the old man standing behind her. 'And you would know, would you?' she asked tartly then cringed at how like Freddy she sounded.

'Aye!' He chewed on his gums. 'But you'll not get a match.'

'What do you mean?'

'Them tiles is too weathered. Put new ones aside them and the roof 'll look like a patchwork quilt.'

'So, what do you suggest?' she asked, not quite believing she was asking the advice of a … *vagrant*.

He wiped away a drop from the end of his nose. 'There's an outhouse out back. You could use the roof tiles from that. Scrape the moss off and you'll have a match.'

She blinked rapidly at the obvious solution. 'What's your name?'

'Joe.'

'Okay, Joe. Would you be able to take the tiles off the outhouse roof and stack them at the front of the house ready for the roofer?'

Joe sniffed. 'Could do. It'll take another week for a job like that though. Then you'll need new tiles and batons for the outhouse roof.'

'Tiles and batons? Right!' Leaving Joe staring at the roof she made her way back into the kitchen vaguely aware that a dirty white mongrel was trotting at her heels. 'Tiles and batons,' she murmured scribbling it down in her notebook. 'What the hell's a baton?'

The skinny teenager was clearing the soup bowls from the table. 'Joe 'll know.'

'What?'

'Joe knows all about building and stuff.'

'Does he now?' There was a pause. 'What's your name?' she asked.

'Tom.'

She rattled the pen thoughtfully between her teeth. 'I'll need to go to the builders' yard, and I'll need to get in extra food. Any idea where the supermarket is?'

'Over the dual carriageway; on the way to the builders' yard.' Tom hesitated before he said, 'If you're not sure about batons you could take Joe with you.'

The idea of taking Joe appalled her but all she said was, 'That's a good idea. Thanks Tom.' And she was surprised to see how his face lit up when all she'd done was thank him.

Abbie soon discovered that Joe carried his own particular brand of body odour which appeared to be a cocktail of alcohol, tobacco, smoke, pee and dust bins. The problem was it soaked into every inch of her BMW from the moment he sidled into the passenger seat.

'Hope you're not a fast driver,' he growled slamming the door. 'Don't like fast drivers.'

'I'm not a fast driver, Joe.' She pressed the window buttons down. 'I keep within the speed limit.'

Joe pulled his trilby firmly over his head as a blast of icy air whistled through the open windows, then clung nervously on to the arm rest as the car slithered down the driveway. Fortunately, she didn't have to drive far. Over the roundabout and a few yards past the supermarket she spotted, *Barry Matthews, building materials*, blazoned across tall iron gates. Oddly enough though, when Joe spotted it, he wrapped his scarf around his mouth, pulled his trilby over his eyes and as soon as she'd parked, he sloped off without a word.

She found Barry Matthews to be a bald, stocky little man with grizzled tufts of hair sticking out of his ears and a round belly that had popped one of the buttons on his grubby brown overalls. There was a good-natured air about him which she liked, and made it easy for her to introduce herself and tell him about her project.

'So, you've bought the Blue House on the corner, eh?' His chubby face lit up. 'It'll be a pleasure seeing the old place coming to life again. Anything you need, let me know.'

After listening to a list of Freddy's negativities, soaking in these few positive words of encouragement was like nectar. 'Thank you,' she said gratefully. 'My priority is fixing the hole in the roof, so I'm hoping you can supply me with scaffolding.'

'Aye, we can do that. Have to be after New Year though.' He jerked his bald head in the direction of Joe who was inspecting the tiles in the far corner of the yard. 'Is he with you?'

'I'm afraid so.'

'Looks familiar.' Taking a pair of heavily framed glasses out of his pocket, he put them on. 'Aye, it's Joe, isn't it? I'd heard he was on the streets.'

She deliberated briefly before saying, 'Actually, he was. I found him and two others in my kitchen this morning. I hadn't the heart to throw them out in this weather, so I offered them food and shelter if they cleared the house for me.'

Barry gave a chuckle of amusement. 'Good for you. You'll be okay with Joe. Him and me worked together on the building sites for years. Best roofer I ever worked with.'

'He's a roofer?' So that's how he knew all about tiles and batons. 'How did he end up on the streets?'

Barry Matthews shook his head. 'Ah, it was a real shame, that's what it was. Joe, Betty and the boy had a nice little place the other end of town, nothing fancy mind you, but nice. Then his lad died of meningitis ...'

Abbie wished she hadn't asked.

' ... Thought the world of the boy Joe did. A real tragedy. That's when he started drinking, and what builder wants to take on an alcoholic roofer? Within two years it had cost him his job, his home and his marriage.'

Abbie tried to stem the familiar wave of grief that rolled in on her like a high tide, bringing with it the heart-breaking memory of her own baby's death. She swallowed hard, trying to shut out the awful vision of his deathly white face the morning she had found him. Yes, she could understand what Joe had gone through. The grief of losing a child was ... unspeakable. She could understand how he had become an alcoholic. She would never forget Freddy's fury at finding the empty wine bottles in her dustbin after .... after ....

Fumbling in her coat pocket she pulled out a paper hankie, blew her nose, and watched Joe picking up tiles and weighing them against the one he had brought with him. His expression was one of total absorption, almost as though the responsibility of choosing the correct tiles for her roof had fallen on his shoulders - because he was the one who knew about such things. And as she watched him discarding one tile for another, Abbie experienced a strange affinity towards this dirty old alcoholic in his shabby coat and his ridiculous tattered trilby. Like ... like a soulmate, she mused. The only difference being she had had the money not to be made homeless.

'There was a day when Joe could have tiled your roof, rebuilt your chimney and replastered your walls,' Barry was saying. 'In fact, Joe could turn his hand to anything,'

Thrusting the paper hankie into her pocket she said, 'Do you think he's still up roofing?'

'I'd like to think so, but I honestly wouldn't know.' He glanced sceptically at her. 'But if you're thinking what I think you're thinking, the biggest problem will be keeping him sober

An hour later, dressed in an old sweater and jeans and with her hair tied back in a ponytail, Abbie was wondering how she'd got herself involved in cooking a meal for four when she was supposed to be renovating a house. She eyed the enormous black kitchen range apprehensively. It consisted of four hot plates, an oven, which looked as though it hadn't been opened for years, and a roasting spit, all supposedly heated by the fire. Concluding that if the Victorian owners had managed to cook on this contraption, then it couldn't be too difficult, she set about heating a pan of bottled water to scrub the long wooden table where they'd be eating their meals. Then collecting her cooking utensils from the walk-in larder, she began making a pan of stew.

There was a gently 'woof' at her side. Glancing down she saw the shaggy mongrel drooling at her feet. His tail was beating a rhythmic tune on the floor, and his liquid brown eyes were peering at her through an unkempt fringe, pleading too beautifully to be ignored.

'Are you still here?' she asked throwing him a morsel of fat.

There was a snap of teeth as the creature caught the fat mid-air and swallowed it in one easy gulp. His yellow teeth grinned up hopefully for more.

'I don't know who you belong to, but you can't stay here,' she told him tossing him another morsel. Her ears tuned into the rumble of a heavy lorry coming up her driveway. 'Ah! That'll be my first delivery,' she informed him and hurried to the front door.

A pinched faced driver built like a featherweight boxer was unloading the skip when she stepped out into the cold. 'Got your hands full doing up this place,' he called above the roar of the engine.

'That's what I keep being told,' she bellowed back.

'Aye!' Then as the skip clattered on to the driveway he added, 'I'll collect it after the holiday's luv. Merry Christmas.'

She was about to close the door, or to be precise, push the door against what remained of the rotten framework, when the Water Board van slithered up her snowy drive. This provider was on the far side of middle age with legs so bandy he could have arrived by horse rather than van. But he was obliging enough to explain what a stopcock was, where it was, and seeing her blank expression, offer to turn it on for her. The only down-side to his kindness was being forced to listen to a dictionary of profanities from under her cracked sink. But at least that was better than attempting to do the work herself, and it was definitely preferable to drilling teeth, she decided. Half an hour later she heard the welcome splutter of water gushing out of the rusty taps and into the sink.

'We're operational!' she informed the mongrel in delight. 'Remind me to buy you a tin of dog food to celebrate.'

The bandy-legged Water-board man peered out from under the sink looking confused.

Her next delivery was a white van with her household tools, garden equipment and bedding. The rest of her furniture was in storage. The only problem was that Big Ben, having seen the garden equipment, took it into his head to clear the garden instead of the house. Then Joe decided he wanted to remove the tiles from her outhouse roof. Unsure how to handle the situation she decided to put the stew on the hob and give Tom a hand herself. But by the end of the afternoon, she was forced to admit that her first stint of house clearing hadn't gone as well as anticipated. In an uncontrollable frenzy of hammering to remove a dangerously swinging curtain rail in the dining room, she not only brought down the rail, and what she assumed was the baton with chunks of plaster, but she lost control of the hammer altogether. The offending object flew through the air, smashed through the window and landed in the skip outside. Thankfully, no-one was around at the time and Tom was kind enough to climb into the skip after it for her.

It was late afternoon and already dark before Joe put in an appearance. 'Canna work no more, cos I canna see and summat's burning on the stove,' he informed her.

The stew!

Rushing into the kitchen she grabbed the pan handle with the sleeves of her jumper and dragged it off the hob. Lifting the lid, she gave a groan of despair. The liquid had evaporated leaving a congealed mess at the bottom of the pan. However, being well practiced in rescuing her cooking disasters, she crumbled a stock cube over the burnt meat and vegetables, poured boiling water over the top and stirred vigorously, hoping her workers would be so hungry they wouldn't notice. She also lit the paraffin lamps and candles, placed them around the kitchen, and threw another log on the fire to create a cosy atmosphere. Not that anyone appeared to notice.

'What are them rooms in the attic where the chimney fell through gonna be?' Joe asked dragging up a chair and diving into his bowl of stew. His hands were filthy. Obviously, the arrival of running water hadn't induced him to wash up before eating.

'My apartment, store-rooms, and rooms for live-in staff.' She grimaced as Joe dipped his used spoon into the pan for another dumpling. 'And the eight bedrooms below will be guest rooms.'

'Huh-huh! What do you know about doing up old houses then?'

Her fork hovered. 'Nothing!' she said after a pause. 'But presumably the builders will, and it's something I ... I want to do.'

'Huh-huh! And what do you know about running a hotel?'

She shrugged guiltily. 'Again, nothing. I was a dentist. But I'm reading up on it. And sometimes you need to make drastic life-style changes, don't you think?'

Joe made no comment so the rest of the meal they ate in silence, and they left her to wash up and rescue the burnt pan while they and the dog sprawled on their mattresses in front of the fire. She was drying the last dish when it occurred to her that she hadn't sorted out her own sleeping arrangements yet. Her heart sank as she glanced outside. It was dark, she was tired, and she had no idea how to turn on the lights or heating in the caravan.

Irritated at her own stupidity, she dragged two duvets, pillows and a flashlight out of the storeroom, and arms full, staggered towards the kitchen door and flung it open. As an icy wind caught her breath she was almost tempted to step back inside and join her lazy workers around the fire. And she might have done so if Joe dragged himself off the rumpled couch. At first, she though he was coming to help her until he said, 'Need to keep the heat in boss,' and giving her a gentle push, he slammed the door behind her.

It was not just the cold wind but the sudden silence that hit her. Silent, other than the hum of traffic on the dual carriageway that is. In a way, the sound was comforting. It made her feel less alone. Shining her flashlight across the stretch of ice and snow between the house and the caravan she slithered cautiously forward, and after fumbling with the caravan key dragged her bedding inside. A ring of circles appeared on the ceiling as she stood her flashlight on the bench.

'So, how do I get light and heating into this thing?' she muttered. Pulling the box of matches out of her pocket she turned the knob on the cooker, struck the match, stood back and waved the flame in front of it. Nothing happened. There wasn't even a hiss of gas. The match flickered and died. Blowing on her rapidly freezing fingers it briefly crossed her mind that she could go to Freddy's, but then she just as quickly dismissed the idea. She could imagine his response if she arrived on his doorstep on her first night.

'Think Abigail! Think!'

Ah! Yes! The gas bottle; didn't the agent say he'd left a half-full bottle on the towing bracket? Picking up the flashlight she stepped outside and clinging to the sides of the caravan slithered around to the front. To her relief it was there, and after careful examination she discovered a wheel on the top. 'What do you do I wonder?' she muttered. Figuring there was only one way to find out, she turned it. A moment later the welcome hiss of gas came from inside the caravan. Slithering back inside she struck a match and reaching out, waved it in front of the cooker. This time the ring flared into life with more of an explosion than a pop. With a squeal of alarm, she leapt back but having achieved success with the cooker gave her confidence to start on the gas lights. After a few alarming hisses she found if she adjusted the pressure that they too worked perfectly.

Standing back, she examined her temporary accommodation with a sense of achievement. It certainly looked smaller than when she had bought it but then, she reasoned, it hadn't been piled high with luggage and bedding but at least it was warming up and after she had given it a good clean it should be ... adequate. She drew the curtains to keep in the warmth then leapt back with a yelp as a disintegrated spider fell on her hair. Shuddering in revulsion she frantically ran her fingers through her hair but once satisfied the creature had gone, she set too making her caravan habitable. That was more difficult than she had anticipated as she had brought far too many clothes to cram into the tiny wardrobe, and there was very little storage space for personal items. After half an hour, she flopped on to the bed, curled her arms around her legs and tried not to dwell on the fact that she had made very little progress – either in the house or the caravan, and would probably freeze to death when she switched off the gas. She examined a broken nail ruefully and tried not to imagine the pleasures of easing aching muscles in a hot bath, or sitting in front of a warm fire watching television. She knew she ought to get ready for bed, but she couldn't remember where she had put her pyjamas. Slipping off her trainers she crawled under the pile of duvets and pulled them up to her chin. Squinting at the luminous dials on her travel clock she was horrified to find that it was only eight o'clock. Eight o'clock? What on earth was she supposed to do for the rest of the evening? Sit alone, like she had night after night since Donald had died? Perhaps Freddy was right and this change of lifestyle was too drastic? Sometime during the evening, she must have switched off the lights. She couldn't remember doing it because Freddy's parting shot had continued to reverberate around her head with annoying persistence. *"You don't know what you've let yourself in for Abigail! You haven't got what it takes to turn this place into a hotel."* And she couldn't help wondering if he was right.

Chapter 3

Charlie was right. It was a long walk, and JD was conscious that he was holding him up. But it was only when sheer exhaustion forced him to stop and lean against a tall stone pillar at the end of a driveway that Charlie made a comment.

'There's still a long way to go, mate,' he said worriedly. He looked around. It was dark and the row of shops nearby were all shuttered up for the night; all except the fish and chip shop next to the stone church. 'We could break into the church for the night,' he suggested.

At one time, JD would have been horrified by such a suggestion, but truth be told, he was past caring what they did. Fortunately, he was saved from having to give his opinion by an unexpected break in the clouds. That was when they saw it; a derelict old house at the top of the driveway. It stood out clear and sharp, like a black pencil drawn sketch against a bright moonlit sky.

Charlie gave a nod of satisfaction. 'That's our shelter for the night. Okay?'

They made their way slowly up the driveway, but as Charlie pushed open the front door and they stumbled into the dark hallway, a light emerged and an aggressive voice shouted, 'What'd you want? This is private property.'

JD felt his heart sink at the thought of trouble. But then he saw a slow grin spread across Charlie's face. 'Private property? Don't give me that.' Barging past an old man in a shabby overcoat he said, 'Come on JD.'

As Charlie clearly didn't see this old man as a threat he followed both men into a warm kitchen with a roaring fire, glowing lanterns, and food piled high on an old-fashioned dresser. Limping his way over to the kitchen range he stretched out his frozen fingers. A skinny lad hugging the fire shuffled nervously back to make room for him. The bigger lad simply stared in revulsion at his bruised and battered face.

'Got yourself a nice little set-up here,' Charlie said admiringly. 'How come?'

The old man threw another log on the fire. 'This lady dentist's turning the place into a hotel. We're clearing out the rubbish in return for food and lodgings.'

Charlie sniffed the air. 'I thought I could smell stew - burnt stew.'

The old man gave a chuckle. 'Aye, that's her attempts at cooking. But if you think that's bad, you should have seen the pig's breakfast she made of taking down the curtain rails; smashed the window and brought half the wall down with her. Forget health and safety with her around.'

Charlie turned his back to the fire to warm his rear end. Ponderously twirling his thumbs behind his back, he said, 'Sounds to me like you could do with a chef and a bit of muscle.'

'Aye! We could.' The old man narrowed his eyes. 'Why?'

'Cos I'm both.'

'You're a chef? A proper one?'

Charlie's mouth broadened into a grin. 'Aye, a proper one.'

'Aye, we need a chef, no doubt about that. I'm Joe, by the way. That big fella's Big Ben and the skinny runt's, Tom.'

'Right Joe. Then me and JD ...' Charlie indicated him with a jerk of the head, '... will need you to convince your lady dentist that we can be of service to her?'

JD wasn't so sure he could, or even wanted to be of service to anyone, but he was only too grateful when Charlie dragged a tatty mattress across the floor for him. He was so exhausted he would have fallen on it if it hadn't been for his broken ribs. Instead, he sank down gingerly, and as the warmth of the fire seeped into his frozen body, he felt sleep washing over him.

He was awakened the following morning by an icy draught, the slamming of a door, and an astonished, 'What on earth ...!'

He struggled to sit up, wincing as his body objected to being forced into action. Joe, Big Ben, and the one he had referred to as 'the skinny runt' were sitting at the kitchen table with bowls of porridge, and standing shivering at the kitchen door was a woman. She looked to be in her early thirties; straight nose, firm chin, thick tawny hair bouncing off her shoulders, and she would have looked quite pretty if it hadn't been for the dark circles under her gentle hazel eyes.

'Got you a chef with a bit'o muscle and a labourer, boss.' Joe said brightly.

'And what makes you think I need either?' the dentist asked coolly.

Joe slurped his tea, apparently unconcerned by her aloof manner. 'Obvious, isn't it? If I'm working on the outhouse roof and Big Ben's clearing the garden, there's only Tom clearing the house and there's too much heavy lifting for a skinny lad like him. Besides – and no disrespect boss – but if your performance of yesterday is anything to go by, we'll still be taking down curtain rails and eating burnt stew till next Christmas.'

'I see,' she said frostily. She pursed her lips thoughtfully, then addressing Charlie who was standing over the kitchen range stirring porridge, she asked, 'Where are you from?'

'Porridge?' he asked turning to her with raised eyebrows.

'What?'

'Would you like porridge for breakfast?' He nodded towards an empty bowl on the table.

She seemed surprised by the invitation, but after a slight hesitation slid on to a kitchen stool. 'Thank you. Yes. What's your name?'

'Charlie.' Charlie concentrated on ladling porridge neatly into her bowl.

'Where've you come from, Charlie?'

There was a slight hesitation before he said, 'Inside.'

'Inside where?'

He banged the ladle on the side of the pan. 'I've been one of Her Majesty's guests for a couple of years,' he smoothly admitted.

Her expression remained blank.

'Prison boss,' Joe intervened. 'He means he's been in the nick.''

Her face reddened. 'Oh! May I ask what for?'

And that was when Charlie flashed her a broad grin, a friendly, foxy grin that lit up his face and filled his startling blue eyes with laughter. If there had been a point where she had seen him as a criminal and a threat, this transformation now turned him into a big loveable rogue. 'Ah! Now there's a question. I've been in and out of jail all my life, see. This last time I went down for a safe job.' He gave her a wink. 'I was innocent of course.'

The dentist gave him a ghost of a smile. 'In other words, you're a thief?'

'I wouldn't go as far as to say that, but if you think I'll nick your stuff, then don't worry; I won't. All I need is a roof over my head and food for a week or so. You give me that and me and JD 'll work our socks off for you.'

'You're not on the run from the police, are you?'

'No ma'am, I give you my word, I'm not,' he said as he handed JD a bowl of porridge.

The dentist twirled her spoon around the bowl before saying, 'It'll not be paying much if I'm feeding you and giving you a roof over your heads.'

'Fair enough,' Charlie said taking the pan over to the sink and filling it with water.

'And we've no electricity so you'll be cooking on that kitchen range.'

'Yes, I know. I've just made porridge on it.'

'Ah! Yes! Of course, you have.' She watched him pour her a mug of tea. 'Leave me a list of what you need each day and I'll shop for food.' She paused. 'You can write, can't you?'

Charlie gave a grin. 'I can even do joined up writing.'

She blushed, unsure whether that was a joke or sarcasm. 'This place was a military hospital during the first and second world wars so there's more than the usual sinks, baths and toilets that'll need dismantling and throwing in the skip.'

Charlie leant back against the dresser. 'Fine!'

And then JD realised she was looking at him, and he was suddenly conscious of his long, mattered and greasy hair, the bandage around his head, another around his neck, and that his face was bruised and bloody.

'JD? What does that stand for?' she asked.

It was Charlie who answered for him. 'That's his name.'

'And have you been released from prison?'

He shook his head.

'But are you fit enough for work because you look as though you've been in the wars?'

'He was mugged,' Charlie answered for him. 'But don't you worry. He'll do his fair share, won't you JD?'

A nod was all he could manage.

Christmas!

This was the time of year she had been dreading. This first Christmas without Donald and her baby. She had tried relegating it to the back of her mind but with Jingle Bells blasting out in every store, Christmas trees dripping with tinsel and baubles, shelves bulging with gifts, children's toys and cards, it was hard to ignore. Deciding that Christmas was going to happen whether she liked it or not she flung a frozen turkey and Christmas pudding into her supermarket trolly, added anything else she could think of that would accompany a Christmas dinner, dumped it all on Charlie and leaving her workers to their own devices, headed into the city for last minute presents for the big day.

Christmas Day at Freddy and Susan's was, as she expected, one of mixed blessings. The blessings were being able to recharge her mobile phone and lap top. It had never occurred to her what a wonderful invention electricity was until she didn't have any. The other blessing was being able to indulge in a hot bath. Freddy was none too pleased when she cried off attending the Christmas Day service merely to have a bath. But then Freddy wasn't pleased with anything she did these days.

'We've always gone to church on Christmas morning, Abigail,' he scolded. 'And believe me, you need a dose of spirituality more than any of us.'

It was her gently supportive sister-in-law, Susan, who having seen her worn out expression had ushered Freddy out of the door claiming they'd be late for church. Freddy hated being late for anything. Abbie had flashed her a look of gratitude before taking the stairs two at a time and turning on the bath taps.

Sliding into hot soapy water was pure ecstasy. She groaned with pleasure as her aching muscles succumbed to the heat. Running her fingers through the foam she breathed in the fragrant luxury of apples, or was it pears? She didn't care. Either way, the aroma was lovely so she allowed herself to drift....

'You need a dose of spirituality more than any of us, Abigail.'

Irritated by Freddy's comment, she rubbed her nose leaving a handful of bubbles on her upper lip, then she ruefully examined her damaged fingernails and made a determined effort not to let his opinion spoil her brief hour of indulgence. She knew why she hadn't gone to church, but she wouldn't dare tell Freddy. Truth be told, she had a problem admitting it even to herself. She draped the hot flannel over her face. It was strangely comforting. Three times this ... this *awful* thing had happened to her; three times, she brooded. The first time was when she was fourteen and her parents had been killed;

the second when her baby had …, then Donald … She fought back the heavy lump in her throat. Each time she had desperately wanted God to understand her pain; to gain comfort from Him, strength, but whenever she had tried to pray her words had sounded flat and empty, as though she had been speaking to herself.

'I'm right out of faith,' she admitted in a whisper, and then, in a sudden wave of bravado added, 'because *You* turned your back on me when I needed You most God.' She didn't care if she was speaking to herself; or that her words were ones of condemnation of Almighty God Himself – if He even existed. The grievances, doubts and disillusionment that had accumulated over recent months gathered momentum.

'*How can I celebrate the birth of Your Son when You've so cruelly taken mine?*'

There! She'd said it!

'*All I ever wanted was a husband who loved me and a child to care for. But You took them both. How could You be so … cruel?*'

Pulling the flannel off her face she opened her eyes. Her lower lip quivered at the concept that not only had she been abandoned by her husband, but now it seemed, by God.

'*Where are You God?*'

She fought back the tears as the silence persisted.

'*You don't even exist, do you?*'

She sank lower in the bath. Her feet touched the taps. Her knees rose; the water covered her mouth.

'*Why shouldn't I turn my back on You? You've turned your back on me.*'

Closing her eyes, she submerged under the water. Her hair floated around her face, and the dull, muffled silence that penetrated her head made her feel she had entered another world. A world without pain or grief. A world of calm, quietness, nothingness... She wanted to stay here ... stay where there was no pain no ...She rose to the surface gasping, and lay, not thinking, not feeling, just numb.

How long she lay in the bath she had no idea. But the water was cool when she heard the front door slam and the chatter of excitable voices indicating Freddy, Susan and the boys were back from church. The numbness faded, and that was when she realised, she was actually relieved to hear them. She needed the company, even though she knew she would have to readjusted her, "I'm absolutely fine!" mask, play with children that were not her own, and make a point of not antagonising Freddy by mentioning the renovation. Unfortunately, to do all that she was forced to drink more than usual to fortify herself, so by the time Christmas Day was over her head was pounding as though an army of Freddy's was marching through it.

An overworked, disgruntled taxi driver picked her up at eight that evening but refused to take her any further than the entrance of her drive, which meant that she was obliged to negotiate the pot-holes in heeled boots, in the dark. It was only when she dropped her Christmas presents on to her caravan bed and lit the gas lights that she became aware of the awful silence around her; silence except for the hissing of the gas lights. An awful loneliness descended and for a split second she wished she had stayed at Freddy's for the night. At least she would have had company. But then she caught sight of a light shining through the kitchen window. On the spur of the moment, she grabbed the wine, chocolates, liquors and Christmas cake from Freddy and Susan, switched off the caravan lights and stepped outside. Her heeled boots sank into the mud.

The paraffin lamp flickered as she opened the kitchen door letting in a blast of cold air. Shutting it hastily behind her she found her workers sprawled out in front of a crackling fire. They looked up curiously as she entered. There was a smell of turkey, beer, Christmas pudding, burning logs, body odours and dog. The shaggy mongrel wagged his tail in greeting but made no attempt to rouse himself from the hearth. She paused by the door, wondering if she was intruding on their Christmas; unsure whether they'd even want her.

'Merry Christmas!' She forced a laugh which even to her ears sounded remarkably like a hyena. But then it always did if she'd drunk too much. Holding up her carrier bags she added, 'Booze and food.'

Dumping the bags on the table she vaguely noted that the old green dresser had been scrubbed clean and the remains of the turkey, crockery and Christmas food was stacked neatly on the shelves. It gave the shambolic kitchen rather a homely feel, she thought. 'We'll have to drink the wine out of mugs I'm afraid. I'm too tired to hunt for wine glasses ...' She furrowed her brow at the sight of a dark eyed girl in her mid-twenties, with short black hair framing an oval face, sitting on the hearth watching her uneasily.

'Meet Sarah, boss,' Joe said casually waving his arm in the girl's direction. 'She's had a bit of husband trouble, so we invited her for Christmas dinner. I told her she could pay for it by stripping wallpaper and washing dishes. I reckoned we could use her while Charlie shifts that chimney what crashed through the roof. That's one mother of a ...'

She raised her hand, 'Watch your language, Joe, and don't call me boss.' She turned to the girl. 'Trouble?'

The girl dropped her eyes. 'I was on my way to the Woman's Refuge when I saw smoke coming out of your chimney. It looked so ... welcoming I decided to investigate.' She was quietly spoken with a hint of a local accent.

'As its Christmas, Sarah you're welcome to stay for the holidays but ...' she frowned at Joe. 'Stripping wallpaper, Joe? I can't remember having said anything about stripping wallpaper.'

'Aye, I know, boss but you've eight guest bedrooms, the attic rooms, the dining room, kitchen, and the two big rooms across that *huge* hallway. Big job stripping walls. It'll take you forever on your own, and a painter and decorator will cost you an arm and a leg. Whereas us, we'll do it for nowt.'

'Hardly for nowt ... nothing Joe. You're getting food and lodgings ...' She ran her fingers through her hair wondering how she'd got into this conversation in the first place. 'Okay Joe. But that's it. I don't need any more workers, and what's not done by ... by ...'

'End of January boss.'

She had a vague recollection she stipulated mid-January, but she was too fuzzy-headed to argue.' What's not done by then has to be left?'

'You're the boss, boss.' His eyes wandered over to the bottles on the table.

She waved her arm. 'Help yourself.'

Her vagrants didn't need a second invitation. Sarah cut the Christmas cake, Charlie poured wine into their mugs, Big Ben threw another log on the fire which spat and hissed in protest, and Tom opened the chocolates. JD, she noticed remained propped up on his mattress, and although he still looked battered and bruised, he did at least look a little less haunted. Joe patted the space next to him on the sofa as an invitation for her to join him. She rolled comfortably into the sag in the middle and it wasn't long before she could feel her face flushing from the heat of the fire – and the wine.

They talked about football, politics, dogs and the house, and they listened to a comedy show on the small portable radio she had brought from the caravan. But nobody talked about their personal lives and she didn't ask. Besides, she would rather not know about the people she would be forced to throw out in mid – or was it the end of January?

It was somewhere round midnight when she discovered she rather liked chocolates and Christmas cake washed down with mugs of warm wine. In fact, by that time, she had come to the happy conclusion that she rather liked her dirty smelly vagrants and their shaggy dog and was wishing she had spent Christmas Day with them rather than her pompous and overbearing brother.

'Cheers!' she toasted her companions sleepily, and the last thing she remembered was Joe covering her muddy boots with his stinking old blanket.

Tom lay on his mattress watching the flames flicker around the kitchen walls. He could hardly believe he'd actually *enjoyed* Christmas day. He'd never enjoyed Christmas day in his life. Although that wasn't strictly true, he conceded. Perhaps when he and his sister were small; before his old man … Pulling his sleeping bag over his head he deliberately switched his thinking back to earlier that day. They'd played cards, read the magazines and newspapers the boss had bought them. Charlie had whistled a tuneless song while he'd cooked the turkey, and then Sarah had arrived.

'Have Christmas dinner with us,' Joe had invited.

Charlie had eyed the girl up warily. 'The boss isn't going to like this, Joe.'

'The boss is away all day and what she doesn't know can't hurt her. There's enough turkey and pudding to go around, isn't there? The lass can at least have a decent Christmas dinner.' He'd squinted at Charlie. 'That is, if it's cooked proper.'

'Cheeky sod,' Charlie had growled but Tom could tell he wasn't really angry.

The only thing that had cast a cloud over Christmas was the recurring image of his fourteen-year-old sister's terrified face when he'd fled from the house.

JD rolled over on his mattress to watch the fire make shadows of the sleeping occupants. He could tell most of them were asleep from their snores. But Tom was awake. He'd seen him tossing and turning earlier. The new girl, Sarah, was also awake; curled up in the corner like a frightened mouse.

It occurred him then that he hadn't given much thought as to what he was supposed to do when Charlie moved on. But then he hadn't given much thought to anything since … well, for a long time. All he'd done was struggle to survive in a world that no longer had any meaning for him. Perhaps all his sleeping companions were the same? Perhaps they were all running away from something or someone. Perhaps?

Chapter 4

Abbie swilled down two Paracetamol with a bottle of water and came to the conclusion that there was absolutely no way she was going to make it through the rest of the day. The continual, thump, thump, thump of her workers dragging sack after sack of chimney rubble down three flights of stairs and the clatter as they hurled it into the iron skip was unbearable. Although, if she was honest, she'd had this darned headache since Christmas Day. Understandable after all the alcohol she'd consumed, she brooded, but the holidays were over now and no amount of pain killers seemed able to shift it. Of course, she hadn't been sleeping too soundly either. The hailstones bouncing off her caravan roof last night had sounded like frozen peas on a drum and kept her awake for most of the night.

She switched on the small battery radio with some vague notion that it might muffle the noise. It didn't; but that was how she failed to hear the knock on the front door. It was the bellowed, 'Hello? Police!' that alerted her.

Police! Her stomach tightened. Rising shakily to her feet she tried to dismiss the flashing images of that awful night when the police arrived to tell her Donald had been killed. She switched off the radio. That was when she realised that all the household noises had stopped. A heavy tread sounded across the hallway. A moment later a burley, middle-aged policeman, oozing authority and with strained uniform buttons suggesting his days of chasing crooks was over, entered her kitchen. He had a pleasantly large face with apple red cheeks and a friendly smile that made his eyes crinkle at the corners.

He must have seen her alarmed expression because his tone was reassuring when he said, 'Nothing to worry about, Mrs Hunter. I'm P.C. Bill Nicholson. Just a routine visit, that's all.' His shrewd blue eyes scanned the pile of dirty dishes in the sink before landing on the mattresses and sleeping bags in the corner. 'I gather you've taken in some of our city's homeless then?'

'Yes. They're clearing the rubbish out for me.'

'As long as that's all they're clearing out.'

'Oh, my personal belongings are quite safe,' she assured him. 'I've locked them in the store-room.'

'Huh-huh! I've never known a locked door deter a thief, Mrs Hunter. Not that I'm suggesting they're thieves, but you never know.' His heavy boots clattered on the floor as he stepped back into the hallway and examined the wide staircase. 'Making it into a hotel your brother told me.'

She leant on the kitchen door watching him. 'Freddy? You've spoken to Freddy?'

'He told us about your er … workers and asked us to keep an eye on the place.'

Abbie pursed her lips. 'I wish he wouldn't interfere,' she said irritably. 'And I suppose you're here to tell me I'm making a big mistake as well?'

He turned to her in astonishment. 'Goodness me, no! It'll be nice to see the old Blue House being licked into shape again.' He ran his fingers lightly over a broken newel on the stairs as if he was investigating a crime scene.

Pleasantly surprised by his approval she asked, 'The old Blue House?'

'That's what the locals call it. The original owners not only painted the front door blue but had a wall of blue rhododendrons stretching from the gate posts to the house.'

'The original owners?'

'Lord and Lady Wheatsheaf. Rich industrialist; made his fortune during the golden reign of Queen Victoria. He owned a cotton factory where the supermarket now stands. Built this house around the 1890's.'

'Wasn't it a hospital at some point? At least that's what the solicitor told me.'

'Aye, it was, during the first and second world wars.' The policeman leant on the banister in a manner that suggested he was about to embark on a history lesson. He was. 'I remember my grandfather telling me that it was Lord and Lady Wheatsheaf's four boys who brought about the hospital. They all fought in the 1914-1918 World War. The eldest two were lost in the trenches, but the two youngest were so mentally and physically broken when they returned that Lady Wheatsheaf and her daughter decided to turn their home into a hospital for wounded military.'

'And Lord Wheatsheaf?'

'Never knew what they were up to, poor man. Died of Spanish flu the same year as his sons returned from war. But then millions died of it. They reckon it had a lot to do with the movement of troops around the world. It swept across Britain like a tsunami and took my great-grandfather with it.' PC Nicholson pushed his cap to the back of his head. 'The Wheatsheaf daughter kept the old Blue House on as a military hospital during the Second World War, but then funds ran out and the NHS came into being.'

'What happened to the Wheatsheaf children?'

The policeman gave a shrug. 'The boys died of their wounds; the daughter never married, and left the house to a pharmaceutical company when she died. Sadly, the place really deteriorated when a succession of smaller companies took it over, then the storm of two thousand and ... whatever, brought the oak tree crashing through the roof.' He paused before patting the banister. 'I always liked this hallway and the sweep of that staircase,' he said admiringly. 'Look at the carvings on those newels – beautiful, absolutely beautiful. I'd guess Lady Wheatsheaf had them specially carved; shame there's a few missing.' He patted the banister again. 'Lovely house you've got here, Mrs Hunter, lovely.'

'Thank you,' she said restraining an irresistible urge to throw her arms around his bulky uniform and kiss him.

The floorboards creaked under his big flat feet as he made his way to the front door. 'Aye, well I just thought I'd pop in to introduce myself as it were and say good luck. Don't hesitate to give me a ring if you have any problems with your er ... work force, will you?'

'I won't, thank you.' And with a brief salute he left and was at the bottom of the drive before the thumping and banging resumed in the house again.

She spent the rest of the morning phoning a lift-manufacturer about installing a lift, booking an electrician, speaking to the gas board, a builder, a glazier and shopping for food. She only got around to thinking about physically working in the house around four o'clock, but by then daylight had faded. Wandering wearily into the dining room she contemplated the mammoth task ahead of her. She was cold, tired, her head ached; her body felt as though it had been dragged through a wringer, and she didn't need scales to tell her she was losing weight. Perhaps she was coming down with something, she brooded. She pulled absently at a torn piece of embossed wallpaper above the dado, and decided it was going to take more than wallpaper stripper to get this stuff off the walls. Her gaze dropped to the dents in the walls below the dado. Bending down she ran her fingers over the dark green paint. There was something rather nostalgic knowing those dints had been caused by hospital beds nudging persistently against the walls. She remained on her haunches, wondering whether any of the soldiers who'd been nursed here were still alive, or whether they even remembered the Blue House.

It was Charlie bellowing, 'Dinner in twenty minutes,' that drove her stiffly to her feet. Making her way over to the door leading into the kitchen, she had her hand on the door knob when something about it caught her attention. It was a simple plain, round knob but it occurred to her it looked suspiciously like … *brass*? She furrowed her brow. Surely not! If it was brass thieves would have absconded with it long ago. Rubbing the mouldy green handle with the sleeve of her jumper she examined it in disbelief. No doubt about it; a brass door handle. She glanced over at the door leading into the hall. It was the same. Brass handles! Unbelievable! For the first time that day her headache took second place to her discovery. Her vision for this room expanded as in her mind's eye she was polishing them up, restoring the grand walnut Victorian fireplace, redecorating the walls in lighter shades, and hanging heavy thick curtains at the long windows. What a wonderfully pleasant dining area this would be, she thought. Probably reminiscent of the days when Lord and Lady Wheatsheaf dined here.

Hugging herself to keep warm she allowed her imagination to fire back over the years and into the life this house used to have. She could almost see Lord and Lady Wheatsheaf, their four sons and their daughter gathered around a highly polished rosewood table. When they had guests, as surely a wealthy industrialist would do, it would be set with silver cutlery, dainty napkins and the best dinner service. Their visitors would be seated on high backed chairs with velvet cushions, laughing as they drank from cut glass wine glasses. Servants would be hovering unobtrusively to serve hot food in silver tureens. They would have had thick red velvet curtains at the windows to keep out the draughts, shimmering candles, and a crackling fire in the grate would have given the dinner party a certain ambience. There would have been laughter, lively conversation, and mild flirtations even. No doubt there'd be an assortment of family photographs sitting in silver frames on the mantelshelf. Pictures of the children at various stages of their lives. Lady Wheatsheaf would have been dressed in …

An unexpected gust of wind rattled the windows and the image faded as quickly as it had materialised. In its place came a deep sadness. It washed over her like an incoming tide as the squalor around her brought her back to reality. There was no highly polished rosewood table was there? No photographs of children. The laughter had long since gone, along with the servants, and a fire had not been lit in that grate for years. Only the torn, faded wallpaper bore witness to the pleasures that had once taken place in this room. All it reflected now was the death of an era long gone, the decay of time, the sad passing of a family… like …like …

Her deliberations unintentionally wandered where she didn't want them to go. To the passing of her own family. There had been times, in the early days of her marriage, when she and Donald had hosted elegant dinner parties. When she had watched him pour wine and laugh with their friends or his business associates. Their mantelshelf too had been filled with photographs of Donald, herself and their baby. But now, she thought bitterly, Donald no longer poured wine for their guests, and those secret smiles he used to throw her when they were in the presence of other people had long since ceased. As for her baby, her lovely baby boy; he no longer gurgled in her arms. Gone ... both of them, along with the guests who had promised to call but never did because they were too embarrassed by ....

It was the frightening silence in her head that brought her face to face with the awful truth. From the day she had put Donald in his grave she had known it. But to acknowledge the shame of it was not an issue she had been ready to look at – until now. But when she did, oddly enough she didn't cry. The last thing she felt like doing was crying. She simply stood in the middle of the cold dark dining room agonising over the shame he had left her with.

It was some time before she realised Charlie was bellowing out his second dinner call.

'Chicken and dumplings folks. Come and get it.'

Still engrossed with her own personal traumas she wandered into the kitchen. She only vaguely noticed that Tom was sitting on the hearth staring into the fire. The dog, who for some strange reason they had named Mutt, was curled up beside him. Charlie was bent over the kitchen range stirring the dinner; Sarah was setting the table and the others were sprawled out reading newspapers. Picking up one of the newspapers she perched on the edge of the couch and stared glassy eyed at the print on the page, trying to stir up an interest in what the rest of the world was doing.

'That fire stinks,' Tom commented to no-one in particular.

'Aye,' Charlie agreed. 'It's not been pulling for a couple of days.'

Discarding his newspaper, Joe struggled to his feet with a grunt. 'Best have a look at it. The chimney 's probably blocked. Shift over, Tom.' Kneeling down he peered up the chimney, his face gradually turning red with the heat. 'Most of these old kitchen ranges had dampers.'

'Hang on! Wait till I've shifted this lot.' Reaching over, Charlie lifted their chicken and dumplings off the hot plate and on to the table.

'Aye, I can see a lever.' Joe picked up the iron bar they'd been using as a poker, thrust it up the chimney and waggled it. Nothing happened. 'What'd you reckon, boss?'

Realising that the problems in this house were actually her responsibility, she grudgingly put down her newspaper and with a sigh knelt down beside Joe and peered up the chimney. 'I don't know, I'm sure, Joe. Give the lever a bang.'

Joe glanced warily at her. 'Dunno about that boss. Last time you started banging things we had smashed windows, fallen plaster, and you nearly killed Tom when 'y hammer ….'

Snatching the iron bar out of his hands, she closed her eyes against the overpowering heat, thrust the bar up the chimney and hammered it fiercely against the lever, three, four times. The hammering rang painfully through her head like the dull clanging tones of a church bell, except that at each strike there was a grinding sound, like cement against cement.

Tom peered up the chimney. 'You've shifted summat, boss; no doubt about …'

It happened so suddenly there was no time to react. There was rumble, as though something was coming down the chimney, before a 'whoosh' of hot ash, soot and flames billowed out into the kitchen. Joe scrambled to his feet in alarm, dragging her with him as shards of burning wood sprayed over them. Tom howled as fiery shards penetrated his hoodie. Mutt fled into the corner. Even JD acted quickly; leaping up to beat out the glowing embers on the floor with his coat. Charlie threw a tea towel over the pan of chicken and dumplings.

'Get out!' he bellowed as smoke filled the kitchen, but no-one needed to be told to run. Joe had already opened the door. Mutt was first out, Charlie last, slamming the door behind him. They stood in the cold dark hallway coughing, spluttering and gasping for air.

'Fire! In the kitchen!' Abbie choked.

Charlie poked his head cautiously around the door. Smoke drifted through into the hallway. 'Nothing's on fire boss, but we need to shovel up the embers in case a spark sets the mattresses alight.'

Holding their hands to their mouths they moved cautiously back into the kitchen wafting away the smoke. Abbie inspected the hearth of her kitchen range. It wasn't only loose bricks and cement that had come down the chimney, but the remains of charred birds, what was left of their nest, and thick lumps of congealed soot.

'Looks like chicken and dumplings are off the menu tonight.' Charlie jerked his head towards the thin film of soot which had added a topping to their chicken dinner.

'I don't suppose we could salvage…' She poked at the mushy mess of chicken, tea towel, soot and dumplings. 'Mmm. Perhaps not.' But then it occurred to her that she was the one responsible for providing food and shelter for her workers. She stood undecided, her brain numbed by pain, pills and tiredness.

'Fish and chips, boss?' Charlie suggested.

No one said that was a good idea, but then no one said it wasn't. They merely switched off the paraffin lamps, snuffed out the candles, made the kitchen safe, then grabbing their outdoor coats, and still coughing, followed Charlie out of the house.

Abbie had never particularly liked the dark winter evenings but tonight she was more than grateful for them. Pulling her hood over her head, as much for protection against the freezing drizzle as from anyone she knew seeing her with her undesirable companions, she led the way down the High Street, past the hairdressers, fruit shop and butchers all closed for the night, to the fish and chip shop. Relieved to find it empty, she stepped inside. It was warm, and bright with mirrored walls and yellow plastic tables.

'Seven cod and chips with mushy peas, please.' Fumbling with the zip of her anorak pocket she added, 'And do you mind if we pull a couple of tables together?'

It was the stony silence from behind the counter that warned her something wasn't right. Glancing up she was alarmed to see an expression of utter contempt etched across the fish and chip man's face. He was a bald-headed man with a round gut hanging over his apron.

He pointed to their mongrel. 'Dogs not allowed.'

Tom hastily opened the door and kicked Mutt outside. The animal stood looking through the window whining pitifully.

'Seven fish and chips?' There was an edge to his voice which she didn't like. 'Can you pay for it?'

'Of course, I can pay,' she said indignantly and tugged at the unyielding zip of her coat.

'Huh-Huh! Then you'll have to take it outside. I can't have the likes of you lot in here. I'd lose my custom.'

'What do you mean, "You lot"? I'm ...' Her voice trailed off as she caught sight of her workers in the mirrored tiles. They had more soot over them than a chimney sweep. Tom's hoodie was singed, JD's coat was blackened and ... She breathed in fiercely as she caught a glimpse of her own reflection. Not only did she have streaks of black running down her face but there were lumps of soot in her hair, and clinging to her anorak, jeans, and hands. Squaring her shoulders in an attempt to regain some form of composure she said, 'Then we'll have them to take away?'

'Let's see your money first.'

She took a deep breath. 'Right!' She knew she shouldn't tug so fiercely at the unyielding zip on her anorak, but she was embarrassed, so she did. The pocket ripped. Cringing, she thrust her fingers through the rip, pulled out four £20 notes and handed them over. The fish and chip man snatched the money from her hand, rang it through the till and slammed the change on to the counter. Unable to think of a thing to say she stood in an awkward silence watching him shuffling fish and chips into individual polythene cartons before drowning them in salt and vinegar. Common sense told her she ought to assert herself; justify her standing in society. In her head she was shouting, 'I'm not a *vagrant* like them you stupid moron! I'm a professional woman. I'm a dentist. I have a house, a car, I have money.' But she didn't, she couldn't. Her tongue seemed to be clamped to the roof of her mouth, and the truth was, she thought, she was no longer a dentist or a professional woman, was she? She wasn't even a wife or mother any more. She no longer wore fashionable clothes or had a fashionable home. She was .... what? What was she? Who was she? She had lost her identity. She was ... nobody. A heaviness landed in her chest as though someone had slammed a paving slab on top of her making it difficult for her to breathe. Silently handing the cartons over to her work-force she followed them outside into the rain.

'Best eat in the underpass or the fish and chips'll get wet, boss,' Joe instructed.

Wordlessly, she trailed after Joe, shivering as a biting wind whistled down the steps of the underpass after them. Tom, with only his thin charred hoodie for warmth, was shaking uncontrollably. Halfway along the tunnel Joe stopped, slid down the wall and crossed his legs. The others followed suite. Abbie sat in the middle feeling like one in a line of coconuts at a fair stall waiting to be shot down. Opening her carton, she began picking at the hot, greasy fish and chips with her black broken fingernails. She did her best to ignore the expressions of disgust by passing pedestrians but it wasn't easy. She knew what they were thinking, and she was ashamed to admit she'd had the same thoughts herself at times. Why don't these people get a job? Why don't they claim benefits? It's probably their own fault they're in such a predicament. Drugs? Drink? Why don't they go to a shelter instead of littering up public pavements?

'Come on folks, move on. You know better than to camp out here.'

PC Bill Nicholson was sauntering down the steps of the underpass towards them. She lowered her head, trying to be inconspicuous. Move on? *Move on?* The law had never moved her on in her life! Her workers struggled to their feet with their polythene cartons, quite unperturbed by the order, but then this was probably a normal occurrence for them. She stood up, hiding behind Charlie as best she could, but then she had the strangest sensation that someone else had managed to get into her body. This filthy dirty creature, smelling of smoke, rejected by humanity, couldn't possibly be her. It couldn't!

'Church doorway.' Joe instructed, and without argument they made their way up the underpass steps to the church doorway, and all the while she tried to ignore the fact that she was now trailing aimlessly around the streets like ... like a *vagrant!*

The steady rainfall which had accompanied them since leaving the house had now developed into an unexpected squall, so that by the time they reached the church doorway it had already soaked through their clothes. Abbie pressed her cold wet body up against the thick wooden doors and slid down on to a step worn from use by worshippers of years long gone. She stared up at the black decorative wrought iron hinges sprawling towards the latch. There wasn't an inch of rust on them, as though some church member regularly cared for the entrance to their church. A sign on the notice board read, '*God is Love*' in bold red capitals. She squeezed her eyes shut, willing herself to feel love, pain, cold; anything but this awful raw numbness.

Joe was chomping his gums in a manner that suggested he was thoroughly enjoying his fish and chips and was quite unperturbed by the conditions, but the last thing she felt like was food. Running her tongue around her cracked lips she was surprised to find them wet, not with rain but with salty tears mixed with soot, but she couldn't remember when she had started to cry. Numbly, she watched her teardrops fall into her fish and chips leaving a congealed black mess in the polythene carton.

'You shouldn't have let my family die, God!' She was shocked by the unexpected surge of anger, and was vaguely aware that her companions had stopped eating and were looking worried by her sudden outburst. Her sobs were growing louder now but there was nothing she could do about it. *'Donald abandoned me, He a b a n d o n e d me.!'*

Her shoulders shuddered and her fish and chips splattered to the ground as she found herself, once again, standing at Donald's graveside with the mourners staring in her direction. Their pitying looks, their wary expressions, their whispered, 'Do you think she knew?' had been the most humiliating experience of her life and would stay with her till the day she died. She knew that. Her weeping was uncontrollable now. It was as bad as the morning she had found her baby boy, white, still and ... dead. Cot death', the doctor had diagnosed.

She moaned as she rocked herself backwards and forwards, vaguely aware that Joe had grasped her hand. And somewhere at the back of her mind she realised he was possibly the only other person in the world who understood what it was like to lose a child, so she clung to him. There was a smell of alcohol, soot and pee about him but she didn't mind.

'Best we go home, boss,' he said gently.

He and Charlie helped her stand up, but her legs were so wet, cold and stiff she could barely put one foot in front of the other, and she couldn't stop crying. Charlie and JD half carried; half dragged her between them. She was vaguely aware that passers-by were staring at them but she neither cared nor wanted their help. No one wanted to be involved anyway, not with what they perceived as dirty homeless vagrants.

She hadn't realised they had reached the caravan until Sarah was rummaging through her anorak pockets for the key. She let her. Her own fingers were too stiff with cold. Then they hauled her inside. The caravan vibrated with movement as Charlie lit the lights, Tom put the kettle on, and she was still sobbing. At some point the men left. Where to she had no idea. Sarah began pulling off her wet clothes, wrapping a quilt around her frozen body, putting her to bed, and by then her crying had reduced to the odd shuddering sob.

She lay on her bed cocooned in her quilt. A faint draught momentarily swept through the caravan as the men came back. She listened to them whispering, excluding her, yet including her because she knew they were talking about her. Someone helped her sit up and a mug of hot sweet tea was thrust into her hands, but they trembled so much that Sarah had to hold it for her. Charlie handed her a couple of pills from a packet. She had no idea what they were, but she took them anyway. Then she rolled back on to her bed with her face to the wall.

The gaslights were hissing, the chill was lifting from the caravan, and it shuddered as her companions moved around, doing what she no longer cared. Mutt jumped on to the bed and curled around her feet and there was a smell of wet dog, wet clothes, brewed tea and soot, and the odd thing was, she found it strangely comforting.

Someone threw a blanket over her and she realised that she had stopped crying. She closed her eyes because they were heavy but her sooty lashes stuck together. She told herself it didn't matter, nothing mattered any more, and if the vagrants were going to rob her, or murder her in her bed, now was the time to do it. But she knew they wouldn't, not tonight, and it was that comforting thought that drew her into an exhausted sleep.

The following morning, she surfaced sluggishly from what felt like a drug induced sleep, and lay for a while, too exhausted to move. But as the fog gradually lifted from her brain the humiliating images of the previous evening emerged. With a groan she rolled over, pulling the quilt around her body like a chrysalis in a cocoon. For months now she had portrayed a brave face to the world to prove what; to herself, to Freddy and her so called friends that she could cope with the deaths of her husband, her child - *and* the scandal? Well, last night, she had proved that she couldn't, could she?

Brass handles!

She blinked rapidly, wondering how, in the midst of a nervous breakdown, brass handles should come to mind. And then she remembered. It was finding those wretched brass door handles that had started last night's ... trauma off. It had been imagining Lord and Lady Wheatsheaf and their family in the dining room that had reminded her of the loss of her own family.

She buried her head in the quilt as the heavy weight of grief rose to the surface. She had been numbed and shocked in the days that followed her baby boy's death and had agonized over whether she could have done something to prevent it; whether she had been in any way to blame. But there had been no time to come to a conclusion, no time to grieve, because less than three weeks later had come Donald's devastating accident …

Finding she needed air she emerged from the quilt gasping. She barely noticed the cold air in the caravan as in her mind's eye she was standing at her husband's graveside again. Everyone was staring in her direction with those pitying looks that mourners tend to have. She could still sense their unspoken comments. "How awful for her; finding out like this." "Do you think she guessed they'd been having an affair?" "Do you think she knew he'd been planning to leave her?" She had wanted to scream, 'No! No! No! I didn't know! How could I have known? I thought we were happy.' In fact, if Donald hadn't said he had to go on an important business trip she would never have known. He had even given her the impression he was concerned over having to leave her so soon after losing their child, but as he promised he'd only be gone for three days she had convinced him she didn't mind. It was when his car had crashed that the awful truth came out. Her best friend had been in the passenger seat when it happened. She and Donald, she discovered, had been having an affair for two years; *two years*! How had she not known? *How*?

Freddy kept telling her to ignore the gossip, put the past behind her and move on but from the moment the truth came out she had felt an overwhelming sense of failure. She hated that word, 'failure' but that's what she had felt like; a failure, she thought bitterly. She couldn't hold on to her marriage; she couldn't hold on to her baby; she couldn't hold on to her best friend, and she couldn't even be a decent Christian and forgive them. What madness made her think she could renovate this old house and turn it into …?'

'I see it! I see it!'

It was the excitable yells in the garden that pulled her away from sinking any lower into her pit of depression. Her curiosity aroused, she rested on her elbow, pulled open the curtain at the head of her bed and was instantly blinded by the bright morning sunshine. It was one of those rare, crisp January days with white fluffy clouds drifting across a pale blue sky. But it wasn't the weather that was her main focus of attention. It was the wire brush waving wildly out of her kitchen chimney pot.

'It's out! It's out!' Tom was bouncing up and down excitedly pointing at the wire brush. It was jiggling around like a dancer sending clouds of black soot across the neighbourhood. 'Pull it back! Pull it back!' he yelled.

Knowing she ought to get up and take control of the situation she swung her legs over the bed, shivering as the cold air wrapped itself around them. Dragging the duvet around her shoulders, she shook the kettle on the gas ring to check it was full. It was. Lighting the gas under it she jumped back into bed.

There was a timid knock on her caravan door before it opened and a multi-coloured pom-pom hat appeared. It was Sarah. 'Just say if you want to be alone, but I saw your curtains open. Do you want me to come in and make you a cuppa?'

'Yes, come in.' Abbie dragged herself into a sitting position but still embarrassed over the previous evening, avoided eye contact. 'What time is it?' Her voice had a crackle to it. She gave a cough to clear it then grimaced as a lump of sooty phlegm materialised.

'Midday.'

'What! Midday? I've been asleep for twelve hours?'

'I guess so.' Sarah closed the door behind her. 'How are you feeling?'

'Better, I think. Did er ... did you all have to sleep in er ... the kitchen?'

'It was cold and the mattresses were sooty but there's worse places.'

'Really?' She glanced up and saw Sarah was smiling. The kettle began to whistle.

'I'll make you tea, shall I?'

'Yes please.' Abbie loosened the quilt from around her shoulders as the gas ring warmed up the caravan. 'Sarah, why is there a brush sticking out of my chimney?'

'Ah! Yes.' Sarah popped a tea bag into a mug and poured boiling water on top. 'Joe went to see the builder, Barry Matthews, and told him we'd had a fall of soot. Barry gave him the name of a chimney sweep, but Joe reckoned a chimney sweep would be too expensive, and that he could do the job himself. So, Barry gave him a brush and poles and said he'd put it on your bill.'

She took a sip of tea. 'I thought they used electric sweepers these days?'

'They do, but we don't have electricity, do we?'

'Ah! Of course.'

'Charlie asked Joe if he knew what he was doing but all Joe said was, "How difficult can it be to sweep a chimney?"'

Abbie viewed the thick billows of soot drifting up Grange Avenue with some misgivings and hoped she had understanding neighbours. She cleared her throat. 'I'd ... er ... like to say ... thank you for last night, Sarah.'

'No problem.'

Abbie ran her fingers through her hair leaving a black film of soot on them. She wiped it off on a sheet already black and sooty.

'I could go to the laundrette for you,' Sarah offered. 'I could also wash your hair if you like. I'm a hairdresser.' She gave an embarrassed laugh. 'Or rather I was before ....'

A loud clatter from the front of the caravan made Abbie jump.

'Don't worry. That's just Charlie fixing a new gas bottle. We had to leave the gas on last night to dry you out.' But then that guilty expression reappeared. 'I'm afraid we had to take money out of your purse to pay for it but... but I've left the receipt and the change on the kitchen table, and Charlie says he'll cook you a meal when you wake up.'

And it was the simple fact that she was being lovingly cared for that brought the first smile to her face.

Chapter 5

The weatherman's sober tones caught Abbie's attention so she turned up her small battery radio. '... *and according to weather records, January has been the wettest month in ten years.*'

'No need to tell me, mate. The water's pouring in through the hole in my roof.' She threw the crust of her toast to Mutt who was drooling at her feet under the kitchen table. 'And what's the point of having scaffolding up if I can't get a roofer?' she asked him then brushed her hands vigorously together as though that would get rid of her problems. 'Take it easy, the doctor said. Take it easy? Huh! How am I supposed to take it easy when I'm in the middle of renovating an old house?'

Mutt twitched his ears sympathetically.

Delayed grief had been the doctor's diagnosis. But then she could have told him that. He was a neat, precise, careful little man with rimmed glasses perched on the edge of a thin pointed nose. He had been her and Freddy's doctor all their lives.

'I haven't been sleeping properly since ... since losing my baby,' she had blubbered. 'But then losing my husband and discovering my marriage had been nothing more than a ... a sham... and that the woman he was having an affair with was my best ... friend ...' She had blown her nose, more to shut herself up than anything. 'Anyway, I know it sounds ridiculous, but I think what triggered this ... episode off was imagining the dinner parties the Victorian owners of my house must have had. It sparked off memories of the dinner parties Donald and I ...' She blew her nose again. 'Now I suppose you're going to tell me I'm being over imaginative as well as a fool for renovating an old house in my state of mind?'

'Am I?' He had peered kindly at her over his spectacles. 'I don't think you're being over imaginative or a fool.' He had steepled his fingers thoughtfully. 'Take your fall of soot for instance. Loose bricks, soot and birds' nests had been stuck up that chimney for goodness knows how long, but eventually the density of it prevented the fire from functioning properly - until you banged on the damper and dislodged it. Likewise, there are times when the grieving process gets stuck. It doesn't move on the way it should because other traumatic incidents in life pile up and cause a blockage. Sometimes it can be years before it's released. And perhaps you're right. Imagining your Victorian family dining together could have dislodged your blockage. It certainly made you face the stark reality of the last few months. And that's good. As for you renovating an old house; if a challenge and a complete change of lifestyle is what you want to help you move on, fine! But a word of caution; you've been through quite an ordeal in recent months, so while you're rebuilding your life – and your house - don't overdo it; be kind to yourself. You're on a journey of healing so take it slow and easy, eh?'

His comments had sounded feasible and comforting, she decided and she had felt better for having talked the problem through with him and realising she wasn't going totally mad. But then he had suggested bereavement counselling, given her pills and ordered rest. She declined the counselling, took the pills, promised she would take it easy and swore him to patient doctor confidentiality as far as Freddy was concerned. But now, listening to the weatherman forecasting worsening conditions for February, a sinking feeling was growing in the pit of her stomach. And she knew why. She had promised her workers they could stay till the end of January, but the very idea of having to throw them back on the streets in what was forecast as atrocious weather was causing her problems. How could she, after all they had done for her? It was Joe who had organised a working schedule for the others when all she had done was curl up in her caravan and sleep; Joe who had plucked up the courage to visit his prosperous mate, Barry Matthews, the builder, and ask for tools to sweep her chimney. And Joe who had organised the scaffolding for the so far non-existent roofer while he doggedly continued retiling the outhouse roof.

And what would happen to Big Ben on the streets, she brooded? Poor lad would never cope. And Charlie? She had grown accustomed to her ex-con's cheerful whistle and lively banter echoing around the house. She would miss that – and she would certainly miss his cooking. And how in good conscience could she throw Tom out? The lad would probably end up on drugs if he was forced back on to the streets. As for Sarah; she had washed dishes, sooty blankets and sleeping bags; she had shopped, cleared rubbish, fed her countless cups of tea, made sure her caravan was warm and that she rested. Abbie's brow clouded over as her thoughts drifted to JD. His face was still discoloured and his throat still swollen so he was a silent worker, but there was a quiet steadiness to his work that she found reassuring. Yes, she brooded nursing her empty mug. Throwing her workers out of the Blue House was going to be a nightmare.

A blast of cold air followed Abbie into the kitchen. Slamming the door behind her she stood with her arms wrapped around herself, shivering. There was a playful banter going on between Charlie and Tom who were sitting at the kitchen table accusing each other of cheating at cards. Sarah looked up briefly and smiled as she tidied up and the others were either reading separate pages of the newspaper or snoozing.

Charlie dragged his eyes away from his cards. 'Thought you'd gone to bed, boss?'

'I had but I couldn't settle.' Dragging one of the chairs over to the fire, she sat down beside Joe. Stretching her hands out to the flames she said, 'I have questions I need to ask.'

'You have? Then fire away boss,' Charlie invited. 'We're all ears.'

She turned to Joe. 'Why don't you claim benefits, Joe?'

Joe blinked rapidly. 'Eh?'

Charlie gave a snort. 'Don't tell me that old sot's benefits are what's keeping you awake, boss?'

She ignored him. 'Benefits Joe. Why don't you claim them?'

'Cos ... it's complicated.'

'How's it complicated?'

'It's the system what's complicated.'

'What do you mean? Even if you're homeless, you're entitled to something, surely?'

'Yes, but you need an address. I was told I could use a friend's address, a hostel or day centre but everyone I know is in the same boat as me, homeless. Besides, I don't have no bank account no more – and ... ' he sniffed. 'Anyway, it's ... complicated.'

Charlie's chair scraped across the kitchen floor. 'What he means is, he can't understand it boss.' Making his way over to the fire he shovelled more coal on to it.

'So, what do you do for food, Joe?'

Joe watched the flames disappear under the black lumps of coal before answering. 'The Sally Army'll give you a shower and a meal but you've got to wait till they open at five o'clock. Then there's not always room and you've got to be off real early next morning. Asides which, they put a limit on how long you can stay. I know where the soup kitchens are, and there's a day care shelter near the arches but I had stuff nicked there once. Don't go there no more.' The old man's jaw muscles drooped and his eyes suddenly looked sad. Leaning forward he stretched out his hands to the struggling flames. Clearly, talking about his life on the streets was upsetting.

'Daft old sot likes it here, don't you, Joe,' Charlie intervened with a grin.

'Aye, I do that,' the old man said softly. 'I like sitting by the hearth of a night, having warm feet, good company and being fed proper food. Even a lumpy settee stinking of soot is luxury compared to a cold concrete pavement. Being homeless in the winter is hell, I can tell y'. The dampness seeps summat terrible into 'y bones.' Averting his gaze from the struggling flames, he narrowed his eyes at her. 'Why all the questions, boss?'

'I had an idea, that's all.'

'Good for you, boss.' Charlie shuffled his cards.

'When Barry Matthews came to erect the scaffolding, he examined the outhouse roof and reckoned you'd made a darn good job of it, Joe. He told me that although you're a roofer by trade you started off as a bricky but you've also had experience as a plasterer. In his opinion, you could turn your hand to almost anything.'

'Barry said that, did he?' Joe gave a sniff of pride. 'Aye, it's true. Been in the building trade since I was Tom's age.'

'Really? Then I have a proposition for you.'

Charlie gave a chuckle. 'You must be pretty desperate to proposition that old soak boss.'

She gave him a withering look before turning back to Joe. 'As I was saying, a proposition, but there are conditions.'

'Aye?' the old man eyed her nervously.

'If you think you can rebuild my chimney, tile the roof of my house and build a well in the cellar for a lift then you can stay till the weather warms up.'

She was suddenly aware that she had everyone's attention. Joe licked his lips. 'And the conditions?'

Abbie gave a long sigh. 'I'll be honest with you, Joe. It's you drinking that worries me. If Health and Safety discover I'm allowing an alcoholic up my scaffolding they'll close me down before I've had a chance to open. So, my condition is, you get help from Alcoholics Anonymous.'

Joe rubbed his whiskered chin. 'Done A.A. Didn't work.'

'That's a shame, because that's one of the conditions for keeping you on. I've even picked up a leaflet telling me when and where the local branch meet.' Pulling a leaflet out of her jeans pocket she handed it to him. Joe studied the leaflet apprehensively. 'I know it won't be easy, Joe but we'll all support you.'

The silence was so pronounced it was almost as loud as a shout.

'*We* boss?' Charlie quietly asked. 'Are you saying you'd keep us all on?'

Dragging a crumpled sheet of paper out of the pocket of her jeans she handed it to him. 'Only till Easter and the weather warms up, and only *if* you can do the work on this list.'

Charlie snatched the paper out of her hand. Joe still appeared to be weighing up the odds. 'I suppose I could try AA again, but I canna promise nowt boss.'

Charlie's long thick finger stabbed at the list. 'I can knock fireplaces out.'

'You've knocked fireplaces out before, have you, Charlie?'

'No. But how difficult can it be to smash a fireplace up?'

To her surprise it was JD who answered. His voice was husky, barely above a whisper and he cleared his throat after every few words. 'Did you know, the fireplaces on the top floor are cast iron, Victorian. They'll be valuable. The Adams fireplaces downstairs are even more valuable.' This was probably the longest sentence she had ever heard from him and to her surprise he was extremely well spoken.

Joe studied him thoughtfully. 'You seem to know a hell of a lot about fireplaces fella?' He wiped the sleeve of his jumper across his nose and adopted a knowledgeable air. 'Aye, well, knocking fireplaces out isn't the problem. It's blocking up the opening that's the difficult bit. You need to know what you're doing.'

'Would you know what you were doing, Joe?' Abbie asked.

'Aye.' He chewed on his gums. 'Me and Barry Matthews knocked a whole terrace of fireplaces out once. I reckon Charlie and JD could manage a job like that if I showed them how.' The old man squared his shoulders, and the years seemed to drop off him as he picked up a lifetime of experience in the building trade. 'Aye, I can keep the lads in hand, boss.' He gave a sniff of self-importance as he officially established himself in the role of site foreman.

'Count me in,' Tom said eagerly.

'And me.' Sarah added. 'I can strip wallpaper, sand down paintwork, shop, anything.' She looked pointedly at JD who was still gazing into the fire. He shrugged his shoulders noncommittally.

'So, the pay's lousy, there's no set contract, the sleeping accommodation's terrible but on the positive side, you'll have food and shelter, a temporary address you can use to claim benefits, and if we pull together there'll be enough work to keep you here till spring.' But then her face clouded over. 'However, I will need you to work. I haven't got an endless pot of money and if you slack off, and I'm forced to call in builders and tradesmen, you'll have to go.' Then, quietly to herself she added, 'And I suppose all I have to worry about now is how much of this I should explain to the tax man, the employment agency, National Insurance, Health and Safety – and … Ah!' She raised her voice and her finger to regain their attention. 'There's one other condition.' She could almost hear them holding their breath. 'You avoid my brother Freddy at all costs.'

There was an audible sigh of relief around the kitchen. *That* they could do.

She knew exactly where she would find Big Ben; in the garden. He was always in the garden. This morning he was raking out mounds of leaves from under the bushes near the house. He was perfectly happy if left to his own devices but didn't seem to mind too much if Charlie or Joe called him into the house when they needed extra muscles for lifting. In fact, he seemed quite proud of the fact that they needed him. She watched him raking for a while before it dawned on her that she had been so busy concentrating on renovating her house that she had failed to notice the transformation that had been taking place in her garden. One side of the drive, from the tall pillars almost to the house itself, had been completely cleared of leaves, twigs, weeds and debris of years gone by. Big Ben had not only cut off dead branches and cut back bushes but made that whole side of the garden light and spacious.

'Goodness! Are those snowdrops I see peeping through, Ben?'

Startled by her sudden appearance he stopped work and looked at her blankly.

'And look, are those daffodil shoots pushing through over there?'

He gave a snort of amusement. 'They're crocuses, not daffodils,' he informed her.

'Ah! Yes! Of course.' She stood looking at the garden wondering how to continue the conversation. Eventually she asked, 'Do you like it here, Ben?'

He nodded.

'What do you like about it?'

He twirled the rake in his hand and looked heavenward as he thought. 'The food; the garden; and no one bullies me.'

'You've been bullied? When?'

'At school.'

'Why?'

'They said I was different.'

Abbie pursed her lips. 'Ignorance makes people afraid of what they don't understand, Ben.'

'My mother said that.'

'She did?'

Ben nodded, 'She told me, autism doesn't mean I have no brain. It just means my brain works differently, but it can also understand things that other people can't.'

'Wise woman,' Abbie murmured. 'What happened to your mother, Ben?'

His face clouded over and he stared down at his rake. 'She died.'

'Didn't Social Services look after you?'

'The Social Worker assessed me. She told Aunty that because I didn't have a severe mental health issue I couldn't go into a special home. She said I was one of those people who had fallen through the mental health gap, but I've no idea what she'd meant by that because I don't remember falling through anything.'

Abbie curbed a smile. 'What happened?'

'Aunty moved me to a bedsit near her.'

'Can you take care of yourself?'

'Mother taught me to cook, but aunty thought I was buying junk food, so she gave me a shopping list.' He frowned crossly. 'I bought salmon. I like salmon so I saved it for a special occasion. But when Aunty opened my fridge, she wrinkled her nose and threw it in the bin. I'd only had it three weeks.'

'Oh dear! What happened to Aunty, Ben?'

'My cousin took her away to live with her because she forgot things. She forgot to make an appointment for me with the chiropodist, so my nails grew long and black and bled when they broke off. Then she forgot to tell Social Services we'd moved.'

'How did you manage for money?'

Ben shrugged. 'I lost the plastic card that I push in the slot for my money. That's when I went to the soup kitchen and met Joe.' He shuffled uneasily, and Abbie could see he was beginning to be troubled by all the questions. 'Anyway, I have to tidy up,' he said abruptly and would have moved away if Abbie hadn't caught the sleeve of his coat. Alarmed, he stepped sharply back loosening her grip.

'Sorry, Ben. I … I … the others are all staying till spring. Would you like to stay?'

He frowned at her. 'Of course! I haven't finished the garden yet.'

As she watched Big Ben's long lumbering strides towards the house, it dawned on her that this was probably the longest conversation she had ever had with him. Now all she had to do was find time to renew his benefits, then find JD to see if he was staying on.

With the sigh of someone who has been handed an endless list of jobs, she grabbed this brief moment of respite, and lifting her face up to the lukewarm sun listened to the hum of traffic on the dual carriageway; a hum because its roar was muted by the trees, bushes and the high wall. It was odd to have the house so quiet, she mused. For once, no-one was clattering rubble downstairs, and there was no cussing or arguing. Sarah was at the supermarket, Tom and JD were sweeping chimneys in the attic, and it was Charlie's turn to taken Joe to what he called his 'drink club', otherwise known as Alcoholics Anonymous. They had decided amongst themselves that left to his own devices Joe would probably make a detour via the pub, and they were worried that if he was fired then they'd all be. So, having been forced into taking a bath in an old tub they found in the outhouse, and having Sarah trim his hair and beard, Joe had proudly set off wearing a new thick worker's shirt, trousers, boots and checked jacket - compliments of his employer - to give him an air of respectability. The outfit also included a bright yellow hard hat which he had insisted on wearing to his drink club.

It was the swish of car tyres turning into the driveway that made her open her eyes. Her heart sank as Freddy's silver Audi pulled up alongside her.

'Hi!' She greeted him. 'Come to check up on me?'

'Not at all,' he answered switching off the engine. 'Has the Building Inspector been yet?'

'Yes, he has. He introduced himself and told me about his staged visits.'

'Good.' Stepping out of the car Freddy leaned on the open door and surveyed the scaffolding around the front of the house with a critical eye. 'Your roofer has found a good brick match for that chimney.'

'Yes, he ....' Following Freddy's line of vision her eyes widened in alarm at the sight of Big Ben stretching precariously over the top of the scaffolding cutting back the overgrown ivy. 'Ah! Yes! He er ... came highly recommended from Barry Matthews.'

At that precise moment, the highly recommended man in question materialised at the bottom of the drive looking quite the professional in his new clothes and yellow hard hat. His minder, Charlie, was with him. Her mind scrambled around for a feasible explanation. 'Actually ... er ... that's not my roofer on the scaffolding, Freddy. It's my gardener.'

Freddy frowned towards the roof. 'What's your gardener doing up the scaffolding?'

'Obviously, he's cutting back the ivy for the roofer,' she answered primly. Raising her voice she called, 'Charlie! Would you tell the gardener there's work to be done in the back garden while I talk to *Freddy*.' She jerked her head towards the scaffolding. It took Charlie only seconds to assess the situation. His expression changed to one of alarm, but to her relief all he did was raised his hand as indication he understood and walk smartly towards the scaffolding.

Taking Freddy's arm, Abbie spun him away from the action. 'That's my roofer,' she said pointing to Joe and hoping Freddy wouldn't remember him as the shabby vagrant he had encountered slurping soup at her kitchen table before Christmas. Blithely unaware of anything amiss, Joe was ambling up the drive as though he'd spent a leisurely afternoon playing bowls instead of at Alcoholics Anonymous.

'You've done a good job finding a matching brick for that chimney,' Freddy commented.

'Eh?'

'Freddy's an architect so he knows a good roofer when he sees one,' she explained Her eyes slithered towards Charlie climbing rapidly up the scaffolding after Big Ben.

'That's kind of 'ya.' Her roofer pummelled Freddy's outstretched hand.

'There's a fresh brew of tea in the kitchen, Joe.' She gave a firm jerk of her head.

Her roofer hesitated, pointedly waiting for more acclaim, but seeing her scowl deepen he wiped his nose across the sleeve of his new jacket and headed towards the house.

Freddy waited until he was out of earshot before asking, 'Who was that rough looking character with him?'

'Ah! That's Charlie; he's er.... he's taking the fireplaces out for me.' A surreptitious glance over Freddy's shoulder assured her that her fireplace remover had reached her gardener and appeared to be trying to persuade him that leaning precariously over scaffolding with a pair of sharp secateurs was not a good idea.

That was when Sarah arrived with the shopping.

'Have you found an electrician yet?' Freddy asked.

'Sort of.'

'What do you mean, 'sort of'? You either have or you haven't.'

'I have but he's never here. I think he's keeping another job going alongside ours.'

'I'll sort him out for you.'

'Thank you, Freddy, but I'd rather do it myself.'

'Huh!' Freddy drummed his fingers on the side of his car. 'So, there are no major problems then?'

'None I can think of.' She tried to lightly in an attempt to curb a squeak of alarm when her gardener, hands up to show he flatly refused to climb down the ladder, backed towards the edge of the scaffolding. Sarah arrived laden with shopping, her eyes a narrow slit between her hat and scarf.

'Who was that?' Freddy mouthed when she had passed them.

'Sarah. I er … decided to employ a housekeeper for er … shopping and household jobs.'

The breath going through Freddy's nose whistled faintly as he pondered on the comings and goings on site. 'Surprisingly enough, you seem to have your tradesmen well organised, Abs. And the plumber?'

A plumber! *She'd forgotten to get a plumber*! 'Sorted,' she lied.

'Who?'

'I can't remember his name off hand.'

'As long as it isn't Susan's father. He's just got out of hospital and we don't want him going back to work yet.' Freddy's fingers continued drumming on the window of his car. 'So, you'll call me if you need me then?'

'I will.' She pecked him on the cheek, noticing over his shoulder that Charlie had managed to get Big Ben's foot on the ladder. All he had to do now was climb down.

'Good. Come for dinner this Sunday.' As usual, Freddy made it sound like an order rather than an invitation.

'Thank you, Freddy.' She firmly resisted the urge to manhandle him smartly back into his Audi before anything else occurred. Fortunately, he was pulling out of the drive before the sound of raised voices warned her there was trouble brewing inside the house. Running up the drive she vaguely registered that Big Ben and Charlie were now halfway down the ladder, but having heard the rumpus in the house, Charlie had obviously decided their gardener could manage the rest of the journey himself, so her chef-cum-fireplace remover was now skimming down the ladder like a fireman's pole. As she raced inside, she heard his heavy boots thudding in the hallway behind her, and Tom and JD's feet clattering down the stairs. Flinging open the kitchen door she found Sarah cowering by the dresser, her arms over her head. Joe was standing over her, the iron poker raised.

Abbie screamed, *'Joe!'* but in three long strides Charlie had crossed the kitchen, grabbed the poker out of his hand and twisted the old man's arm behind his back.

'Leave off her y' drunken old sot.'

'Mind 'y ...!' Joe gave him a violent kick on his shin with his new hard tipped boots. Their chef swore, and clenching his fist delivered a sharp punch to the old man's jaw. Joe staggered back. Unfazed, he lowered his head, and with a roar charged Charlie like a rampant bull with a yellow hard hat.

JD dived in between them but Charlie shoved him roughly aside. Darting over to the fire, Abbie grabbed the coal shovel and banged it on the kitchen table sending clouds of dust into the air. 'Stop it! Stop it! Or I'll fire the lot of you,' she bellowed.

The fighting stopped so abruptly it reminded her of the game of 'statues' she used to play when she was in the Brownies. No one spoke, no one moved. It was like a still picture shot. Joe was the first one to react. His shoulders sagged. Staggering over to the kitchen chair he sank down. 'I need a drink.'

Abbie found her hands were trembling. 'No, you don't, Joe.'

Sarah scrambled to her feet. 'This is all my fault,' she said shakily. 'I thought I'd wash Joe's old clothes while he was wearing his new ones.'

Joe glowered at her. 'They're *my* clothes. Stupid bitch! Now the coat 'll have no shape, the jumper 'll have washed out and the pants 'll have shrunk.'

Charlie wiped the dust off the kitchen table with the damp dishcloth. 'Y' daft old goat. That coat never had any shape in the first place, there were more holes in that jumper, than jumper, and I've never smelt anything as bad as the pee on your pants.'

Joe stared sullenly at him. 'I need a drink,' he repeated.

Charlie thrust a mug and a teabag angrily towards him.

'I mean a real drink. If this drink club was working how come I lost it cos my clothes have been washed? My nerves are all on edge. ' Joe dropped his head in his hands and his yellow hard-hat slipped down to his nose. 'I'm not like Charlie here. I'm not violent, and I've *never* raised a hand to a woman in my life. That's what coming off the drink does for you.' He pushed his yellow hard hat to the back of his head. 'I didn't mean to get mad at you lass. I'll get back on the drink and I'll be fine.'

'No, you won't.' Pouring boiling water into the mug, Charlie thrust the tea across the kitchen table towards him. Some of it slopped over the edge.

'Tea's no cure,' Joe said sullenly.

Charlie studied the roofer carefully before lifting a jar of honey from their groceries on the dresser and banging it on the table. 'Not on its own, no, but adding honey is.'

'Eh?'

'Trust me. I'm a chef. I know about these things.'

Joe sniffed in disbelief, but Abbie noticed he picked up the honey jar and studied the label anyway. 'Tea with honey? Why haven't they mentioned that at the drink club then?'

'It's a trade secret.'

Joe squinted at the label. 'Get off! Doesn't say nowt about that here.'

'Course not 'y stupid old sot. I told you. It's a trade secret. Imagine the rush on honey if all the drunks knew about it. The bees 'd never be able to keep up production.'

Abbie struggled to keep a straight face as Joe began to read the small print on the label. 'Trade secret, eh?'

'Yeh! Me telling 'y about it; call it a peace offering.'

'Yeh?' Opening the jar, Joe hesitantly spooned a large dollop of honey into his tea.

'I'm sorry, Joe,' Sarah said in a small voice.

'That's OK me luv.' Joe watched the honey dissolve in the tea. 'They probably needed a wash anyway.'

Abbie flopped down on one of the sofas overcome by a sudden wave of exhaustion. 'Thank goodness we've got that ... ' With a gasp she leapt to her feet again.' We've left Big Ben up the scaffolding!' As she raced out of the kitchen, she was plagued with the terrifying image of her gardener lying dead on her driveway and wondered how she was going to explain that to Health and Safety.

As it happens, Big Ben wasn't lying dead on her driveway. Instead, having heard the rumpus in the house, he had obviously decided he was safer at the top of the scaffolding, so had climbed back up and had continued to trim back the ivy.

With a groan of despair, Charlie climbed back up the scaffolding after him.

JD hadn't intended inspecting the room across the hallway, he was merely giving himself a break from Charlie's hammering. Besides, it was quieter in this room and he needed time to think about whether he should stay – or move on. The boss wanted an answer, and soon. He pursed his lips. It was a long time since he had planned ahead. It had been impossible after .... JD checked his train of thought and brought it back to the Blue House. No doubt about it, since staying in the Blue House his injuries had improved, he was eating better and growing stronger every day. There was no reason why he should move on. He was safe here. No-one would find him here. Besides, being hungry, cold, and facing the dangers of sleeping on the streets again filled him with dread. He tried not to think of the day he'd caught a glimpse of the long-haired, bearded, scruffy individual staring back at him through the shop window. That was the day he had grown so depressingly low he had considered ending it all. But he hadn't, because that was the day he'd been mugged, and Charlie had dragged him out of that pit of despair and into the Blue House.

His thoughts were briefly distracted by a strange odour. He sniffed, twice. The room had a musty smell of decay to it. Glancing around his eye fell on the tell-tale signs of cotton-wool mushrooms poking up behind the cracked skirting boards below the broken windows. Dry rot? If it was, it was likely to have spread under the floorboards, and would soon spread throughout the whole house. He thrust his hands defiantly into his pockets. Why should he care? It wasn't his house.

His gaze drifted over to where a ray of late afternoon sunshine had landed on the dark oak bookshelves either side of a magnificent carved oak fireplace. He breathed in softly and moved unhurriedly towards the empty bookshelves. His boots crunched on broken glass, but he barely noticed. Of course; this room would have been the library, he mused gazing around. A room for reading, books, encyclopaedias, a room of learning and culture. JD unexpectedly found himself identifying with this room; identifying with the master of the house, a businessman, who would have retired here after his evening meal. There'd have been a thickly piled carpet, comfortable wing chair where he would relax in front of a roaring fire with his brandy, cigar and his evening paper. JD felt a stirring deep inside himself. 'It's who I am,' he murmured. The revelation was comforting rather than surprising, yet reassuring to say it out loud. It was if he was reaching out to grasp back a bit of himself. But then the shaft of sunlight faded, the image disappeared and in its place was the smell of dry rot and the draught from the broken windows. Yet strangely enough, identifying with the spirit of learning and intellect in this library stayed with him.

He ran his fingers thoughtfully over the oak panelling below the bookshelves, then his fingers stopped. Oak panelling! A new train of thought pressed in. He studied the oak panelling carefully for a moment before leaving the library. Making his way across the hallway to the dining room he examined the walls with growing curiosity. The area above the dado was covered in a heavily embossed wallpaper. Below, had been painted dark green. No oak panels. Running his fingers over the green gloss paint he furrowed his brow. That was when he spotted a tack sticking out near the skirting board. Kneeling down he removed the hammer from his belt and gently prized it out. Then removing the tack in each corner, he pulled away the sheet of green hardboard and breathed in sharply. Oak panelling. Who in their right mind would want to cover up oak panelling?

He felt a sense of urgency as he made his way back into the hallway. Kneeling down he examined the walls at the bottom of the stairs and discovered a small crack. Pulling out his hammer he carefully prized more boarding away from the wall. Underneath? Dark oak panelling. He was so engrossed in what he was doing he didn't hear Joe's approach until their roofer gave a low whistle.

'Hey boss. Look at this.'

JD heard her coming across the hall, but he didn't turn around.

'Oak panelling? You've found oak panelling, JD?'

It was the excitement in her voice that helped him find his own voice. He cleared his throat. 'There's more in the dining room and library,' he huskily told her.

She gave a cry of delight. 'Really? You mean, I've got oak panelling in all the downstairs rooms? I could have that restored, couldn't I?'

Joe sucked in his cheeks in a manner that suggested he was about to import vital information. 'A joiner 'll cost you a pretty penny to do that, boss.'

'A specialist then, and stop calling me boss.'

Joe stroked his chin as if giving the problem his due consideration. 'I wouldn't like to say what a specialist 'll charge 'cos it'll be a time-consuming job removing all that hardboard.'

JD heard the slightest hesitation in her voice before she asked, 'What do you think, JD? Do you think you could remove it; if you decide to stay, that is?'

He hesitated, wondering why she was asking him, because to answer would be to commit himself and he wasn't sure that he wanted to do that, but then he didn't know what he wanted to do, did he? 'You could make enquires about treating oak panelling by going on line, or you could ask Barry Matthew,' he found himself saying,

'Any chance you could take on that task; you could use my computer – after I've charged it up at Freddy's?'

He swivelled slowly around to face her. 'I suppose so.' He paused. 'And while I'm about it, I could find out how to deal with the dry rot I suspect you have in your library.'

Chapter 6.

'A two-year-old could lay bricks better than ......!' Fortunately, the rest of the argument was lost when a heavy thud shuddered the attic floorboards.

'What the ...!' Sid the plumber bumped his head off the rafter as he squeezed out of the narrow crevice where he was installing the new hot water cylinder.

Tom grinned at the plumber's alarm. 'It's only Joe and Charlie fighting again. Charlie's bricking up the fireplaces and Joe's complaining about his work. He says he's fed up at having to plaster over his mistakes. Go on with what you were saying, Sid.' Tom wrapped his arms around his knees and watched the plumber slide his long lithe body back into the narrow crevice again. What he liked most about working with Sid, was that he took time to explain what he was doing and why, and he'd even given him a few plumbing tasks.

'Aye. I was saying, what Abbie needed was a big enough boiler to cope with a hotel this size, but this one should do the trick. Hand me that wrench over there, lad, so I can tighten up this joint.'

Tom handed him the wrench, pondering on the fact that he hadn't even known what a wrench was until Sid arrived. 'How do you know all this stuff, Sid?'

'Been a plumber since I was your age, lad. Interesting job. Every house is different.'

'Do you think I could ...?' Tom chewed nervously on his nail.

'Could what, son?'

'Nothing …'

'Go on, spit it out.'

Spitting out what was left of his nail, he asked, 'Do you think I could be a plumber?'

Sid emerged from the crevice with a hairy black spider scuttling across his thick white hair. Unconcerned, he brushed it off. 'No reason why not. There are courses you could attend, or you could go to college.'

'So, there's a lot of studying and ….'

'Deliveries!' the shout echoed up to the attic from the hallway.

Sid made a move to respond but Tom laid a restraining hand on his arm. 'It'll just be the plasterboard and insulation, and it's Big Ben's job to help the drivers unload so he can keep the deliveries in neat tidy piles in the hallway. He's obsessed with neat tidy piles. If they've brought your copper piping, I'll fetch it up later. Go on, Sid.'

Sid parked himself on the top stair. 'Where was I? Oh aye, from what I remember, the last apprentice I took on needed his City and Guilds Technical Certificate, and the Basic Plumbing Certificate, NVQ level 2. That told him all he needed to know about plumbing systems, pipe work, joining and the like before he advanced to Level 3. Course it might have changed a bit since then but there's leaflets that'll tell you.' Sid pursed his lips thoughtfully. 'On the other hand,' he said after a pause, 'If you got yourself a plumbing apprenticeship, you'd learn the practical and technical sides of plumbing far quicker. And judging from the work you've done for me I reckon many a firm would be glad to take you on.'

Tom face flushed up with pleasure. 'Would they? You're not just saying that?'

'I don't say things I don't mean, lad.' Sid studied his big boots intently before adding, 'Of course, if you were serious, you'd have to get off the streets - and the drugs,' he added with a sly glance in his direction.

'What do you mean?'

Sid gave a wry smile. 'I'm not completely senile, Tom.' He gave a snort. 'Although I wish someone would tell that to our Susan.' Seeing Tom's puzzlement he added, 'My daughter Susan is married to Abbie's brother, Freddy, so you can imagine the grief I get with those two. And it's got worse since being on my own then having a heart op. They're forever nagging me to stay in the office. Bless them, they mean well enough, but it would be the death of me sitting behind a desk all day. I like working hands on. Besides, I'm fond of Abbie, and when she couldn't find a plumber for a job this size, I felt sorry for her.'

'So, it's your plumbing business, is it, Sid?'

'Aye, it is. The rest of my lads are out on other jobs, that's why you're giving me a hand.' He gave a chuckle. 'There'd be ructions to pay if Freddy and Susan discover what we're up to. But they won't. Abbie's going to tell them that all I'm doing is supervising, and I'll keep mum about her using you lot till Easter.' He shook his head. 'Families, eh? You got a family, Tom?'

'I ... yeh! I suppose.'

'You going back to them when you're finish here?'

'Not likely!'

'Where are you going then?'

'Dunno. Back on the streets, I suppose. What choice do I have?'

'There's always choices, lad.'

'Aye, I know, and the choice I made was getting as far away as possible from my old man.'

There was a long pause before Sid asked, 'And your next choice is ...?'

'Eh?'

'What's your next choice?'

Tom shrugged his shoulders. 'Dunno. Haven't thought about it.'

Sid ran his finger over his neat white moustache. 'Well, you better get thinking, because if you were genuinely interested in plumbing, your next choice should be to ask me to get you leaflets about courses, apprenticeships and benefits.'

And for a brief moment, Tom caught a vision of himself fixing pipes, installing boilers, diverting water from one place to another, and in years to come being able to point to the old Blue House on the corner and saying, "See that hotel? I did the plumbing for that." And he'd feel proud at having achieved something. 'Aye, I'd like to be a plumber, Sid,' he said softly. 'I'd really like that. But what's the point of leaflets and telephone numbers. Even if by some miracle I got accepted for training I'd have to live somewhere, and we're out of here at Easter.'

'And you definitely can't go home?'

'No way! Last time my old man beat me up I rang the coppers. When they arrived, he told them I was a druggy, and he was trying to warn me off with a beating. So, the coppers told *him* to take it easy and left *me* with a warning. *Me! I'd* been the one to ring *them*!'

Sid's face soured and it was a while before he said. 'I suppose you could make a start by seeing what's involved in plumbing. If it doesn't work out, then it doesn't. You'll be disappointed but at least you 'll have given it your best shot. And you'll be no worse off that's for sure.'

Tom studied his hard-bitten nails thoughtfully. 'Aye, I'd be no worse off that's for sure.'

'Good lad.' Sid slapped him on the back then, using his shoulder as a crutch, got to his feet. 'I'll get those leaflets for you. Now go and see if that delivery van has brought our copper piping. I'll need a couple of lengths to start off with.'

Choices! Tom mused as he ran downstairs. Sid said there were always choices. Was qualifying as a plumber one of them, or was he reaching too high? No doubt about it, he'd never been as happy since Sid had asked him to help with the plumbing, and Sid said he was good at it, except ... Tom slowed down as he reached the hallway, his thoughts invariably turning to the only person in his life who actually meant something to him; Ellie, his fourteen-year-old sister. His fingers tightened on the banister. He had been at home watching a late TV show the night he had heard her crying. Alarmed, he had taken the stairs two at a time to find out what was wrong. That was when he had seen his father leaving her bedroom. When he saw his son he had looked decidedly guilty and he had avoided eye contact.

'Getting too pretty for her own good,' his old man had muttered defiantly.

'How long has this been going on, Ellie?' Tom had asked when they were sure his old man was out of hearing range, but all his shivering sister had done was clutch her nightgown to her chest and shake her head. That was when Tom had lost his temper. Grabbing Ellie's tennis racket, he ran downstairs and smashed his old man over the head with it. And for his gallantry he had received the thrashing of his life. His mother had done nothing to stop the violence, but then she never had.

'I've told you, don't annoy him. Keep out of his way,' she'd whined. And when his father had caught him sleeping outside Ellie's room as protecting, the beatings had got worse. So he had taken his mother's advice and got out of his way. In fact, he'd got out altogether, leaving, to his shame, Ellie to fend for herself. Tom picked up the copper piping and slung it over his shoulder. So, what was he supposed to have done, he brooded making his way slowly back up the stairs? He could hardly have taken her with him. The authorities would only have sent her back. He needed money to protect her and he didn't have any, did he? All he had was a meagre wage from the boss and the few quid Sid had slipped him as a plumber's mate. That wouldn't get them far unless ... he stopped abruptly on the landing, trying to juggle a sudden wild idea into a clear and comprehensible plan. It was Friday, wasn't it? Pay day for his old man. If he could get his hands on that, and the money his mother kept hidden in tea caddy, plus his own wage; then if he claimed benefits, and if Ellie could get a Saturday job, they might be able to afford somewhere cheap till he qualified as a plumber. Would the authorities allow that? Tom felt a sudden surge of excitement. Aye, Sid was right. There were always choices if you looked for them. He found himself thinking and planning about little else for the rest of the day.

It was dark when he left the house. Not wanting to waste money on fares to get him from one side of the city to the other, he jumped the barrier at the train station, and once in the city walked the rest of the way. Then making his way through the council estate to Walker Road, he stayed hidden in the shadows of the newsagent's doorway, watching the door of number 27.

Hugging himself to keep warm he dispassionately surveyed the estate where he had lived all his life. Overgrown gardens, dumped chairs, flaking paintwork and filthy windows was all Walker Road had to offer. He stamped his feet to keep warm until it occurred to him that he might be drawing attention to himself. So, he stopped, and waited silently in the draughty doorway. The drone of a low flying aeroplane turned his gaze up to the dark night sky. Its lights flashed at him from the darkness, and he felt a sudden surge of resentment against the rich holiday-makers who were able to fly away from their troubles and spend their days in the sun. The drone of the plane gradually faded leaving him with only the moon for company. It hung high above him like the white crest of a thumbnail in an inky black sky.

The minutes dragged by. Peering into the newsagent's shuttered shop he saw from the clock inside that it was two minutes to eight. Not long now. He tucked his hands under his armpits for warmth. Shortly after eight fifteen the front door of number 27 opened, and his old man's short solid figure was silhouetted briefly against the hall light before he slammed the door behind him. The pub, that's where he'd be going. That's where he went most nights, except Tom knew he'd stay there longer on Friday because he'd been paid – and he'd have left the housekeeping money on the kitchen table

Tom watched his father kick open the garden gate, thrust his hands in his pockets, slouched off down the road and felt not a flicker of affection for him, only relief that he would be out of the way for a couple of hours at least. He waited until his old man had rounded the corner before pulling his hood over his head and running across the road. His trainers barely made a sound on the pavement.

Number 27 Walker Road was a mirror image of its neighbours. Overgrown garden, broken fences and overflowing bins stinking of rubbish. No-one took any pride in their property, not around here. He found the door on the catch, as usual. Silently slipping inside he was greeted by the pungent smell of fried onions and the low hum of a television reality show. Nothing had changed. He stood listening, wondering whether Ellie would be watching TV with their mother, or in her bedroom. He was about to make his way upstairs when he was surprised to spot his old man's wallet lying on the hall table. Picking it up he rifled through the flaps. To his amazement it was full of money. Obviously, he had gone off to the pub without it, and judging from the amount the housekeeping money hadn't been handed over either. Tom didn't hesitate. He thrust all the notes into his pocket without the slightest trace of guilt. As far as he was concerned this was survival money for him and Ellie.

'Tom?'

Startled he almost dropped the wallet. Ellie was running lightly down the stairs towards him in her bare feet. Flinging her arms around his neck she clung to him. He could feel her trembling in his arms.

He didn't want to ask but he knew he had to. 'It's got worse, hasn't it?'

She dropped her arms from around his neck and stepped back, her face flushing up in embarrassment.

'Ellie?'

'Yes,' she whispered. 'It's when he comes back from the pub. You know how he gets with the drink in him.'

Tom nodded; milk bottles falling over, doors slamming; his old man stumbling up the stairs, then the beatings began.

'I locked my door, like you told me, and put a chair under the handle but he got mad when he couldn't get in. So mad that ...' She gave a nervous sob in the back of her throat. 'There's a hole in my door,' she said shakily and dropped her head as though she was the guilty one.

He gripped her cold hand. 'I shouldn't have left you, Ellie. I shouldn't,' he whispered.

'You had to. He said he'd kill you if he ever set eyes on you again.'

'But this time I've a plan. I know how to get us out of this.'

She raised her head, hopeful. 'How?'

He pulled his hood back. 'We go, now, tonight.'

Ellie's eyes widened in alarm. 'But, we've no money? And what about school? If a fourteen-year-old goes missing, they'll only bring me back.'

'And that's when you'll tell the police, social workers and school, what's going on.'

Ellie gasped, horrified. 'I couldn't do that. I couldn't! What'll my friends say?'

'You can't think like that, Ellie. You can't! I've worked it all out. The worst that can happen is they'll send you to a foster home till you're sixteen. After that you could get a place with me.' He squeezed her hands. 'That's not long to wait, is it? Less than eighteen months. Meanwhile, I'll be training as a plumber and then I'll have money enough for us both. At least you'd be free of this place.'

They looked up startled as the living room door opened.

'I thought I heard voices.' Their overweight mother leant on the door jamb, pulled on a cigarette and blew smoke across the narrow hallway. Her hair was in curlers and she was wearing the same stained jogging pants, baggy green jumper and down at the heel mules she'd worn when he'd left. 'So, you're back, are you?' There was no warmth in her greeting and her dull blue eyes were completely lacking in love. 'You better not let him catch you here.'

'I wondered how you and Ellie were doing, that's all mam,' he muttered.

'So now you've seen. You're not back for good, I hope?'

'No, I ....'

They froze as a footstep scraped on the doorstep. The handle turned, and to Tom's alarm the front door burst open letting in a blast of cold air - and his father. He loomed threateningly in the doorway. If he was surprised to see his son, he didn't show it.

'Ah-ha! What have we here?' He smiled, but not with his eyes, and his misshapen front teeth gave the impression of a hungry crocodile. 'The prodigal returns, eh?' He swaggered into the passage, kicking the front door shut with the heel of his boot. 'Good job I came back for my wallet, otherwise I would've missed this happy family reunion.'

Tom glanced at his mother. Not that he expected her to do anything. She never did.

'I came to see Ellie, dad.' He pushed Ellie behind him.

His father continued blocking the doorway, a sadistic grin spreading across his face - until he saw his wallet in Tom's hand. The grin faded and his knuckles cracked as he clenched them into fists.

Tom knew what was coming. 'I don't want no trouble, dad,' he said uneasily.

His father began unbuckling the belt around his trousers. 'You should've thought of that afore you came back to rob me,' he spat pulling the belt slowly through the loops of his trousers.

Tom threw the wallet back on to the hall table praying his father wouldn't check inside. 'Here! You can have it. I'll not come back again. Okay?'

Obviously, it wasn't okay. His old man began wrapping his belt around his fist, and for a split-second Tom wondered whether there was time to dive through the kitchen and out the back door, but he quickly abandoned that idea. If the key wasn't in the lock he'd be trapped. He backed away slowly as his father moved deliberately towards him swinging the belt.

'Dad! No dad!' Helpless to defend himself in such a narrow hall he raised his arms to protect his head, but as the brass buckle sliced across his ear, he let out a cry of pain.

Ellie screamed, 'Mam! Do something!' But predictably, his mother's only response was to dart into the living room, slam the door and turn up the volume on the TV.

Tom yelled, 'Upstairs Ellie! Barricade your door.' And was relieved to hear her bare feet pounding obediently up the stairs.

'So, you think you can just walk back in here….'

'I'm going, dad. I'm going!' He saw the fury on his old man's face, heard the belt whirl through the air again, and ducked - but not quickly enough. As the belt ripped across his cheek, he stumbled over the hall table. Unable to save himself, he fell, cracking his head against the bannisters. He lay, momentarily stunned, but then his survival instincts kicked in. Realising the only way to get out of here in one piece was through the front door he scrambled to his feet. He heard the belt whirling again. This time he didn't hesitate. Covering his head with his arms he lunged forward like a charging bull. His father's bulky form barely budged as their bodies collided. But then, by some miracle he was through. One, two, three paces to the front door. He heard the 'whoosh' of the belt; his hand reached out for the door latch but the belt swung around his neck as though he was being lassoed. He gagged, panicked as his breathing was restricted, but with both hands occupied pulling at the belt he was unable to protect himself from the fist that rammed into his side. He grunted, his knees buckled, and the passageway swam in front of him. When the second blow came it was to his groin. Terrified of what would happen if he lost consciousness he fought against the descending blackness. But then, he found a moment of respite as he heard Ellie screaming, 'Leave him! Leave him alone, dad!' and realised she was hurling tennis balls down the stairs at their father.

'What the….?' Otherwise occupied by a barrage of tennis balls his father tentatively loosened his grip. That was all it took for Tom to unwrap the belt from his throat. Gasping for air he groped for the front door latch. Turning it, he flung the door open and stumbled outside. For a split second he thought he'd got away, thought he was free, until a heavy blow to the side of his head sent him sprawling across the concrete path. There was a buzzing sound in his ear and a brick landed beside him. Stunned, he struggled to his feet and staggered down the garden path. How he managed to negotiate the gate he had no idea. He could barely see it for the blood blurring his vision.

It was only the sound of his father's heavy breathing advancing down the drive after him that spurred him on. Willing his legs into action, Tom lurched away from number 27 Walker Road, trying to widen the distance between them. By the time he reached the end of the road his lungs were at bursting point.

People! He knew he'd be safe around people. His father wouldn't dare do anything in public. So, he headed towards the High Street. It was the sound of traffic pounding through his head like a herd of stampeding elephants that made him realise there was something seriously wrong with his hearing. Leaning momentarily against a lamppost he sucked oxygen into his bursting lungs. And it was only the fear of staying in one place for too long that forced him hobbling towards the late-night shoppers congregated around the department store. Occasionally he glanced behind, but only occasionally as the action of turning his head made him dizzy. But as far as he could tell his father had given up the chase. There was a bus shelter ahead. The only other occupant being a middle-aged woman in a fur coat, a Russian style fur hat and arms bulging with carrier bags. Making his way over to the far corner of the shelter he leant heavily against the clear plastic partition and made a pretence of trying to read the bus timetable. Not that he intended catching a bus. The money in his pocket had been too hard won to spend on bus fares, but the rest momentarily helped ease the pain in his lungs. It also made him conscious of a warm sticky substance running down his neck from his ear. He touched it, gingerly, and was horrified to find his fingers mattered with blood and hair. It was the shock of so much blood that made him throw up. The woman with the Russian hat turned away in disgust. Wiping what was left of the vomit on the sleeve of his hoodie he decided he better move on in case the woman called the coppers. Pulling his hood over his bloodied head he staggered away from the bus stand.

Dazed, he wandered around in the dark. How long for, he had no idea. At some point he must have left the High Street and then he vaguely remembered finding himself somewhere near the arches; at least he guessed that's where he was. He slunk into a darkened shop doorway, slid down the wall, and tried to pull his scattered thoughts together.

The Blue House. He'd be safe at the Blue House was his only clear thought. But how did he get there? That was when he caught a glimpse of himself through the shop window. He stared at the image, horrified. His hoodie was drenched with blood, and his cheek had a deep gash from his eye to his jaw. If he was seen in this condition, he'd have the coppers on him unless …. Ah! Yes! If he was near the archers, he'd ne near the public toilets. He could clean up there before heading home. He had a sudden urge to laugh. Home! How could anyone in their right mind call the Blue House home? There was no electricity, no furniture, no TV, and he slept on a manky old mattress on the floor. And yet, that was where he wanted to be more than anywhere else in the world; the Blue House.

It was that thought alone that brought him to his feet. He swayed as the ground tilted. Clinging on to a lamppost he waited until his vision had steadied before stepping out of the shop doorway.

'Tom?'

A blurred but vaguely familiar figure was standing outside the cinema doors.

'Andy!' He stumbled towards his dealer with relief. Andy was a thin young man with the complexion of a candle. 'Good God! What's happened to you?'

'Don't ask.' Tom realised his voice was barely above a whisper. He tried clearing his throat; it stung like crazy. 'Anywhere round here where I can clean myself up?'

'No problem, mate. Come with me.' Andy took his arm and led him down the street. 'You look as though you've been in the wars.' His eyes shifted uneasily towards the queue at the cinema. He dropped his voice. 'I've some good stuff on me, not your usual crap; higher purity level they told me. Expensive though.'

Tom shook his head. 'I need the money for ... for me and Ellie.'

'Money? You've money on you?' His dealer pulled him into an alleyway.

'Where's the loo, Andy?' He pushed him away when he realised Andy was fumbling in his pockets. But he was too late. The stolen money fell to the ground.

Andy whistled through his teeth as he bent down to retrieve it. 'Whew! You can have a few wraps for what you've got here, mate.'

Tom could feel his legs buckling under him. 'Aye. I need to ... sit...'

'This stuff 'll deaden the pain that's for sure.'

'No, I ...' Tom wavered.

Sometime later, how long he had no way of knowing, he found himself slumped against a cold brick wall with a warm glow flowing through his body leaving him with an overall sense of peace. It was like being wrapped in a warm, woozy cocoon. A cocoon that shut out the loud rumble of traffic, deadened the pain in his head, and eased his sore throat. But what was equally good was feeling his inner torments diminish into obscurity. As the drowsiness washed over him, he wondered whether to take the other packet? Why not, he asked himself? And receiving no answer opened the second packet.

'Still no sign of him?'

Abbie was pouring herself another cup of tea when their worried plumber entered the kitchen. 'None, Sid. I've rung the local hospitals and no one answering his description was brought in. I even rang P.C Bill Nicholson, our local bobby, to see if he'd been locked up but he hasn't. Maybe he's just had enough and gone home.'

Sid pulled up a stool and joined the rest of the Blue House workers around the breakfast table. 'I canna see him doing that, lass. He was adamant that returning home was out of the question. Besides, he was too keen to explore this plumbing course.' He dropped a handful of plumbing leaflets on the kitchen table. 'No one knows where he used to live, do they?'

'First time me and Big Ben clapped eyes on him was under the arches,' Joe said.

Abbie sipped her tea. 'I suppose we could start by looking there and then we could ... I don't know, scour the city centre perhaps?'

'Damned kid!' Charlie snapped. 'When we get him back here, I'm gonna kill him.' He glanced hesitantly at Abbie before saying, 'He's a user boss. That's what he spends his pay on. My bet is he's got caught up with his dealer, otherwise, he'd be back by now.'

Abbie twirled her wedding ring absently around her finger. But then she stopped. Frowning, she considered the ring before pulling it off her finger and pushing it into the pocket of her jeans. 'OK Charlie, so where can I find a drug dealer?'

'Eh?' Charlie's eyes widened in alarm. 'Y' can't go looking for drug dealers, boss.'

'Why not? It's better than sitting around here doing nothing.'

'Aye, but ....'

'But what, Charlie?'

'You don't know who you're getting mixed up with when it comes to drugs, boss. Dealers can be a nasty bunch and drugs are a fool's game. I had a sister what died of drugs.'

'All the more reason for finding Tom. Don't you agree?'

'Not really, boss. The lad's a free agent. He can do what he likes.'

'He's seventeen, Charlie.'

'And he's had it rough at home,' Sid added. 'His old man used to beat him. That's how he ended up on the streets. I'm with Abbie here. I think we should try to find him.'

Charlie looked uncomfortable. 'For my part, I'd rather *not* go into the city, if you catch my drift, boss. Besides, I've no idea who's dealing these days and it wasn't my scene anyway.' But then he gave a low growl deep in his throat which sounded not unlike Mutt when he was having a bad dream. 'Okay! Okay! I suppose we shouldn't be sitting on our backsides doing nowt.' Resting his elbow on the table he stroked his chin with his finger and thumb. 'If he's not back by this evening, JD and me 'll ask around the clubs.'

'Any other ideas folks?' Abbie asked.

Sid rattled his van keys. 'If Joe could show me where the arches and the local shelters are, we could check them out.'

'Are you sure you're up to it, Sid?'

'Don't you start fussing, lass. You sound just like your Freddy and my Susan.'

Abbie smiled crookedly over their shared family problem before glancing sideways at Sarah. 'Would you mind staying here with Big Ben? If Tom does arrive home, we'll need someone here.' And she didn't miss the look of relief that crossed the girl's face. 'Besides,' she added, 'I have the lift manufacturers coming to inspect the site.' She lowered her voice. 'And I don't want to leave the electrician doing the rewiring alone. I wouldn't put it past him to scarper off for the afternoon.' She planted both hands on the table. 'Right! So that's our action plan then, and if any of you find him ring me on my mobile and I'll come and get you.'

Charlie gave her a quizzical look. 'And how are we supposed to do that boss when none of us have mobiles?'

'Ah!' She pondered a while before adding, 'Actually, that's immaterial. I have to go to the hairdressers anyway.'

Charlie scratched his head. 'I'm confused. What has the hairdresser got to do with this?'

She splayed both hands. 'And where else can I recharge my mobile?'

To her surprise JD gave a hint of a smile. She'd never seen him smile before. 'What?'

'You could buy a portable charger,' he suggested.

There was silence around the table.

'A ... what?'

'A portable charger. Otherwise known as a power bank. It'll give you extra juice through the week for your phone.'

Charlie raised an eyebrow at him.

'I didn't know there was such a thing,' Abbie said. 'Where would I buy one?'

'I'll make enquiries if you like?'

And then she smiled at him as though she was seeing him for the first time. 'Thank you, JD?'

Tom had no idea how long he had been in the alleyway. The initial euphoria had long since gone leaving him cold and in pain. His ear hurt like hell, and there were times he felt as though he was fading away into nothingness. He wondered if this was what it was like to die.

He was vaguely aware that day came – and went, and night came – again. His money had gone, his dealer had gone, and for hours his head had been telling him he ought to eat, and he would have done if he'd had any money, and if the pains in his stomach would stop. He wanted ... he wanted ...what did he want? He wanted .... It dawned on him gradually. Yeh, he wanted to get back to the Blue House and learn how to be a plumber; that's what he wanted. He tried opening his eyes but one eyelid was so swollen it wouldn't open, and when he tried forcing the other one, he found the world around him so blurred he closed it again.

'Hey kid.'

The voice sounded far away, muffled, but then the sound of traffic, and the music from the night-club across the road sounded muffled too. It was all because of his ear, it hurt; it hurt real bad.

'Hey Tom! Tom!'

He opened his one good eye slowly, blinked, and then shrank back with a cry of alarm. The vile apparition in front of him had facial features that contorted into odd shapes like the 'Hall of Mirrors' at the fairground. Its forehead bulged and there was a tail growing out of the back of its head. Its arms were alive with slithering snakes reaching out for him, their forked tongues ready to strike. Hell! He was in hell.

'Tom! Wake up Tom!' The vile apparition had big hands and was shaking him. 'Come on kid. Get to your feet.' Then the voice shouted. 'JD, he's over here.'

JD? JD? The name registered but he couldn't remember how. Narrowing his one good eye he found to his surprise that large white flakes were drifting down from an inky black sky. It was beautiful, absolutely beautiful. Maybe he wasn't in hell after all. Maybe....

'It's Charlie. Remember? Now move kid! You'll die if you stay here.' Although the voice was muffled there was no mistaking the urgency in it. Another heave from those big hands and he found himself on his feet. He cried out in pain as his half-frozen legs took the weight of his body, but then another pair of hands emerged from out of nowhere and supported him from the other side.

'That's it, Tom. Now walk!' This voice was posh but hoarse. Walk? Why did he need to walk if he was in hell? But … he wasn't in hell, wasn't he?

'Charlie? JD?' The words came out in a whisper.

'That's us kid. Put your arm around our shoulders. We'll get you home.'

'No! No! Can't go home. My old man …'

'No Tom. Back to the Blue House.'

'The Blue … Blue House?' Tom tried to clear the jumble of images in his head but the cold air penetrating the gash on his ear felt like an ice cube on toothache and made it difficult to concentrate.

'We'll never get him back like this, Charlie. We should ring the boss.'

'And how are we supposed to do that?'

'The nightclub over there. They'll have a phone and it'll be somewhere warm for Tom while we wait for her.'

Tom felt his legs buckle from under him more than once as JD and Charlie hauled him across the road to the nightclub. He could tell the snow was coming down thicker now because he could see the imprints of his trainers. And then he felt a rush of warm air on his frozen face as the nightclub door opened and they came face to face with the bouncer.

'W' canna let him in here, mate. Look at the state of him?' The declaration was firm.

'Ten minutes, my friend. That's all the time we'll need to make a phone call for the lad here to get help. We'll find a quiet corner.'

JD's calm reassuring tones must have done the trick because a moment later he heard the drone of voices, and he was clinging on to JD and Charlie as his frozen feet tried to negotiate a narrow staircase. There was the boom, boom, boom of heavy metal music pounding though his head, and flashing lights across the ceiling and walls, closed in on him and made him dizzy. There was a smell of beer, the sound of laughter, and the dance floor quivered beneath his feet with the gyrating of human bodies, but it was warm. Oh, so beautifully warm.

He allowed himself to be guided to the back of the nightclub simply because he had no choice in the matter. His rescuers slid him into a corner seat with a sticky leather covering, and through his one good eye he watched them rummaging through their pockets for change. Pulling a few loose coins out of his pocket, JD left them to speak to the barman, signing a telephone with his clenched hand to his ear. The barman pointed to the corridor.

Hot breath blew into his good ear as Charlie shouted. 'JD's gone to ring the boss. She'll be here shortly. Hang on, kid. We'll soon have you home.'

Tom raised a chewed thumb as indication he'd heard. Nodding his head was out of the question. Cautiously leaning back against the cracked leather seat, he closed his eyes. A deep rustic voice penetrated his darkness.

'Hey Charlie! Long-time no see. Where' you been man?'

Tom guardedly opened his eye. The speaker was an imposing six-foot black man with heavy facial features, an excessive amount of frizzy hair and a black silk shirt with patches of sweat under the armpits.

'Doing a bit 'o time, haven't I?' Charlie murmured.

'Folks is looking for you. You know that?'

'Really!'

'So where 'll I tell them they can find you; if they asks me?'

'Around.'

'Around where man? Is you working?'

'Sort of.'

The big fellow's face twisted as he scrutinized Tom. 'Looks like your mate here's been in the wars, Charlie. Looks like he be needing a hospital.'

There was silence from Charlie. But then a familiar voice cut in.

'OK Charlie?'

JD stood in front of them, the collar of his long black coat up, his hands in his pockets.

The black man grinned. 'OK Charlie, my man. I'll telt your friends you around, eh?'

Tom watched him swaggering back to the bar until he lost sight of him in the crowd.

'Who was that?' JD asked sitting down.

'The last person on earth I wanted to bump into,' Charlie said grimly. 'How long's the boss gonna be?'

'I had to give her directions but …' JD ran his tongue around the front of his teeth. 'Goodness knows if she'll find her way through the one-way system. If you need to get out of here, I suggest we give her ten minutes then go and stand at the door.'

Sometime later, Tom found himself negotiating the stairs again with Charlie and JD either side of him, and discovering that going up was considerably harder than coming down. But what he found even more unpleasant was the icy blizzard conditions outside that penetrated through his thin hoodie and sent a searing pain through his ear. In fact, if it hadn't been for JD holding him upright, he suspected he'd be flat on his back. Charlie was pacing up and down near the road leaving big footprints in the snow.

Tom closed his eye, that was how he heard rather than saw the BMW arrive, but he knew it was the boss's car from the sound of the engine. Next thing he knew, he was being shuffled into the back seat with Charlie. He heard the boss gasp, 'Oh my goodness, Tom!' And then the warmth of the car washed over him. He could feel leather seats under his frozen fingers and smell pine from the dangling cardboard tree hanging on the mirror.

'It's all right, Tom,' the boss spoke reassuringly, and the hand that reached over to squeeze his was comforting. 'Don't worry. We'll soon have you home.'

Home! In his mind's eye he conjured up a faded blue front door, copper pipes under floorboards, cylinders, Charlie cooking dinner over a roaring fire in the kitchen, Mutt lying under the table, Sid...

'Move it, boss. We need to get out of here.' There was an urgency in Charlie's order.

'What? You're making me sound as though I'm a getaway driver, Charlie.'

'Actually, you are,' Charlie said. 'I bumped into an ex-con I'd have rather not bumped into. Nasty piece of work. Hopefully he didn't see us getting into your car.'

'What!' The tyres squealed and Tom winced as his head bounced off the leather upholstery.

'No need to get over-excited boss,' Charlie murmured grabbing on to the door handle.

Eventually, convinced that danger wasn't imminent, the car settled into an easy rhythm. Tom listened to the drone of their conversation. They were discussing him, he knew that, but he didn't care because he knew he was in safe hands. He heard the crunch of gravel as the car swung into the drive, sensed Charlie leave his side. The car door slammed behind him, and then to his surprise they were off again, the boss and JD in the front and him alone in the back. Where they were going, he had no idea and he felt too ill to care. He heard the roar of traffic and the wail of sirens, so he guessed they were heading along the dual carriageway and into the city again. But eventually, the car slowed down, crawled a few yards and stopped. Forcing open his eye he squinted at the bright sign,

"Accident and Emergency", and the massive three-storey building in front of him. They'd brought him to the hospital? They must think he was in a bad way. The car doors opened and JD and the boss helped him out.

'Come on Tom,' the boss coaxed, the way she did Mutt when she wanted him out of the kitchen. 'JD and I will stay with you while we see the doctor.'

From then on, he found himself in a dream world. He had a vague recollection of sitting in a wheelchair and being pushed through corridors smelling of antiseptic, being helped on to a trolley covered with blue paper, then crying out in pain as someone in a white coat messed about with his ear, then his eye, then examined his stomach. And all the while the boss squeezed his hand and made reassuring noises. At least he assumed they were reassuring because she smiled a lot, but her voice was muffled, far away. The last thing he remembered was curling up in a bed and sleep drifting over him.

He woke once through the night. He knew it was night because it was still dark, and JD and the boss were sprawled out on chairs either side of his bed, fast asleep. The second time he woke he could feel sunshine on his face and hear subdued voices. He kept his eyes closed.

'That was a nasty beating he took, Mrs Hunter.' Tom guessed that was the doctor who had treated him earlier. 'We've put stitches between his left ear and his jaw but it's his hearing that gives us cause for concern. It's too early to tell whether it's been affected permanently, we'll have to see how it goes, but the swollen eye should heal up in time.' There was a slight hesitation. 'Our greatest concern is the effect of the drugs. Fortunately, he still had the remains of what he'd taken screwed up in silver foil, so it gave us an idea of what we were dealing with. It was bad stuff. He's been lucky is all I can say. Naturally, we've had to inform the police.'

The boss took a deep breath. 'I see. So, what now? Will you need to keep him in for observation or could we take him home?'

'You can take him home, but we'll need to make an appointment with him at outpatients for his ear and I strongly advise he attends the Drug Dependency Unit. We can do our part with medication, Mrs Hunter but what that boy could do with is a solid network of support. Can you supply that?'

There was only the slightest hesitation before the boss gave a decisive, 'Of course. Yes. We can do that.' But once the doctor had left the room, he heard her flop down on his bedside chair and let out a groan of despair. 'What on earth possessed me to say yes?' she muttered to herself. 'I'm housing a boy with a mental health issue; an alcoholic, a criminal, and now a drug addict and all I can offer him is a smelly mattress on the kitchen floor and a house without hot water or electricity. A solid network of support? Yeh! Right!' And he hadn't stirred an inch when she had picked up his nail bitten fingers and given them a gentle squeeze. 'But we'll give it a try, won't we Tom?' she whispered, and that was when he had felt like crying.

At some point that morning the doctor reappeared to inform her the police were waiting for him to wake up so they could question him. Tom shuffled gingerly down the bed, afraid to face the police, afraid to tell them what had happened to him. But then it occurred to him. Ellie! He could tell them about Ellie. He had to do something for her. Neither of them could avoid the problem forever.

It was a relief to find the policeman who came was PC Bill Nicholson. Tom had seen him from the windows of the Blue House on one of his many visits. He wasn't as scary as Tom had expected, and it was comforting to find the boss and JD were allowed to stay while he was being questioned. Tom found his voice rasped when he talked and his story came out in a jumble of incoherencies but he guessed the copper made sense of it because he patted his hand reassuringly when he'd finished taking notes.

Towards the end of the day, with a bag full of pills, creams and plasters, and with the overnight snow melting on the roads, he found himself being driven out of the city hospital by the boss and JD. But it wasn't until he drove between the tall pillars of the Blue House and heard the wheels crunch on the gravel that he felt safe again. He sat forward, his arms resting on the seats in front, and stared at the magnificent old house with its blue front door hanging off its hinges and allowed himself a closed mouth smile. To an outside observer the Blue House might appear empty, ownerless, forsaken and neglected, but they were mending it; Charlie, Joe, JD, Big Ben, Sarah, Sid the plumber, the boss … and him. Broken things could be mended.

Chapter 7

It was the hammering that woke Tom. He didn't open his eyes but lay wallowing in the warmth from the kitchen fire, comforted by the companionship of Mutt lying in the curvature of his legs, twitching in his sleep. At first, he thought the noise was Joe and Charlie sound-proofing the attic floors but then he realised the hammering was coming from across the hallway. Puzzled, he rolled over on his mattress, wincing as the stitches around his ear pulled sharply. Mutt grumbled deep in his throat at being disturbed. The dry rot specialist, that's who it would be, Tom decided. He was a smug faced rotund little man who had stepped through their front door in spotless navy overalls, proudly announcing that he had come to replace their rotten floorboards in the library, and telling them in no uncertain terms that they had better keep out of his way. Joe had taken an instant dislike to him.

'Who gave him the authority to tell us who goes where in this house?' he'd complained to anyone who would listen. 'And I have grave doubts he knows what he's doing. He's supposed to be spraying odourless chemicals over the mould for a start but he's stinking the whole house out.' The boss had told Joe to ignore him. But Joe hadn't, judging from the argument drifting through from the hallway.

Tom tuned his ears to the other noises in the house, relieved that the doctor had been right and his hearing appeared to be gradually improving. 'Rest!' had been his advice – so that's what he'd been doing. Although, if he was honest, he was getting a bit bored with all the resting. He tuned his ears to the glazier in the dining room calling out window measurements to his assistant. There was the rattle of piping from Sid upstairs and ... Sid! Tom bit his lip, embarrassed that Sid was having to do the plumbing on his own. He should be helping instead of lying here. Stupid! Stupid! He'd let the whole house down. How much work had been lost while they'd been out looking for him?

He forced his swollen eyelids open, his spirits lifting slightly when he saw the mid-day sun streaming in through the kitchen window. At least he could now see through both eyes. He lay for a while, trying not to think about his injuries, trying not to feel guilty, trying not to fret over what had happened to Ellie, but his thoughts had an uneasy habit of drifting back to his sister. PC Bill Nicholson had called yesterday morning to tell him she'd been taken into care. Despite the fact that he was pleased the authorities were taking action, he couldn't stop worrying about how she was coping without him. Then he'd had the surprise of his life. The boss had walked into the kitchen with her later that day. She was still in her grey school uniform with her hair tied back into a pony tail, but with a badly bruised face.

'The old man?' he'd asked, and she'd dropped her head and nodded.

'But I'm okay,' she had assured him. 'I'm staying with Janice Jordan. She's the year above me at school. Her parents foster teenagers who are in ...difficulties.'

'And dad?'

'Mrs. Kennedy, the social worker, told me there'd be a court case and a ...a ...' she had glanced across at the boss.

'A restraining order,' Abbie had volunteered. 'That means that if he comes near either of you, they'll lock him up.'

Tom had made no comment, simply because he couldn't imagine anything like a restraining order stopping his old man from doing what he wanted.

Then Ellie's face had brightened. 'But Mrs Hunter said I can come here any time and visit. Isn't that great, Tom?'

'Yeh, Ellie. Great!' he'd agreed but all he'd been able to think about since was the impending court case looming ahead of them.

He raised himself up on his elbow as Charlie came into the kitchen. Their chef didn't say anything at first but set about boiling the kettle on the fire and scrubbing his hands before preparing their lunch. But then realising the invalid was watching him he said, 'Right kid! I think it's about time you got your lazy butt out of bed. Rest time is over. There's work to be done round here and Sid needs his assistant back.'

And Charlie's words were like music to his ears.

Arriving for breakfast later than usual, Abbie found her workers clearing the table.

'Ah! Good! I wanted to catch you all before you started work. There's been so much going on lately I feel I'm losing track of things, so I've decided to make up a schedule.'

Big Ben placed his spoon neatly in his empty cereal bowl, licked the white moustache around his upper lip and wordlessly got to his feet. Picking up his black anorak he headed for the back door.

'Obviously Ben doesn't like schedules,' Abbie murmured as the door closed behind him. 'So,' she continued looking around the room. 'What I'm trying to do is get us back on schedule so that …' She frowned. 'Charlie, what are my food scales and measuring spoons doing on the dresser? I thought they were in my cupboard; the *locked* one?'

'Ah! Yes boss. Explain about that later. But can I suggest you get on with what you were saying before Sid arrives. I think he wants a word with you.'

'He does? What about?' She waved her hand dismissively. 'Never mind. As I was saying,
What I'm trying to do is get us back on schedule.'

'Didn't know you had a schedule, boss.' Joe said dumping his cereal bowl in the sink.

'I haven't, not exactly.' She flicked through her notebook as though she was looking for something. 'Right! Now where was I?'

'Planning a schedule?' Charlie volunteered.

'Ah yes. Firstly, I want to talk to you about Easter.'
There was silence in the kitchen.

'I know the plan was that you should move on at Easter, but it occurred to me that, other than a few personal hiccups, we're not doing too badly. So, I'm thinking that, if you want to stay until we've finished gutting the place, then you can.'

'You mean you'd keep us on?' Charlie asked.

'Not permanently, Charlie. Only until the work is beyond your capabilities, then I'll get skilled workers in. But I think we can keep going like this till the end of April, don't you? However, if you are wanting to move on and you need references ….' She trailed off, trying to think of what she could possibly say in a reference.

"He/she has made good progress since coming off the streets; started Alcoholics Anonymous; stopped drinking; stopped taking drugs; was released from prison …"

Joe broke the silence. 'There's a mountain of work we can still handle boss.'

'I know there is Joe, and top of *your* priority list is building that lift shaft in the cellar, but whenever I ask you about it you make excuses.'

Joe glared at her, offended. 'If you want me to work in the cellar boss, top of *your* priority list will be getting that miserable old sod of an electrician to fit me lights down there. I canna work in the dark.'

'Ah! Good point!' She scribbled, "*Electricity in the cellar*" in her notebook. 'Fine! I'll have a word with him. Next item. Sid says I'll need to bring in the builders to erect timber and stud partitions in the main bedrooms and the staff quarters in the attic so he and Tom can get on with the plumbing.'

Her roofer pursed his lips. 'I think I could handle that boss.'

'Don't you *think* you have enough to do with the lift shaft, Joe?'

'Course I have, but if you get a builder in it'll cost you a pretty penny, and I've erected stud partitions 'afore now.'

'You have?' She rattled the pen between her teeth before making another note in her notebook. "*Ask Barry Matthews: Can Joe erect stud partitions? – And: order timber for stud partitions!*" 'So, what else is going on?'

Joe raised his eyes to the ceiling. 'It's your house, boss. Don't you know?'

'Vaguely,' she admitted. 'Although, at the moment, everyone else appears to be more in control of what's going on than I am. So?'

Joe began ticking the items off on his fingers. 'The chimney's up, the roof's finished, me, Charlie and JD are insulating the top floor, and JD's treating the oak panels downstairs in between times. But if you're wanting them timber stud partitions erected boss, you and Sarah 'll have to crack on stripping them walls.'

'It's using a chemical solution in this cold weather that's the problem,' she said. 'Our hands are freezing. What we really need is a steam wallpaper stripper.'

'And y' can't get one of those till we've got electricity, boss.'

'Yes, I realise that. I think I'm going to have to take a firm stand with that electrician, don't you? It's not good enough his keeping two or more jobs on ....' She knew something was wrong by the way Sarah's mouth dropped open like a fish, and her eyes widened in alarm. 'What? What's wrong? What did I say ...?'

'Er ... stay still boss.' Charlie rose slowly to his feet and inching towards the kitchen range slowly picked up their coal shovel. 'Stay perfectly still.'

It was the menacing way her chef advanced towards her brandishing the coal shovel that unnerved her. 'Why? Why must I stay still?'

'Because there's a rat on the bench behind you.'

'*A ... RAT!*'

Staying still was not an option. Lunging towards the chair Charlie had just vacated she leapt up on to it. '*Where? Where is it?*'

'Calm down boss, you'll scare it.'

'*I'll* scare *IT?*' She inhaled sharply as her eyes lighted on an enormous dark brown rat sitting on the bench, his piercing black eyes glaring at her, his whiskers twitching angrily as though she was the intruder in *his* house rather than the other way around. There was a rattle by the fireplace as JD picked up their iron poker. Joe advanced with their broom. Tom rolled up a newspaper and jumped up on to the sofa, and Sarah grabbed a pan with both hands as though she intended to do something with it, but what, she wasn't sure. Instead, she clambered on to the kitchen table.

Seeing the advancing army, the rat must have decided he'd had enough. With a whisk of his tail, he suddenly became a blur as he ran down the bench, flashed across the floor, under her chair and into the open larder.

Abbie screamed. *'Kill it. Kill it!'*

Mutt, probably obeying the first order in his life, dived into the larder after it in a frenzy of barking.

'The door!' Charlie yelled. 'Shut the door, boss.' But, seeing his boss was totally incapable of doing anything, he leapt over the settee and slammed the larder door shut himself. Mutt, realising he was locked in a pitch-black larder with a large brown rat, switched his aggressive barking to fearful whimpers.

'Where's the other one?' Joe asked looking around the kitchen.

'*Two*? There are *two* of them?' Abbie scrambled up on to the table with Sarah. It was higher than the chair. It groaned in protest.

'Where the hell is it?'

'*Find it! Find it*!'

Joe rattled a pan on the kitchen sink. 'Come on little ratty ....'

A sleeker, larger version of its mate flew across the kitchen floor towards the larder. Charlie whisked the door open. A terrified Mutt shot out and an equally terrified rat dived in. Charlie slammed the door. 'Gone!'

'*What do you mean, 'gone?*' Abbie screeched. Even to her own ears she sounded like a demented diva in a bad opera. '*We've got two rats locked in our larder.*'

'Not quite correct boss,' Charlie said looking around the kitchen.

'What do you mean?'

'Well, if you get down off the table, I'll tell you.'

'Tell me what?'

'I think the rats have had babies.'

'*The rats have had babies!*'

'Stop repeating everything I say, boss. Why don't we get back to your meeting?'

'To hell with the meeting. How can I remember what we were talking about when we have rats in the larder?'

'I can remember,' Charlie offered with a grin. 'You were about to offer us work in this rat hole?' Amused by his own humour, he chuckled as he returned his shovel to the kitchen range. 'Tell you what folks, how about *rat*atouille for dinner tonight?'

'Very funny, Charlie,' she said scrutinising the kitchen floor before making her descent. But once on the floor she couldn't resist smiling because, clearly pleased that his ratatouille joke was a source of amusement, Charlie began churning out rat jokes faster than his pancakes, each one slightly more vulgar than the last. Tom sprawled out on the old sofa convulsed in laughter, and then they were all at it. Even JD had the merest trace of a smile on his lips. And laughter was such a rare occurrence in the Blue House she hadn't the heart to interrupt them.

It took a while for the hilarity to calm down, but when it had Charlie said, 'I've an idea, boss. While I'm putting down rat poison, and blocking up holes, why don't you let me do a thorough job in that larder. I could put up shelving, buy a new door and paint it.'

'Good idea, Charlie.' Pulling her notepad out of her pocket she scribbled, "R*at poison – trap - paint – shelving – brackets – larder door*".

'And I had another idea.' Opening the kitchen door into the garden, Charlie stepped outside. They all trailed after him. Abbie rubbed her arms. There was a nip in the air this morning. 'Joe and I called in at the builders' yard yesterday after his drink club, and they have a sale on,' Charlie examined the back of the house thoughtfully. 'If we're lucky, we might get two outside doors for the price of one.'

'They're not a supermarket, Charlie,'

'No, but it would make sense to replace these knackered back doors. I'll fix them.'

'And I suppose you know how, do you?'

Charlie gave a nonchalant shrug 'I'm not an expert but I've a good idea.'

Joe popped a strip of chewing gum into his mouth, the latest of his habits along with honey in his tea to stave off his craving for drink. 'I'll keep him right, boss.'

As her workers stood viewing the back of the house she scribbled, "*doors and frames for back of house*".

'A patio with a seat in the sun would be nice,' Sarah ventured.'

'Aye, that's an idea,' Charlie agreed. 'If the patio stretched the width of the house and up as far as the outhouse it could be used for bins, deliveries and stuff.'

Abbie drummed her pen on her notebook. 'Expensive though. Which reminds me,' "*check my bank account*," she jotted down.

Joe sucked in his cheeks. 'Aye, you're right there, boss. Cost you a pretty penny to hire a gardener to lay slabs. But don't you worry, I know how to lay slabs.' He jerked his head towards her notebook. 'So, make a note; slabs – sand– cement - and seat.'

'You do realise laying slabs isn't in my schedule, Joe. Actually, it isn't in my budget.' Abbie sucked the end of the pen thoughtfully. 'I'm not even sure if it's on my plans.'

'Excuse me, Mrs Hunter.'

Their thin lipped, sour-faced, 'waste-as-much-time-as-you-can' electrician with grey unsettling eyes and receding red hair was standing at the kitchen door. 'I've installed a switchboard with circuit breakers, so you've got lights in the kitchen.'

Abbie beamed at him. 'You have? Brilliant! And how about lights in the cellar and the rest of the house?'

'I'll get on with it after the holidays.'

'Holidays?' Her mobile rang. Flicking it open she saw it was her brother. 'Hello Freddy! Guess what? I've got electricity in my kitchen so I can now plug in my lap top and …. Easter? Gosh, Freddy, I've been so busy I'd clean forgotten I'd agreed to go to the church service on Easter Sunday with you.' Her mind whirled like an eddy for a reasonable excuse. 'Actually, is there any chance I could see you Easter Monday instead? I've made plans to er … to go to a nice little church around the corner.' She flinched at the blatant lie. 'You're sure you don't mind? Lovely! See you Easter Monday.' Turning, she saw her workers had been listening. 'So, it's Good Friday tomorrow,' she said flinging her pad and mobile on to the table. 'I love all your ideas for the house. I really do, but how about we take time off to celebrate?'

'Celebrate what?' Charlie asked. Clearly the religious aspect of Easter had never crossed his mind.

'For a start we have electricity in the kitchen,' she said. 'Secondly, we haven't had a day off since Christmas, and thirdly ... I can't think of a thirdly other than it occurred to me I'd rather be making plans with you lot than drilling teeth. So, let's have roast lamb and wine or something special over the holidays. Okay, Charlie?'

Joe chomped on his gums a couple of times, and appeared to be thinking the idea of a holiday through. 'Aye, good idea, boss. If you give me your list, I'll measure up for a job lot of outside doors then head off to Barry Matthews. I wouldn't mind a morning browsing around the builders' yard. I'll take Big Ben with me and we can have a trip to the garden centre while we're about it. He likes looking at the plants.'

Abbie tried to keep a straight face as half an hour later Joe strutted out wearing his yellow hard hat closely followed by Big Ben.

Abbie stared thoughtfully out of her caravan window, her chin propped up in the palm of her hand, her elbows resting on the small table strewn with bills, invoices, delivery notes and bank statements. The sun shone encouragingly on yellow daffodils and red tulips poking their heads through the conglomeration of weeds not yet dug up in the back garden. In front of them, Tom sat on a sawn-off stump of the old oak tree browsing through his plumbing leaflets and application forms. The house was unusually quiet. Charlie and Sarah were at the supermarket buying food for their Easter dinner, and Joe and Big Ben were at the builder's yard. Of JD, there was no sign.

Having decided to make the most of a quiet house to sort through her bills she was beginning to wish she hadn't bothered. It had certainly put a dampener on her buoyant mood of earlier. Shuffling through her papers she deliberated whether there couldn't be an easier way to deal with her administration. This present system was turning out to be a nightmare. If she was honest, it was Joe, Sid, and even Barry Matthews who were running this job for her. They were the ones who were prompting her when, and what to order in the way of building materials. If it hadn't been for them, she'd have been in a mess. But there was nothing written down, no actual schedule in place, and in her opinion the hardest part by far was keeping track of delivery notes, invoices, what bills had been paid and what was outstanding. Fortunately, the money from her house sale, her savings, and Donald's private insurance was keeping her buoyant, but it was alarming to see how rapidly her bank account was diminishing. The figures might not have looked so bad if Donald's business partners, having agreed to buy out his share of the company, hadn't been so slow in settling up. Even having the insurance from the car accident would have made a difference. She'd been relying on both to get the work done, and she knew if they didn't settle up soon, she'd be in a mess. She shuffled the papers around the table once again, hating to admit, Freddy had been right when he warned her that renovating an old house took organizational and administrative skills; skills she was beginning to realise she clearly didn't possess.

Turning away from her depressing paperwork she rested her chin on her hand and stared moodily out of the window. Tom was wearing a puzzled expression as he examined his application forms. Pushing his thumb between his teeth he began biting his nail. She watched him for a while before grabbing her cardigan and making her way into the house.

She found JD sitting on an upturned crate stripping down the library door. Wondering why, when the rest of her workers had taken time off, he had chosen to work, she stood for a moment watching him scraping off the sticky substance he'd used to shrivel up the paint. It was a slow laborious task but he seemed engrossed in it. Abbie had noticed he always fell back to doing this or the oak panelling when others weren't demanding his help. It was almost as if he was finding the renovating of the wooden doors and panels in the Blue House therapeutic. She cleared her throat to announce her presence.

'That looks like a tedious job,' she ventured.

JD didn't turn but kept on with what he was doing.

'Isn't there a quicker way?'

There was a long pause before he said, 'There is. But according to Barry Matthews, the mechanical and heat methods of stripping lead-based paint from doors can produce fumes. So, I opted for the safer method, a chemical stripper and scraper.'

'Is that so?'

JD continued scraping at the door.

'I expect you've scraped years of paint off those doors?'

Silence.

'Any interesting colours?'

'Dark blue, brown, black.'

'Goodness! Who on earth would paint a door black?'

'The Victorians. They went in for deep colours.'

'Did they? When did we start using more conventional colours?'

He paused. 'During the war.'

'Really?'

JD removed his goggles and mask and swivelled around on his crate in a manner that suggested he'd given up trying to find a quiet time for himself. 'Did you want something?'

'I did. JD, can I ask a favour?'

He regarded her warily. 'Go on.'

'You're an intelligent man.'

'What makes you say that?'

'You're well-spoken for a start.'

'Ah! And from that you assume I'm intelligent?'

'No. I notice you barely flick through the sensational newspapers Charlie goes for but you're quick to pick up my Times and turn to the political or financial pages.'

He regarded her steadily. 'You're very observant. So, what is it you want?'

'It's not for me, it's for Tom.' Abbie glanced around to make sure their youngest member wasn't within hearing distance. Then pulling up another crate she sat down and wrapped her arms around her knees. 'Sid got him an application form for a plumbing course at college. The course starts after Easter so he's late getting his application form in. But Sid's had a word with the principle about his situation, and I've asked Ellie's Social worker to do the same. The trouble is, he's struggling to fill the form in so I wondered if you could help?'

'And you can't do that because …?' JD raised his eyebrows.

'At the risk of sounding sexist, because plumbing is still very much a male dominated trade, and I don't want to embarrass Tom by offering my help'.

'What about Sid?'

'It's the holidays and Sid's not here.'

JD dropped his head as if he was considering her request. It was difficult to see his expression with his long hair hanging over his face, but Abbie wasn't fazed by the silence, rather she was beginning to recognise someone who thought before answering, so she waited.

'Where is he now?' JD asked.

'In the garden gazing at his form and looking lost.'

JD nodded slowly. 'Right!' he said.

Chapter 8

'OK boss? You look at bit frazzled.' Charlie stopped and frowned at his boss as he passed her on the stairs. He had a roll of insulation over his shoulder, a hammer sticking out of his belt and was forced to shout above the hammering, clattering and whine of drills.

Unwilling to say what was really troubling her she simply shouted back, 'The lift manufacturers have rescheduled - yet again - and the noise in this house is driving me mad today.'

'Y' canna lay insulation without taking up floorboards and hammering them down again boss, and y' canna have radiators plumbed in without a few clatters and bangs. If you wanna blame someone blame them glaziers. They're making more noise than the lot of us put together w' their whistling. Or blame Sarah; heat gun, drill, hairdryer, anything electric and she can't wait to get her hands on it.' He gave a half laugh as though the idea of Sarah and electricals amused him. He was about to continue upstairs when a thought occurred to him. 'By the way boss, Barry Mathews is delivering the back doors and paving slabs this morning so we thought we'd work outside this afternoon. Looks like it's gonna be a nice day.'

'See? This is exactly what I'm talking about. What's the point of me trying to keep to a schedule when....?' The rest of her sentence was lost by the whine of a heavy power drill in the attic. 'It seems to me there are too many jobs being started around here but not finished.'

'Hello! Deliveries!' The bellow came from the hallway.

Waving her hand dismissively at her chef she hurried down the stairs to catch Mick, Barry Matthew's lorry driver, with a load of deliveries and last month's bill.

'New back doors Charlie ordered,' Mick shouted. 'But I only had room for half the slabs for your patio. Not enough room by the time I'd loaded on the fibre insulation and stud partitions for Joe.' Leaning forward he dropped his voice. 'Barry says Joe 'll have no problem erecting stud partitions, but if you're worried about him reading the architect's plans, he'll oversee the work; make sure he gets the measurements right.'

Abbie gave a nod of satisfaction. This wasn't the first time Barry Matthews had surreptitiously helped out. Not only was he genuinely interested in the development of the Blue House, but they both knew that his other interest was keeping an eye on his old workmate so that Abbie could keep him employed and off the streets.

'Thanks Mick. I appreciate it.'

It was noon. The time of day when silence descended on the house like a shroud as workmen, resident and imported, disappeared for lunch or congregated in the kitchen. The resident inmates had barely finished lunch when there was a knock on the front door. Their regular visitors such as Barry, Mick, PC Bill Nicholson, and the postman all announced themselves with a bellow, so having someone knock politely on their front door was a rare occurrence. Leaving the table, Abbie stepped nimbly over the deliveries in the hallway and opened the door. It shuddered on the wooden floor.

'Mrs. Hunter?' The caller was well-spoken, had slicked back brown hair, a tan coat, highly polished brown shoes and a smile that never reached his eyes.

'Yes! I'm Abigail Hunter.' She examined his two companions warily. One had spiky red hair, chewed minty gum in a failed attempt to hide bad breath, and was sizing the place up in a manner that suggested he could have business here in the future. The other had a nose that appeared to have lost a fight with a heavyweight boxer, a pock-marked face, and his baggy jogging pants looked as though they had seen better days. That was when it occurred to her that it might have been sensible to fix the front door before concentrating on the back doors.

'I understand Charlie Marr works here?'

'Charlie Marr?' She realised this was the first time she had heard Charlie's surname. 'He does. If you wait here, I'll call him.' She was making her way back into the kitchen calling, 'Charlie!' when Mutt growled from the bottom of the stairs. Swinging around she was alarmed to see all three men had stepped uninvited into her hallway.

'Yeh boss?' Her chef sauntered through from the kitchen wiping his hands on a checked green towel. When he saw their visitors, his face hardened. 'What do you want?'

It was Charlie's abrasive greeting that decided Abbie to remain in the hallway. The man in the tan coat spread his arms, his smile revealing a row of straight polished teeth. 'What way is that to greet old friends, Charlie?'

'Yeh? Last time I was greeted by old friends like you I ended up in jail.'

Abbie tried not to appear alarmed.

'I'm here to collect my money, Charlie. Nothing more.'

Charlie gave a one shouldered shrug. 'No can do, Mr. Carter.'

Carter dropped his arms, and the pleasant expression vanished. 'You owe me, Charlie.'

'I don't think so.'

'You misunderstood our deal, Charlie.'

'I don't think so.'

A clatter by the kitchen door interrupted the growing hostility. Glancing behind, Abbie saw Joe bending down to pick up a wrench. It wasn't hard to guess he'd been eavesdropping. Sauntering up to the deliveries in the hallway he made pretence of inspecting them. JD appeared, a hammer in the belt of his trousers. Folding his arms, he leant casually on the kitchen door listening to the conversation.

Carter's gaze flickered across the hallway towards them, but all he said was, 'There's still the interest on the loan you owe, Charlie. Otherwise ....'

'Otherwise, what?' Charlie snapped. 'You'll send these two goons along to collect?'

The gum chewer with the spikey red hair and bad breath stepped forward thrusting his face up to Charlie's. 'Who're you calling a goon?'

Charlie grimaced and wafted his hand between their faces. 'You!'

'Is that so?' The goon stabbed Charlie aggressively in the chest with his forefinger. 'Then let me tell you mate ...!' A rattle of copper piping from the top of the stairs stopped his threat mid-flight. He looked up. Sid was sitting on the top stair looking down at them.

Abbie swallowed hard, wondering whether she ought to intervene to cool things off a bit.

Carter glanced over at JD, then Joe, then up at Sid and spread his hands in a reconciliatory manner. 'Whoa! Let's not get carried away here. All I'm after is what's owed me. I wouldn't want to see you back inside Charlie, not with your record.'

'That sounds like a threat, Mr. Carter.'

'I'm sorry you see it that way, Charlie. Pay up. That's all I ask.'

Bracing herself, Abbie moved over to Charlie's side. He was, after all, one of her employees – in a manner of speaking. 'Don't worry, Mr Carter; I don't want my chef back inside any more than you do, but your call is unexpected to say the least. Obviously, Charlie needs time to consider what you've said and to raise the money, if he does in fact owe you any,' she added and looked pointedly up at her chef. 'Isn't that right, Charlie?'

There was a slight hesitation before Charlie answered, 'Right, boss.'

'Will that suit you, Mr. Carter?' she asked lightly.

Judging from the expression on Carter's face it wouldn't but there was little he could do about it with a decorator, plumber and roofer, armed with the tools of their trade and making a point they were in support of their chef. 'No rush, Mrs. Hunter. I can give Charlie time to raise the cash. I can't say fairer than that now, can I?' He paused, his eyes narrowing. 'You wouldn't try running out on me again, would you, Charlie?'

Charlie glowered at him. 'I don't run from nobody, Mr Carter.'

'Glad to hear it.' Carter's gaze roamed the hallway. 'Nice little set up you've got here, Mrs Hunter. Must be costing you a bit to restore it?'

'Must it?' Brushing past her visitors she marched purposefully across the hallway and flung open the front door, at least she would have flung it open if it hadn't shuddered helplessly across the floorboards. She glared pointedly at her guests. 'It's been a pleasure meeting you gentlemen, and perhaps next time you call there'll be a few less threats?' She kept her gaze steady as the spikey haired, gum chewing goon, the flat faced, broken-nosed boxer and their smooth-talking boss sauntered out. She only wavered uncomfortably when Carter sized her up before stepping out into the spring sunshine. The front door shuddered on the floor as she slammed it behind them.

Charlie blew softly through lips. 'Whew! Thanks boss.' He grinned awkwardly at his workmates. 'Nice one, thanks.'

'Okay Charlie, what's this about you owing money?' she demanded planting her hands on her hips, then swore under her breath as there was another knock on the door. She flung it open. 'What!'

A pale-faced, skinny little man with round spectacles, stepped back in alarm. 'Oh! Sorry! So ... so sorry to bother you, Mrs Hunter,' he stammered. 'I'm the double glazier. We have a problem with the installation of the library windows. Can you spare a few minutes?'

She took a deep breath. 'Fine!'

Her mobile rang. It was Barry Matthews. She held up her hand to the glazier indicating five minutes before giving her full attention to the builder's merchant. 'Yes Barry.'

'I've got Big Ben here at the yard, Abbie.'

'You have? I assumed he was in the garden. Is there a problem?'

'I'm not sure,' Barry said slowly. 'He's arrived here with two huge boxes of plants for your garden.'

'Really? Where did he get the money to buy those?'

'His wages, I think.'

'His wages? Good heavens! What's he doing at your yard?'

'Ah! That's the problem. He's bought himself work trousers, shirts, boots, a jacket, and a yellow hard hat like Joes. Apparently, he's heard you tell my staff to put all purchases for the Blue House on your account, so he's done just that. His bill comes to a couple of hundred pounds or so. When I told him to put the stuff back, he got distressed. I'm afraid I'm not used to handling folk with er … whatever it is he's got; autism, is it?'

Abbie pinched between her eyes. 'Tell you what, Barry, go ahead put the clothes on my account.' Her thoughts flashed uncomfortably back to her rapidly diminishing bank account. 'As for the plants, I'll sort that out when he comes home.'

It was a desperate need to get away from her mounting problems, and the unbearable noise of drills and Joe and Charlie arguing over slabs that drove her out of the house that afternoon. She wandered down to the shops hoping the fresh air would ease her headache, but the moment she walked through the stone pillars at the end of the drive, she found the roar of traffic on the dual carriageway and the smell of fumes unbearable. That's what drove her into the blackened stone church sandwiched between the fish and chip shop and the greengrocers. That, and guilt. Having told Freddy she intended going to the Easter Sunday service she knew she ought to at least have a look inside the church so that she could give him a description, even if she hadn't gone to the service.

As the heavy wooden doors slammed behind her, she found what she had been looking for. Silence! The absolute peace and tranquillity of a church. Her footsteps sounded loud on the wooden floor and the pew creaked as she sat down but as she leant back and breathed in deeply there was a fragrant smell of beeswax and flowers. She looked around. It was an old, high-ceilinged church with dark wooden pews and a silver piped organ standing above the pulpit. A tall wooden cross decorated with yellow daffodils from the Easter celebrations still stood in the centre of the dais. Above it, a rainbow of light streamed through a coloured window pane depicting prophets from the Old Testament, and another depicting Christ and his apostles. It might be in a weird situation on the High Street, but was a beautiful church. Guilt niggled at her motives for being here just to prove to Freddy that she had. It certainly wasn't to pray, especially when she'd spent the last few months ignoring God.

A side door quietly closed, and the vicar or priest of whatever denomination this church was, walked smiling up the aisle towards her. He was a neat little man of around the age of sixty, with thinning white hair, a freckled face and owlish glasses.

'Can I help you with anything or would you prefer to sit quietly on your own?' His Irish lilt sounded like a gentle ballad echoing around the cavernous church. There was a good-natured air about his greeting which she liked.

'You can help if you know anything about renovating old property,' she said with a grimace. 'I started off with a vision but it's rapidly fading with all the work there is to do.'

'Ah! You'll be the lady renovating the Blue House on the corner. Mrs Hunter, isn't it?'

She was more than a little surprised. 'You're well informed.'

'That's my job. How's the work progressing, or is that what you've come into God's house to get away from?' He beamed at her like a cherub and she couldn't resist smiling back.

'It is,' she answered, and then, because he seemed so kind blurted out, 'What do I do when my convict chef owes money to his shady friends, my roofer's an alcoholic, my plumber's mate's a drug addict and I have an autistic gardener who's bought himself a whole wardrobe of work clothes which he's charged to my account.' She raised both hands in a gesture of hopelessness. 'I dread to think what stories my other two workers have to tell, and my own story is non-too brilliant either. My money is rapidly diminishing because neither my husband's partners nor his accident insurance have paid up yet. So … so, where do you suppose I can find God in that mess Reverend er …?'

'Reverend Padstow, but folk around here just call me Paddy'. Settling himself in the pew in front he swivelled around to face her, his arm on the back of the pew. 'I've no idea, Mrs Hunter. Where've you looked?'

'Nowhere, I've been too busy investigating National Insurance and Benefits for my workers.' She gave a long sigh, relieved to have unburdened herself to someone who was not family or associated with the house. 'It's a nightmare. The lift manufacturers keep putting me off, the electrician comes when he feels like it, my glaziers have hit a problem with the library windows and my workers do what they want, when they want.'

'Mmm.' There was a brief pause.

Abbie wondered later that if there hadn't been that pause, and if he hadn't added, 'Is that it or is there more?' she might not have blurted out, 'No, my... my baby died a year ago ... today.' She choked on the last word.

He gave her a moment to compose herself before softly saying, 'Ah, my dear Mrs Hunter, I'm so sorry.'

And because he sounded so genuinely sorry, and the church was quiet, and she was unlikely to see this nondescript little Irishman again, and he was probably bound by confidentiality anyway, her story poured out. All of it; the loss of her baby; Donald's death; his affair with her best friend; her shame; it spilled out all over the empty church.

When her garbled tale and her tears had dried up, Paddy stroked his chin with his fore-finger and thumb giving an indication he was pondering on her story. Eventually he said, 'Forgive me for asking, but why do you always refer to your infant as, "my baby" or "my child"? Didn't he or she have a name?'

Abbie focussed on her thumbs twirling around each other in her lap. 'Yes, he did. But I suppose I thought that by not using his name it would feel less painful at having lost him.'

'But you have lost him my dear Mrs Hunter,' he said gently. 'You have lost him and you feel the pain anyway.'

'Abbie; please call me Abbie. No-one calls me Abbie any more. I'm either boss, Abigail or Mrs Hunter. I seem to have lost my identity along with my husband, my child, my home and my profession.'

Paddy smiled at her. 'See how important a name and an identity are?' His gaze wandered around the church. 'I wonder ....?

She waited.

'Do you think it would help if you gave your child back his name?'

'What do you mean?'

Paddy thought for a moment before he said, 'A member of my congregation lost her little girl some years ago and was struggling to come to terms with it, so I suggested she write her daughter a letter. At first, she thought it was a silly idea, but then she found that once she started writing, "*My precious* …whatever her child's name was, it slips my mind for the moment, she discovered a flood of things she had wanted to say. Most of all she had wanted to say that she loved …ah! Yes; Marianne; that was the little girl's name. In her letter the mother told Marianne, that she was part of her and always would be. She filled page after page with precious memories of the day Marianne was born, the day she brought her out of the hospital and the happy times they had together. Then she asked Marianne if she remembered the big white polar-bear she took to bed with her; described how her big sisters had made her a bright mobile and how she had loved making it spin. The grieving mother talked about their trip to the seaside and how Marianne squealed with excitement when the incoming tide touched her toes. There were pages and pages of good memories before she wrote about the awful morning that they discovered God had taken her to be with the angels.' Paddy raised his eyebrows. 'Your little boy was called …?'

Her voice was strangled when she answered, 'Nathan.'

'Nathan, a lovely name, and I'm sure he'd love to hear it from your own sweet lips, and to know his mother will always love him, and that no matter how many folks come and go in your life that he alone has a special place in your heart. Would it help to write and tell him that do you think?'

'I don't know. It ... might.'

'Coming to terms with the death of a child is not easy so don't be afraid of the tears that 'll come with the precious memories.' He was silent for a moment watching her shrewdly as if wondering if there were any more revelations. Concluding that there weren't he added, 'You could even try that same writing technique on your husband, if you think it might help. And if you're having difficulty believing in our Lord during this difficult time, don't fret, Abbie. I shall pray for you. It could be when you've come out of this emotional turmoil, you're likely to find He hadn't left you at all. He was with you all the time. You simply couldn't find Him through the fog.' The little man of the cloth sat for a while before rising to his feet. 'It's been real nice meeting you, Abbie. Come back any time you want, either for a little chat or to sit in peace and quiet.'

And then his footsteps were walking silently back down the aisle. And through all that had been revealed in the last hour or so, Abbie found herself wondering whether he wore trainers or slippers to make his footfall so quiet.

JD was conscious that the atmosphere in the kitchen was unusually sombre so he stayed hidden behind an old National Geographic, although he wasn't reading it. Abigail Hunter had come back from her walk in a solemn mood and was now sitting with her elbows on the table, chin in the palm of her hand, staring into space. Tom was at the other end of the table gnawing worriedly on his thumbnail, and Charlie was preparing their evening meal, although judging from the banging of pans, one word out of place would send him into a rage. Only Sarah, laying out knives and forks, and Big Ben, lost in his comic, appeared at ease. Joe shuffled in from the hallway. Picking up the newspaper from the top of the shopping bags he scowled at his workmates.

'What the hell's up w' you, miserable sods?' he demanded sinking into his settee.

'Shut it, Joe, just shut it!' Charlie snapped. Banging a can of peas on the table he twisted the can opener as if he was wringing someone's neck. JD surmised it was probably Carter's.

'Worried about your court case, Tom?' Sarah asked quietly as she set a knife and fork in front of him.

JD's eyes drifted over the top of the magazine.

'Yeh! But ... it's not that. It's this plumbing course,' he said soberly. 'Sid's brought me a load of books he thought might help but there seems an awful lot 'o learning. Dunno if I'm cut out for this.'

JD lowered his magazine slightly. He noticed that although Abbie had been lost in a space capsule of her own making, Tom's comment had drawn her back to earth.

'What makes you think that?' she asked.

'I'm no brain box and I think there might be a lot of reading, and I never read.'

'Maybe that's why you're not a brain box, because you don't read,' she said.

'We never had no books in our house.'

JD lowered his National Geographic an inch more. 'Have you been in the library across the hallway?' he asked casually.

'Not since the dry rot specialist put that smelly stuff down.'

'Go and examine the room later. The walls are covered with bookshelves that would have held not just novels but books on a variety of subjects.'

'How do you know?'

'I don't, for certain, but I'm guessing the owner of this house was a well-read business man, a man of substance. How else could he have afforded a house like this?'

'Suppose, but that was him. This stuff I'll be expected to learn at college is like a foreign language. I don't understand none of it. It's beyond me.'

'How do you know it's beyond you till you've tried?' Abbie asked.

Dropping his reading matter on to the table, JD rose to his feet, meandered across the kitchen, threw a log on to the fire and was surprised to find himself saying, 'I'll give you a hand if you like?'

Tom narrowed his eyes. '*You* will? Why?'

JD made a point of not looking around as he could feel the eyes of the rest of the household on his back. 'No reason. It's up to you.'

'What do you know about plumbing?'

'Not a thing.' He returned to his seat. 'But then I had no idea how to treat oak panels or remove a build-up of paint until I went to the local library and read up about it. What I didn't understand I asked Joe or Barry Matthews. They're the experts in the building trade. But by the time I've finished treating oak panels and doors I'll be an expert myself. Reading and asking questions, that's the secret.'

'I'm not clever, you know?'

'Nobody's clever until they're taught or make the effort to find out.'

'I'm a hopeless case.'

'Who told you that?'

'My old man.'

'And you believed him?' JD shook his head, picked up the magazine but didn't open it. 'You've been given a rare opportunity to have a trade, earn a living and make a life for yourself. It's up to you whether you take it or not.'

Tom moved on from biting one nail to another. 'I suppose.' He examined JD through half lowered lids. 'If you're so clever then why are you on the streets?'

JD flinched inwardly. 'We're not talking about me, Tom. This is about you and what you want out of life. You say you want to be a plumber. Is it just talk or are you willing to put in the hard work to get there?'

'I want to but ...'

'Then we'll browse through your books after dinner.' JD opened his National Geographic again, but he was aware that while the others had lost interest in the conversation, Abigail Hunter had her chin on her upturned hand and was staring at him curiously.

Chapter 9

'Ahh!' Abbie curled her stubbed toe, winced, then glared at Joe, sitting on the doorstep with his mid-morning mug of tea. 'I thought you were supposed to be in charge of this paving project, Joe?'

Joe squinted up at her against the bright May sunshine. 'I am.'

'Then perhaps you could ask your workers not to leave the slabs strewn haphazardly along the back of the house where folks can trip over them,' she snapped, and then she felt guilty. She wasn't usually snappy, but she was still annoyed at being rudely awakened the previous morning with her caravan bouncing across the ruts in the garden. Falling out of bed with a scream, she had staggered to her feet and flung open her curtains to find Joe, Charlie and Big Ben pushing her mobile home across the back lawn.

'Need to make room for a delivery of slabs,' Joe had informed her alarmed face at the window. Levelling the caravan out again hadn't seemed to have occurred to them, so she had spent an uncomfortable night with the blood rushing to her head. This morning, she had insisted they use their spirit level on her caravan, but up to now, nothing had been done. Casting an irritated eye over her work-force she saw JD and Charlie had dug down to the damp-proof course outside the kitchen door, and were now levelling out the foundation mix with their boots.

Limping into the kitchen she dropped a heavy catalogue on to the kitchen table. 'Am I being horrible when I say I can't help hoping it'll rain so they'll get on with working indoors, Sarah?'

Sarah was at the top of the ladders fitting a new lightbulb into the pendant. 'I guess they think laying slabs might as well be done while the weather's fine.'

'I suppose they're right. Anyway, the good news is, the glazier tells me they'll have the attic windows in by the end of the week so I'll be able to decorate my new apartment.' Pulling up a chair she sat down and opened the catalogue. 'I'll be glad to get out of that caravan I can tell you. I can't wait to have my own things around me again.' Her finger stabbed the page in front of her. 'What do you think of these, Sarah?' She pointed to a picture of rustic, cream and beige curtains with a sample of material alongside it.

Cautiously descending the ladders with the old lightbulb, the girl pulled up a chair beside her and leant over the catalogue. 'They're lovely. Are they ready-made?' Seeing her blank expression, she added, 'You know, are they ready to hang or do you have to make them up?'

'I have no idea. My sister-in-law, Susan, picked the catalogue up because the company have gone bust. They're selling off bales of curtain material and bed linen at half price, and she wondered if I'd be interested.'

'Then I suspect you'll have to make the curtains up yourself. None of the windows in this house are a conventional size anyway.' She fingered the material. 'It's good quality.'

'Make them up? Oh dear! I've never been much good with a needle and thread.'

'I could make them up for you, if you like?'

'You can sew?'

'I love sewing. I've made clothes, curtains, anything. Do you have a sewing machine?'

'Ah! No! Any time I've needed to sew anything I've taken it to a shop or Susan.'

'I have a sewing machine but ...' She bit her lip.

'But what?'

She shook her head and continued flicking through the catalogue. 'I see they're selling towels at half-price.'

'And greatly reduced duvets.' Abbie rubbed her chin between her thumb and forefinger. 'It's definitely worth a visit, isn't it?'

'Yes, but we'll need to measure up the windows to see how much material we'll need first.' The pages of the catalogue stopped flicking over. Abbie glanced sideways at her.

'Problem?'

'I wish I had my sewing machine with me, that's all. It's right what you said about having your own things around you. It's not an expensive machine but it's reliable. My father bought it for me when I was debating whether to go into hairdressing or tailoring, so I guess it has a sentimental as well as a practical value. My greatest success was a friend's wedding dress.' The pages began to turn again, more slowly this time, leaving Abbie with the impression her mind was elsewhere. It was a while before she spoke again. 'If I'm going to make up curtains for the Blue House then I think I'd like to use my own sewing machine - if that's okay with you?' She closed the catalogue.

'It certainly is.' Abbie ran her fingers over the cover and chose her next words carefully. 'Although isn't a sewing machine rather heavy? Because, and this is purely a suggestion, after measuring up the windows we could drive into town and see what this company has to offer. I'd value your expertise on that anyway. Then we could pick up your sewing machine and any other belongings you want. What do you think?'

The silence was a long one.

'Of course, I don't know what your home situation is, so if you'd rather go alone, I quite understand. Whatever you want.'

Sarah breathed in deeply. 'What I want,' she said soberly, 'is to go into town, shop in department stores, or even go for a walk without *him* demanding to know where I've been. And you're right. I want my belongings around me, not necessarily furniture, but personal items – like my sewing machine, clothes, books, sentimental pieces of jewellery and photos. That's what I want.'

'Who is *him*?' Abbie queried then raised a hand. 'Don't tell me if you don't want to.'

Sarah thought for a while before she answered. 'Vince, my husband.' She sat back and folded her arms. 'It started not long after we were married. I'd made myself a new dress for my friend Doreen's birthday party and was saying how much I was looking forward to having a girls' night out when he started to sulk. "Why would you want to go gadding about the city without me?" he demanded. "Marriage means doing things together, not separately." In fact, he made such a fuss about my night out that I ended up telling Doreen I was sick and couldn't go.'

Charlie clattered into the kitchen in his boots, made his way to the sink and began scrubbing his hands before preparing food for lunch. She thought Sarah might clam up in front of him, but she didn't.

'Then Vince started coming into the hairdressers during his lunch break. The girls thought it was romantic but I knew he had an ulterior motive. If he caught me cutting a male customer's hair there were repercussions when I got home." I saw you laughing with him." "How often does he come in?" "Why've you been given men's hair to cut?" I plucked up courage to speak to the doctor about it once, and he suggested Vince's possessiveness came from his own insecurities. In a way it helped me to understand his moods, so I tried to be more tolerant and to reassure him that I loved him. I even tried suggesting he visit the doctor himself, but that didn't go down too well.'

Charlie dried his hands on the towel, and then set about cutting bread on the dresser.

'In fact, he refused to speak to me for almost a week. But then the same applied if I was late home from work, or I hadn't finished the ironing, or his favourite shirt hadn't been washed, or if I left dirty cups or newspapers lying around. He never physically beat me, but twice he locked me in the spare room. It was when he began to criticise my clothes, my weight, my make-up, and my friends, and degrade me verbally in front of his family that I woke up to the fact that for almost three years I had been living in a constant state of fear, and that I had lost all confidence and respect for myself.' She dropped her head.

'What about friends; someone you could confide in?'

'I lost most of them because he didn't like me going out without him. There was Doreen at work, but she expected bruises to back up my story of abuse and of course there weren't any. Vince can be Prince Charming himself, and as Doreen only saw his charm, she thought I was being paranoid.'

'Why didn't you walk out sooner?'

'I did, once. I went to a Woman's Refuge. They offered me a place of safety, emotional support and advice. But then he came to the hairdressing salon in tears begging me to return, and because I still loved him, I did.' Sarah shook her head. 'That was a big, *big* mistake. When we got home, he grabbed my throat and pinned me up against the wall. "You run away from me again and I'll kill you, and anyone who helps you. Got it?" Sarah slumped in her chair. 'Oh yes. I got it all right. That was when it dawned on me that I was nothing more than a prisoner in my own home and that violence was his next step. So, Christmas Eve, when I knew he'd be taking presents to his brother's house, I left. I was terrified he would come looking for me, so I made detours on my way to the Woman's Refuge. Then I saw the smoke drifting out of the chimney of the Blue House. I stood behind the tall pillars on the driveway watching it for ages. There was something ... safe, quiet ... welcoming about it. It dawned on me gradually that somewhere safe, quiet and out of the way was exactly what I needed. I was pretty scared coming up the driveway, believe me. After all, I had no idea who or what was in the Blue House. But then I met Joe.' A slow smile spread across her face. 'The last thing I expected was to be invited for Christmas dinner, I can tell you.' She gave a decisive nod of the head as if she had come to a decision. 'But now I think it's about time I got my life back on track again. So, in answer to your earlier question, yes, I'll help you measure up the attic windows then we'll drive into town and see what this company has on sale. And, if it's okay with you, I'll take you up your offer to pick up my sewing machine and my personal belongings from the house while Vince is at work.'

'This is crazy, absolutely crazy! You're mad, both of you. What if he comes home unexpectedly?' Charlie stopped mid-flight in his argument to watch Abbie turning his kitchen upside down. 'What 'y looking for boss?'

'My car keys.'

'Then would you mind putting things back where you found them. I try to keep an orderly kitchen round here. Tell them JD. Tell them they're mad for picking up Sarah's things without taking me along.'

JD was standing at the kitchen sink stirring a pot of primer to start painting all the newly fitted back doors. He didn't even look up when he said, 'I think you're doing a pretty good job of that yourself, Charlie.'

'Look boss, what's wrong with taking me with you?'

'Why? Just so you could have a go at Vince? We'd all end up in jail.'

Charlie removed the newspapers Abbie had slung across the table in the search of her keys. Placing them neatly on the arm of one of the sofas he said, 'I can't believe I'm saying this, but if there's any trouble you will ring the cops, won't you?'

'There won't be any trouble. We've told you; Vince is at work.' She vaguely wondered how her cut glass fruit bowl overflowing with apples and bananas was sitting on the dresser. She could have sworn she'd left it in her locked cupboard. But being too pre-occupied in finding her car keys she only vaguely wondered.

'You could take JD with you,' Charlie persisted. 'He might not be much good in a fight but he'd be darned good at threatening Vince with long sounding legal words.'

Abbie saw a flicker of amusement cross JD's face. 'No Charlie,' she answered. 'Sarah and I will be fine.'

With a shrug of despair, Charlie switched his argument to Sarah. 'This is your party I know, but I don't like the idea of you going back there, not after what I overheard.'

The girl's face flushed with embarrassment but all she said was, 'The boss is right, Charlie. With Vince at work, it shouldn't take more than twenty minutes to pick up what I need and get out of the house.'

'Ha!' The boss rattled her keys. 'Got them!'

Charlie gave a deep sigh. 'Thank God for that! So, you'll be leaving me to clear up the mess you've made in my kitchen, is that the idea, boss?'

'You've got it, Charlie.'

The front door shuddered on the floorboards as they left the house.

Browsing around the fabrics in the warehouse and visualising what both her apartment and the staff bedrooms in the attic would look like made her feel her project was actually making headway. They bought a job lot of good quality half-price duvets and pillows which they arranged to collect the following day, then squashed four bales of reduced curtain material into her car. Satisfied with their buys, Sarah then gave her directions to the west end of the city and a long row of shops on a busy main road. Squeezing her BMW into the only available parking space, Abbie switched off the engine.

Examining the girl's downcast expression she said, 'Nervous?'

'A little,' Sarah murmured viewing the shops. Turning, she added, 'You can come in with me, if you like?'

Recognising the need for moral support, Abbie picked up her bag. 'No problem.' Locking the car doors, she followed Sarah into a brightly lit salon with all manner of hairdressing products on display in the window. The door-bell tinkled as they entered.

A shapely young woman with long black stockinged legs, a short black leather skirt, pink overall and purple streaks in her hair glanced up, her face lit up when she saw them. 'Sarah? Wow! Sarah!'

'Hello Doreen,' Sarah appeared a little embarrassed as she indicated towards Abbie. 'This is Mrs Hunter.'

Doreen gave her a nod of welcome. 'Hi, Mrs Hunter. Sarah, it's great seeing you. Hang on love, I'll just finish setting Mrs Jessop's hair before we chat.'

Mrs Jessop, her greying hair half in rollers, towels around her shoulders viewed the visitors with eyes hungry for gossip. 'So, Sarah. You're back, are you?'

'Not for good, Mrs Jessop. Only for my spare door key. It's in my locker.' She paused uncomfortably before turning to Abbie and adding, 'This is Mrs Jessop. She lives two doors down from where I used to live.'

Doreen's comb hovered in the air. 'Used to live? You're leaving him, for good? Why?'

'Yes why?' Mrs Jessop eyed her critically through the mirror. 'Why leave a charming man like that? It's not as if he beat you up or anything, is it?'

'There are things equally as bad as a beating.'

'Like what?' Doreen asked.

'Yes, like what?' Mrs Jessop asked curiously.

'All I know is he misses you, Sarah.' Doreen combed through another strand of Mrs Jessop's hair. 'He still pops in on his way from work to ask if we've seen you, doesn't he Mrs Jessop.'

'Yes, he does. Lovely man, lovely.'

Doreen scratched her head with the handle of the comb. 'I know I shouldn't tell you this but he says if you hadn't been so depressed you might not have had that affair.' Her face took on that crumpled look of compassion. 'Why don't you see a doctor, Sarah love? Or a counsellor. It might help.'

'You can't merely have an affair because you're bored with your marriage,' Mrs Jessop twittered. 'You have to stick …Ouch!' Doreen rammed a clip through the curler.

Sarah's eyes widened. 'What affair?'

'There! I knew I should have kept my trap shut.'

Sarah bristled. 'I have *not* been having an affair, Doreen, and I certainly don't need to see a doctor for depression. The police for protection maybe, but not a doctor.'

'Eh?' Doreen looked up, startled.

Abbie moved over to a vacant chair next to Mrs Jessop and sat down.

'I need my spare key, Doreen. It's in a bag in my locker.'

'Your er …' Doreen took on a shamefaced expression.

'Don't tell me you let him into my locker?'

Doreen nodded uncomfortably. 'I was trying to help. We thought something in your locker might give a clue as to where you were.' She glanced curiously across at Abbie. 'Where are you living by the way?'

'The Blue House on Grange ….'

Abbie crossed her legs, nudging her new seamstress with her foot as she did so. Sarah's jaw snapped shut. 'I'll write the address down, Doreen.'

Doreen pulled the dryer over Mrs Jessop's head and turned up the heat dial. 'Tell you what I do have.' Grabbing a floppy flowered cloth bag from her locker, she began rummaging inside until she found a bunch of keys. 'Ta-ra!'

'So? What good are your keys to me?'

'Because my friend ...' Doreen struggled to remove a key from one of the rings with her long pink nails. 'I've been carrying this key to your front door ever since you asked me to let in a delivery of furniture.'

Sarah took the bunch of keys from her and removed the one she wanted. 'He'll be at work, is he?'

'Vince? Yes, I saw him passing first thing this morning. Why?'

Abbie noticed Mrs Jessop had lifted the noisy hairdryer and was watching them intently through the mirror.

'Because I'm collecting my things while he's out.' Pushing the key into her pocket she turned to Abbie. 'Ready?'

'You will call again, won't you, Sarah, and give me your address?' Doreen asked. Sarah simply gave a non-committal nod as they left the salon.

It was a short journey to Sarah's house, walking distance really, but they drove. Abbie found the red brick terraced house was one of many on a new estate with small neat gardens and crisp white front doors. Sarah pointed to one with semi-closed blinds at the windows. 'I hope he hasn't changed the locks.'

He hadn't.

Abbie's initial impression was that the house was so orderly that even the cushions seemed obliged to sit regimentally along the settee.

'This is how he lives,' Sarah explained when she saw her line of vision. 'Everything has to be in order from the books in the bookcase to the knives and forks in the drawer and *even* the dirty ones in the dishwasher. It's ridiculous!'

Abbie followed her upstairs, finding, once again, the main bedroom clutter free with neatly drawn back curtains and a white unruffled duvet on the bed.

'That's my wardrobe.' Sarah pointed to a plain white built-in wardrobe. 'Would you mind bundling my clothes into these plastic bags while I get the sewing machine from the other bedroom? Don't waste time folding them. I want to get out of here as quickly as possible.'

As Abbie opened the wardrobe doors, she gave a sharp intake of breath. 'Sarah,' she called. 'I think you better have a look at this.'. Taking a pale pink flowered dress down from the rail Abbie held it up. As Sarah came back into the room her hands flew to her mouth. Not only had the bodice of the dress been ripped but the skirt had been cut into long neat strips. Too shocked to say anything, Sarah examined the other clothes in the wardrobe. All of them had been cut to shreds and then hung tidily and colour co-ordinated up again.

Sarah fingered one of the ruined dresses. 'This is what I wore for my brother's wedding. And this one,' she took down a cream silk blouse with the sleeves cut off. 'It's my favourite. I wore it for his baby's christening before they moved to Australia.'

Abbie didn't know what to say. But then there was nothing to say. She simply watched a dry-eyed Sarah silently taking down her ruined clothes and laying them on the bed. Vince had done a good job. There wasn't one item that could be salvaged. 'What sick mind would do such a thing?' the girl murmured.

Leaving the wardrobe, she moved over to a dressing table and opened the top drawer. Her underclothes were shredded, all of them. Her hand trembled as it moved up to her jewellery box but as she lifted the lid her breath came out in short judders of relief. Holding up a silver chain with a pearl at the end she said, 'It wasn't expensive but it was my mothers.' Laying the silver chain on top of the dressing table she led Abbie across the hall into what she took to be her sewing room. Sliding a family album out of the bookcase, she flicked through the pages.

'Oh Sarah!' Abbie's stomach churned. All the photographs of Sarah, her parents and brother had been defaced with a thick black marking pen.

Slamming the album shut, Sarah surveyed her small sewing room coldly. 'I couldn't come back, not after this,' she said quietly. 'Let's take the sewing machine and go.'

Returning to the bedroom she sadly fingered her trashed clothes on the bed as if she was saying goodbye. 'I would have liked my photographs, especially the ones of my mum and ....' Her eyes widened in alarm at the sound of a key turning in the lock downstairs.

'Vince!' she whispered.

Abbie's mouth felt unexpectedly dry. After witnessing what this man could do to Sarah's belongings, she began to wish she'd taken Charlie up on his offer.

Footsteps ascended slowly up the stairs.

'Have you come home to me, Sarah?' His voice was smooth, friendly even, and when he appeared at the bedroom door Abbie saw he was an inch or so under six foot, wearing a crisp white shirt, red tie and Italian pointed shoes, shiny as glass. He glanced down at the sewing machine, 'Ah, I see you're here to remove your belongings, and you've brought Mrs Hunter with you.'

A cold chill ran down Abbie's spine that he knew who she was. Sarah didn't answer. She appeared to be frozen like a statue.

Vince surveyed the littered clothes on the bed and the open drawers and the smile vanished. 'I can't remember you asking my permission to remove your belongings, Sarah?' The voice now had a ring of steel to it.

'Sarah doesn't need your permission to remove the things that belong to her, Vince,' Abbie said with a calmness she was far from feeling.

Vince's hard green eyes moved deliberately in her direction. 'I can't remember inviting you to take part in this conversation, Mrs Hunter. This is between me and my wife. We have issues we need to discuss so would you …'

The front door slammed. Vince's jaw muscles worked in annoyance as feet pounded up the stairs.

'Sarah!' The arrival of long-legged, purple haired Doreen was a welcome sight indeed. Her gaze swivelled from Vince to Sarah to Abbie and back again. 'What's going on?'

There was the slightest hesitation before Vince raised his hands as if in despair. 'What's going on? I'll tell you what's going on, Doreen.' Striding across the bedroom he picked up one of the ruined dresses. 'Look what I've found. Torn, ruined, all of them.' He picked up another. 'See this? And this one? This time she's gone too far. I ask you, is that the act of a sane woman?'

Abbie could hardly believe what she was hearing. Doreen glanced uneasily from her to Vince. Then edging past Vince, she made her way over to the bed, picked up one of the torn dresses and examined it, unmistakably horrified by the state of the garment. Returning the dress to the bed she addressed her next comment directly to Sarah. 'I know you're a fast worker with a pair of scissors girl but even you'd have had to be going some to have cut up this lot since we saw you fifteen minutes ago.' Turning to Abbie she said, 'He called in at the shop not long after you'd left, and that busy-body Mrs Jessop told him where you were, and who Sarah was with, so I thought I better check.'

Vince's mouth twitched in annoyance when he saw who Doreen was backing. Picking up one of the ruined dresses he smoothed it down and then hung it neatly up in the wardrobe, making sure the torn strips weren't overlapping and the hanger was facing the correct way. And then he did the same with the next dress, and the next one. The three women watched him in silence. 'Look at this mess,' he said closing one of the open drawers. You know how I hate a mess, Sarah.'

Abbie squeezed Sarah's hand. It was sweaty and trembling. 'And from what I've heard, if it got too messy, you'd lock Sarah in the spare bedroom to teach her a lesson. Isn't that right, Vince?'

'Eh?' Doreen looked aghast.

'I like order and Sarah deliberately set out to provoke me.'

Abbie wondered if it was the warmth from her hand that sparked a flame of life back into her new seamstress because after a deep breath her posture straightened and she appeared to regain her confidence.

'I wasn't provoking you when I was cutting men's hair at work, Vince. You just didn't think it appropriate for a woman to be doing the work of a barber, did you?'

Vince was still absorbed in tidying up. 'You're a married woman. You shouldn't be cutting men's hair.'

Doreen's jaw dropped. 'Eh?' she repeated.

Sensing she was gaining support, Sarah continued, 'It wasn't proper for a married woman to have a girl's night out either, was it? That's why you wouldn't let me go to Doreen's birthday party.'

'I know what you girls get up to when you have a night out. I've seen them in town.' Vince's movements were methodical, controlled as he replaced the clothes. 'Sordid behaviour, foul language; you don't need such things in your life.'

'I've told you Vince,' Sarah spoke softly. 'All I wanted to do was celebrate Doreen's birthday with a meal, a few drinks and a laugh with the girls at the salon.'

Doreen closed her mouth long enough to whisper, 'He's mad.'

Vince slammed the wardrobe doors shut. 'I beg your pardon, Doreen?'

Abbie touched Doreen's arm. 'I think now would be a good time to make a move, don't you?'

Vince stepped into the doorway, baring their way. 'Make a move? Where to?'

'Home Vince,' Sarah said quietly. 'I'm going home.'

'You are home.'

Sarah shook her head. 'A home is a place where you're loved, where you can relax and be yourself. This place,' she viewed the bedroom with disgust. 'This place has been my *prison*.' She spat the last word out.

'You belong here, Sarah; with me!'

'Let us pass, Vince.' Abbie moved deliberately towards him. She could feel Doreen clinging on to her jumper.

Vince's head twitched nervously but he made no attempt to move. Reaching out for Doreen's arm, Abbie gently pushed her passed him and into the corridor. The girl clattered down the stairs. Keeping her eyes on Vince, Abbie reached behind again and grasped Sarah's sweaty hand. Side by side they edged towards the bedroom door. Vince still blocked their exit.

'If you don't let us through Vince, Doreen will call the police.' Abbie raised her voice. 'You hear that, Doreen?'

'I did!' Came the reassuring shout from the bottom of the stairs.

Vince tilted his head endearingly to one side. His expression changing like a chameleon from aggressor to victim. 'Stay Sarah?' He pleaded. 'I need you. Please stay.'

She shook her head. 'No Vince. Pleading won't work. Not this time.'

Abbie's spine tingled with revulsion as she squeezed passed him into the corridor.

He laid his hand on Sarah's arm. 'Please, Sarah?'

Sarah wavered. Abbie held her breath as Vince's expression lightened to one of hope as Sarah stepped back into the bedroom. But all she did was pick up her mother's pearl necklace and the jewellery box before making her way into the sewing room. Abbie followed closely behind. Unhurriedly picking up the sewing machine she handed Abbie a sewing box and they made their way down the stairs. Vince stood at the top of the stairs watching them. The nerves on the back of Abbie's head tingled in case he hurled some heavy object after them, but she resisted the temptation to glance back.

She half expected Sarah would burst into tears when she slammed the front door, but she didn't because Doreen beat her to it. She wrapped her arms around Sarah's trembling shoulders.

'I'm so sorry I didn't believe you, Sarah. I'm so sorry.' She paused before clenching her teeth and adding, 'And the next time I get hold of that Mrs Jessop she's not gonna know what hit her when I've finished with those curling tongs!'

JD placed his knife and fork neatly on his empty dinner plate, sat back satisfied, and listened to Joe's rising list of complaints.

Their self-promoted site foreman was waggling his finger in the direction of their boss. 'And that's another thing, boss. Your apartment. I told you not to rush painting till the plaster had dried out. You should've listened cos you've made a right pig's breakfast of that ceiling.'

Sensing a row about to erupt, Tom hastily snatched up his college books and retired to the sofa, Charlie picked up the playing cards, Big Ben joined Tom on the sofa and lost himself in one of his comics, and JD picked up a newspaper.

Abbie glowered at her roofer. 'What do you mean, I've made a right pig's breakfast of painting my ceiling?'

'Have you looked at it?'

'Of course, I've looked at it. I've been painting it.'

'Call that painting, boss? There's paint running down the walls, splashes on the floorboards, and if you look in the mirror, if we had one, the rest is on you, *and* you still haven't ordered the tiles for your bathroom.'

'That's my fault, Joe.' Sarah was collecting the empty dinner plates from the table. 'She's been busy helping me sort out my divorce proceedings.'

Abigail waved her hand dismissively. 'Or it could be I'm just a rotten painter, and stop calling me boss, Joe.'

'Then why don't you leave the painting to JD, Sarah or even Tom.' Joe asked.

'Tom has enough to do with his course work, the rehabilitation centre, and helping Sid with the plumbing. And you've been nagging Sarah for weeks to finish scraping wallpaper so you can erect your wall panelling in the guest rooms. Now I've got her making up curtains.'

JD knew what was coming. Sure enough, Joe swivelled around in his chair and stabbed his finger at his newspaper. 'That leaves you, JD.'

'Fine!' he agreed. He didn't particularly care what he did, although … he was jerked into an odd thought. Perhaps that wasn't exactly true, he deliberated. Not anymore. He did care what he did. He stared at the print on his newspaper without reading it. Strange, but he was actually enjoying sanding down and painting the new back doors and oiling panels. It had been a long time since he had found pleasure in anything. In fact, he was even enjoying helping Tom with his course work.

That was the moment the kitchen door swung open and a startled Mutt leapt to his feet barking as a clean-shaven man in a crisp white shirt, blue striped tie and with Italian pointed shoes sauntered in, his jacket slung casually over his shoulder. 'I'm sorry. I didn't mean to alarm you. I did knock but clearly you didn't hear.' His smile was charming, apologetic even, and his unblinking eyes danced around the occupants of the kitchen until they landed on Sarah. 'Hello Sarah, darling. Aren't you going to introduce me to your friends?'

Sarah remained rooted to the spot, the empty dinner plates in her hands. Vince raised his eyebrows, waiting. She blinked rapidly and then, in a pathetically small voice said, 'This is Vince, my husband.'

JD laid a restraining hand on Mutt to stop him growling and inspected Vince curiously. Having been as horrified as the rest of the Blue House occupants when the women had returned and told their story three days ago, the idea that the culprit himself had found them was not a pleasant one. Folding his newspaper, he laid it on the table and watched their employer casually make her way over to Sarah, clearly marking her support. He noticed her eyes had widened, the way they always did when she was ill at ease, but she had fixed a friendly smile across her face. He guessed her intention was to keep this visit pleasant so she could get this chap out of her house as quickly as possible. He was right, because her opening sentence was gracious.

'I'm sorry we didn't hear you knocking,' she said. 'A new front door and bell are still on our agenda.'

Vince gave her a boyish grin that JD suspected usually won people over. He'd come across that type before when … he gave a slight start as an uncomfortable memory from not so long-ago crept in. His policy these days was to never look back. He took a fleeting look around the table. Everyone looked uneasy but it was Charlie's expression that warned him of trouble. He'd seen that expression before, usually before Charlie lost his temper. He was concentrating on laying his playing cards down on the table, Queen of hearts on the King, six of clubs on the seven. But his mouth was set in a hard, thin line and he was working his jaw.

'What can we do for you, Vince?' Abigail asked.

'Actually, I came to see Sarah.' Vince gave a gentle laugh. 'We had a slight er ... shall we call it a 'domestic? We were both at fault but I'm here to apologise.' His gaze flittered around the occupants at the kitchen table, 'if you would be kind enough to give us a private moment.'

Abigail turned to the girl. 'Do you want a private moment with your husband, Sarah?' Sarah's face was white. She stared numbly down at the dirty dinner plates. 'Sarah?' Abigail murmured. 'You don't have to do anything you don't want to. Understand?'

'I'm sorry Mrs Hunter.' A flicker of irritation crossed Vince's face. 'I would appreciate you *not* putting pressure on my wife. Sarah will do the sensible thing, which is to talk to me - in private. Won't you, Sarah? I am her husband.'

JD glanced across at Charlie, but Charlie was still playing cards, working his jaw.

'And I'm her employer.'

'Employing her to do what exactly?'

'Sarah is a member of my staff. She's helping me renovate my house.'

Vince gave a snort of contempt. 'Renovate a house? Sarah wouldn't have a clue where to start. She's just a hairdresser.'

'*Just* a hairdresser?'

Shuffling up a completed set of cards Charlie murmured, 'She does other things.'

Vince's eyes narrowed. 'What other things?'

Dropping the pack of cards on the table, Charlie stood up with slow easy movements. 'She's a scamstress, she strips wallpaper, shops, sands down doors and helps me in the kitchen. I'm the chef around here.' He sauntered around the table and joined the boss behind Sarah. 'I'd ... we'd miss her if she left,' he said coolly. 'On the other hand, if she wants to go back to you, we wouldn't stop her. She can do whatever she wants.' He laid a hand on Sarah's shoulder. 'Do you want a private moment with this ... *moron?*'

JD groaned inwardly. He could see where this was heading. Yet Charlie's support seemed to have given the girl courage because she laid the dinner plates down on the kitchen table.

'No Vince,' she said firmly. 'No private moments.'

Joe rose from his seat, shuffled across the kitchen, picked up a dishcloth from the sink and wiped a ring of spilt milk off the table. 'Don't think our Sarah wants no private moments,' he muttered addressing his comment to no one in particular.

Sarah ran her tongue over her teeth. 'I don't want to talk to you, Vince because you don't talk, you threaten, and I'm tired of being threatened.'

Joe flung the dishcloth back in the sink. 'That's 'm' girl.'

Abigail glowered at her roofer. 'Shut up, Joe!'

Lifting her chin in a blatant show of courage, Sarah addressed her husband. 'I'm worn down with your jealous rages, Vince. I'm scared of being locked in the spare room and I'm lonely because you don't allow me to have friends.'

'You seem to have found plenty friends here, Sarah.' Vince was staring ominously at Charlie.

'I have. They listen to me. They value my opinion.'

Vince gave a contemptuous, 'Ha! What opinion of any value could you possibly have? Besides, I listen to you.'

'No, you don't, Vince. You never listen. You demand, you bully, you control and you dictate, but you never listen. For years I've been forced to suffer your ... *abuse*! Yes, that's exactly what it is, mental and verbal abuse. You've driven me into being a ... a shell of the person I used to be. You've demeaned me in public, you've squashed my ideas, and physically, you've treated me more like a caged animal than a wife.'

Vince was clearly taken aback by this unexpected onslaught. 'Aw Sarah, come on. That's a gross exaggeration.'

Charlie gave Sarah's shoulder a squeeze and her pert little chin jutted out. 'I don't exaggerate, Vince, and you know it. I've tried making excuses for you; tried to understand your insecurities and the reasons why you act the way you do. I've tried to love you, I have. But you refuse to acknowledge you've a problem, let alone address it. I've reached the point where I've had enough of living like ... like a prisoner, with you as my jailor. That's why I've decided I want... I want ... out of this marriage. I've talked to a solicitor and you should get the divorce papers any day now.'

Vince's mouth hardened and his nostrils flared. 'You want out of our marriage so you can have him I suppose,' he snapped, and the glare of pure hatred he threw at Charlie would have flayed most men, but not Charlie.

'No Vince, so that I can be free to make my own choices in life.'

Vince's voice shook with anger when he said, 'I promise you, you will live to regret this decision, Sarah.'

'I doubt it.' She glared back at him.

His face took on a crazy look, like that of a wild animal under threat. Slinging his jacket on to the stool by the door he lunged towards her. 'You ... slut....!'

Not even JD could predict Charlie would have moved so swiftly. Their chef leapt forward, grabbed Vince by the knot of his tie and slammed him back up against the wall. Their faces were so close their noses were almost touching.

'And you might live to regret the day you walked in through our front door, *mate*,' he hissed. His clenched fist warned JD it was about to deliver a few ultimatums of its own.

Darting forward he grabbing Charlie's raised fist. 'Enough, Charlie! Enough!'

Charlie's breathing was heavy, his anger raging, but JD's intervention was enough to force him to step back. Nevertheless, JD kept firmly hold of the fist. Vince had slumped half-way down the wall, red faced and badly shaken. His gaze drifted nervously from Charlie to JD, then back to Charlie again before struggling into an upright position. Tucking his shirt back into his trousers he attempted to regain his composure.

'I shall be in touch, Sarah. We have unfinished business,' he said shakily.

Cautiously removing his hand from Charlie's fist, JD moved towards the kitchen door, picked up Vince's jacket and was about to hand it to their unnerved visitor when Charlie snatched it from his hand. Crumbling it into a heap he thrust it into Vince's chest. The man staggered back.

'Take this with you, and don't come back!' Charlie hissed through gritted teeth, and his eyes followed him through the hallway until the front door slammed – or at least shuddered across the floor as far as it would go.

JD studied their boss. He wanted to say, 'Are you okay?' but he didn't. He wanted to commend her on the way she had handled a difficult situation, but he didn't do that either. He kept his comments to himself.

It was Joe who broke the silence. 'I could do with a shot of whisky after that.' Catching Charlie's glare, he hastily added, 'perhaps a cuppa would do just as well. Met his sort before, they're the worst. It's all under the surface.' He banged the jar of honey on the kitchen table and patted Sarah's arm. 'You're well shot of him love. Have a spoonful of honey. It's good for the nerves.'

Sarah's legs give way from under her and she sank down on to a chair. 'But am I? Shot of him I mean, and how did he find me?' She dropped her head in her hands.

'Mrs Jessop, remember?' Abbie said. 'You would have given Doreen your address if I hadn't stopped you.'

'I said the Blue House, didn't I? Stupid! Stupid!' she moaned.

Tom joined them at the table. 'That's two threats from Vince. Two! For that, I reckon that you could get a restraining order on him, Sarah. Ask your solicitor.'

Sarah's face softened. 'Thank you, Tom.'

'Tom's right,' Abigail agreed. 'We'll speak to the solicitor about it tomorrow.'

Charlie was still red in the face after his encounter with Vince. 'All the same, it might be safer to stick close to the Blue House till this is settled, Sarah. What do you reckon boss?'

And that was how they spent the next hour, discussing Sarah's divorce, and what to do about Vince's threats. Needless to say, Charlie's contribution, which appeared to involve a form of violent mob tactics, was firmly shot down, but it did bring a watery smile to Sarah's lips.

Chapter 10

Bored with scraping off wallpaper which seemed determined to cling to the walls, Abbie decided to take a leisurely walk to Barry Matthew's builders' yard. Her excuse, if indeed she needed one, she was after all the boss she reasoned, was that Joe insisted they needed another steam wallpaper stripper as the first one had broken. And as he was also nagging her to choose the bathroom tiles for her apartment, it seemed a good opportunity to take a walk on this lovely warm sunny June afternoon and wear her favourite pink silk blouse, newest jeans, wear make-up and feel like a woman again instead of a labourer. Besides, if her labourers claimed they needed to finish laying slabs outside in the back garden, then she could find an excuse too.

After browsing around Barry Matthew's showrooms, she settled on a plain white tile, and a slimmer grey tile to create a delicate patterned border. Pleased with her choice, she then meandered over to the garden centre for a coffee before sauntering home through the underpass. As she came out at the other side, she found herself facing the heavy wooden doors of the stone church. That was when it dawned on her that despite the chaos of the last few weeks, she had actually felt much better; physically and mentally; happier even, thanks to the Reverend Paddy Whatshisname's advice. She frowned. What was his name again? On the spur of the moment, she stepped inside the church.

The man in question, in jeans, tee-shirt and minus his dog collar, was flicking through the bible on his communion table the way Charlie flicked through the sports page when searching for the football news. When he saw her, he raised a hand in greeting and came beaming up the aisle to greet her as though they were friends of long standing.

'Hello Abbie. How are you my dear? You look nice and fresh today. Sit down, sit down. Tell me how the renovation is going, and how you yourself are doing.'

She slid into a pew, surprised he had remembered her. "I've just called in to say thank you,' she said awkwardly.

'The letter writing was helpful then?' Taking the pew in front he slung his arm casually over the back, giving the impression he had nothing else in the world to do but talk to her.

'It was.'

'Difficult though?'

'Very difficult.' She hesitated. 'But oddly enough, once I started writing, "My dearest darling Nathen," I felt … I suppose I felt like I was actually communicating with him again. It felt … good – sort of.' She paused, recalling those long evenings alone in her caravan pouring over her exercise book. 'Everything I ever wanted to say, but never had the chance to, seemed to flood out into my letters. I told him how much I loved him; I recalled our happy times together, the toys he had, the lullaby I sang to him. Then I told him how desperately I missed him and how there would always be a special place for him in my heart that no-one else could ever fill. And you were right. It was exhausting. I cried a lot. The writing stirred up so many unexplored emotions. But then …'

She cleared her throat self-consciously, and stared towards the simple wooden cross on the altar. 'But then it dawned on me that, and I don't understand how, but I had found comfort drawing close to Nathan again. By acknowledging him, and saying what I needed to say I was finally able to acknowledge he had … gone. Closure I think they call it, don't they?'

Paddy nodded his head wisely. 'So, I would call that progress, wouldn't you? What about your husband? Did you try that same letter writing technique on him?'

She pulled a face. 'I did. I had a pile of bills, statements and letters I'd been meaning to go through, but when I saw Donald's signature again, I was furious. I began scribbling, "*HOW DARE YOU DECEIVE ME.!!!*" in bold black capital letters across the bills.' She gave a nervous laugh. 'You wouldn't believe the language I used.'

The reverend gave a chuckle. 'Oh, I think I would Abbie, my love. I think I would. And that's perfectly fine. It's getting rid of all the negative stuff inside you, that's the important thing. Do you think you did that?'

She tilted her head to one side. 'I'm not sure. My letter to Donald was filled with reams and reams of angry accusations over what his infidelity, deceit and his lies had done to me, and found I kept asking him the same question over and over. "*Did you love me at all?*"'

'And did you get an answer?'

She shook her head. 'Not really. I came to the conclusion that he probably did, in the beginning, in his own obscure way but I'll never know for sure, will I? That was why I knew I had to work at letting that question go, otherwise I would drive myself crazy. That's been the hardest part, but whenever I find myself chewing over it, I force myself to focus elsewhere. As for my friend, the one who had the affair with my husband, I wrote her a good long angry letter, then I set it on fire and decided that was the end of her.' She smiled awkwardly. 'So, thank you. That's really all I called in to say. It felt good laying my thoughts out on paper instead of having them rattling around in my head.'

'Overall, it sounds like progress.'

'It was, I think.'

'And how are your workers?'

She gave a short laugh. And there was something rather pleasant about sitting in the cool of the church with the sun streaming through the windows, telling him about the rats, their unwanted visitors, and the progress of the house. But the Reverend Paddy was a good listener, and there were so many amusing anecdotes, that when she did eventually get up to leave, she was surprised to discover that she had been there for well over an hour.

She sauntered back up the sunlit driveway of the Blue House humming some tuneless pop song she'd heard on the radio that morning. It was the colourful splash of pink flowers on the bushes that brought her to a standstill. Weren't those the bushes Big Ben had cut back so severely in January, she mused? How had she never noticed they had come into bloom before now? Her eye travelled over to the red and pink roses, then up to the front door where Ben had placed bright green miniature fir trees in big pots. He had even made use of their inherited cracked stone troughs by filling them with red geraniums and draping white and electric blue lobelias over the cracks. She smiled quietly to herself. She may have had the vision for the Blue House, but Big Ben it seemed had a vision for the garden. Even now he was on his hands and knees making a 'brick on edge' division between the garden and the driveway.

'You're transforming this garden, Ben,' she said standing over him, and was amused to see that although he didn't look up, his enormous face reddened with pleasure. 'Is there anything else you need for it?'

There was a long pause before he muttered, 'Can I have new gravel for the driveway?'

'Of course, you can.' She made a mental note to write it on her works shopping list.'

Tom was sitting on the doorstep beside the cracked stone troughs, his head buried in a plumbing manual. He glanced up when he heard her footsteps. 'Hi boss. Next time you're at the builders' can you get more rat poison? Me and Sid think there's still a rat in the cellar.'

Even that disturbing news couldn't dampen her good mood. 'I shall write that on my shopping list; and don't call me boss.'

'Excuse me!' The call came from above.

Shading her eyes, she squinted up at JD on the ladders, his black tee shirt was daubed in white. 'If you're shopping, I could do with more paint for these windows.'

'Right!' She called back, wishing her workers had told her all this before she'd visited the builders' yard. Gravel, rat poison and paint, she murmured to herself, and made a mental note to write all three down as soon as she reached the kitchen. Picking her way around the building materials in the hallway she was surprised to hear the whirring of a sewing machine in the dining room. Opening the door, she found Sarah perched on a crate, her sewing machine whirring away on an old door propped up by bricks and surrounded by sheets. The whirring stopped when Abbie entered.

'Ta-ra!' Sarah gestured towards her make-shift table. 'Compliments of Charlie. I've started to make up the curtains for your apartment. They'll be ready to hang as soon as you've finished the painting.'

'Brilliant!' Abbie pointed suspiciously to the sheets. 'Where did you get these?'

'Charlie! He told me he had just the thing to keep the curtain material clean,'

'I bet he did,' Abbie said grimly. 'That's the bedlinen from my locked store-room. I shall have words with him.'

The words she was going to have with Charlie never did materialise, nor did she remember to write down the extra items needed at the builder's yard, because as she stepped on to their sun-lit patio she was pleasantly surprised to find that it was completely finished and that to celebrate, Charlie had prepared an elegant summer buffet. One of her best linen tablecloths covered what she presumed was another old door propped up on bricks. In the centre stood a cooked ham surrounded by bowls of salad, new potatoes, beetroot, garlic bread, and jugs of lemonade. 'Charlie! This looks delicious.' Her eye fell on a new wooden bench against the wall. 'Where did this come from?'

'Hope you like it, boss. Present from me.'

'Goodness! I couldn't possibly let you pay ....'

Charlie dismissed her with a wave of his hand.

She sat down on the new bench next to Sid. Living on his own, Abbie had suggested he might as well have his evening meals with them. 'Nice bench, eh Sid?' Resting her head back against the wall, she gave a sigh of contentment as she soaked in the late afternoon sun.

'If you look at it more closely, you'll discover it has the Council's logo on the back,' he whispered.

'*What*?' She sat bolt upright.

Sid laid a restraining hand on her arm. 'I wouldn't say anything, Abbie lass. It's just Charlie's way. He means well enough.'

'But Sid; *stollen property*? I could get …'

But then Joe switched on the radio, and she found Charlie's thieving got lost in a pleasant evening of eating, drinking and listening to 'The Archers', and somehow it seemed wiser – or perhaps easier - to take Sid's advice and just let the matter of where the bench came from, drop. She considered the cloudy mixture in her glass with a furrowed brow. 'Charlie, how have you made this without a blender?'

'Ah! Well, it's like this you see, boss.'

'Don't tell me. You've broken into my storeroom again.' She shook her head. 'Why break in, take my blender, then go to all the bother of re-setting the padlock? Why don't we keep the padlock off then you can basically use whatever you need?'

Charlie sucked in sharply through his teeth. 'Can't do that boss.'

'Why not?'

'Got to keep my hand in somehow.'

She shook her head at him, enjoying the easy banter. It continued through the evening and until the sun had drifted behind the trees, the air had cooled down, and the birds had sung their last lullaby.

Sid was the first one to make a move. He grunted as he stood up. 'Ah well. I suppose I better say goodnight.' He opened the back door into the kitchen. 'See you all ….' what sounded like a 'whoosh' of air came from inside the house. They stared at each other in alarm. Charlie was the first to react. Leaping to his feet he and Sid raced through the kitchen, the others close behind. But as he flung open the door into the hallway, they were forced back by a blast of hot air and billows of thick black smoke. Abbie covered her eyes, but not before she had registered a heavy-set intruder in a combat jacket and balaclava. He had a can in his hands which he was splashing over their deliveries - and judging from the smell and the flames licking up her walls - it was petrol. Momentarily, she froze. The whole scene seemed surreal, as if she was watching a crime thriller on TV. It was their intruder, seeing their arrival and making a dash for the front door that brought her to life again.

'No! Not ... my ... house!' she heard herself screaming. She lurched forward. What she intended to do she had no idea. Save her deliveries? Tackle their intruder? There wasn't time to do either. The sudden 'whoosh' as the petrol ignited forced her sideways, in the direction of the front door – the same direction as their intruder. The intruder, non-too pleased at seeing a crazed woman attempting to block his escape, barely stopped as he raised his hand and lashed out at her. The blow was forceful. It sent her reeling across the hall and crashing against the stairs.

For a moment she lay stunned, a searing pain in her shoulder. Her stinging eyes blinked rapidly through the smoke-filled hallway at their intruder. He had stopped by the front door. Turning, he hurled the whole petrol can at her advancing workers to keep them at bay. It had the desired effect. Not wanting to be soaked in petrol they backed off. Those few seconds were all he needed. Flinging open the partially closed front door - which was a miracle in itself as the front door had never been in a state to be 'flung' before – he fled down the steps. The sudden draught caught the flames.

With another 'whoosh', they licked up the petrol on the sheets of plasterboard, and rolls of insulation causing billows of black smoke. In an attempt to save her deliveries, she staggered to her feet and stumbled forward. Somewhere in the background she heard Charlie yelling, 'Back off boss! Back off!' But it was the intensity of the smoke that drove her back, not Charlie's warning. Gasping for air she made for the open door in time to see Sid chasing their intruder down the driveway.

'No! No Sid!' She screamed, but after smoke insulation her shout brought on an uncontrollable spate of coughing. Someone shoved her roughly to one side. It was Joe. He was charging out of the door with the petrol can held at arm's length. Through a blur of tears, she saw JD and Tom unravelling the yellow hosepipe.

Then Sarah was bellowing, 'Boss! Here!' And she felt a wet towel thrust into her hands.

What? What …?'

'Beat out the flames with it.'

She glanced outside to see if Sid and Joe were okay, but there was too much smoke to see clearly. So, shielding her face against the heat she began to beat out the flames. It soon became apparent that they were making little impact against the fire. But then came a welcome bellow from Charlie at the kitchen door.

'*Move your ass, boss*!'

It was followed by a loud hiss of water which hit the burning materials with such force a roll of burning insulation rolled precariously close to her and Sarah. But then, to her relief, the water began dowsing the flames, and for a split second she felt a glimmer of hope - until Charlie lost control of the hosepipe. She watched in horror as the yellow hosepipe snaked wildly around the hall before the full force of the jet hit her on her back. Propelled forward, she slithered across the wet floor, and would have fallen if a firm hand hadn't landed on her shoulder and hauled her back to the staircase. She found herself dumped on the bottom stair. JD was standing over her.

'Your phone; where's your phone?' he shouted.

She rubbed her stinging eyes, wondering stupidly why JD would want her phone. She pointed to the landline.

'Burnt out. I need your mobile.'

Tapping the back pocket of her jeans she looked helplessly up at him. 'I left it on the kitchen table. Why ....?'

He raced into the kitchen.

'Where's Big Ben?' she shouted after him, but whether he heard or not she had no idea. And then she spotted Big Ben through the open kitchen door. He was banging his head on the wall and howling in distress.

Tom yelled, 'Boss! The new door, boss! The new door!' And he was trying to prise their new front door away from the flames. Slithering across the wet floor she grabbed the other end, both of them crying out in pain as the heat of the wood burned their hands. Between them they staggered outside and dropped it on the gravel. That was when she saw her plumber. Sid was sprawled face down across the driveway with Joe leaning over him.

She vaguely heard Charlie shouting, 'I think we've got it under control!' as she raced across the garden, but her heart was pounding too loudly in her ears to be sure.

'Is he alive?' she shrieked. 'Is he alive?' She fell on her knees next to Sid's motionless body. Joe shook his head. And in that terrifying moment all she could think was, 'This is my fault. My fault! The fire; the house; it was too much for him.'

Tom dropped on to his knees beside her. 'Sid! Sid!' His cry was strangled.

JD arrived. Between them, they rolled their plumber gently over on to his back. There was a groan from the body. Then to her relief, she saw Sid open his eyes. His gaze was blank until it landed on her, then he gave a crooked smile. 'Sorry lass. He … he knocked me out.'

With a sob, Abbie cradled the plumber in her arms before studying the blackened faces of her workers. 'Are you all okay? Where's Big Ben?'

'Sarah's calming him down,' Tom informed her.

The welcome blare of two-toned horns in the distance made her look up. Blue flashing lights were approaching. A moment later an enormous red fire engine pulled into her driveway. That was when it occurred to her why JD had wanted her mobile phone.

Trouble was, there was an ominous silence from her workers when they saw it was followed by two police cars.

Abbie found Station Officer Alan Holmes to be a kindly, capable Fire Officer with shrewd brown eyes trained to pick out the slightest hint of a spark. He ordered his crew to remove all the building materials out of the house, and then, seated on the bottom stair, she watched him and his colleagues make a thorough inspection of the walls, ceiling, floorboards and upstairs until he was convinced the fire was thoroughly quenched.

'All clear, Mrs Hunter,' he assured her in manner that made her feel she was in safe hands. Taking his iPad out of his jacket pocket his face sobered up.

'So, what's the bad news?' she asked brushing a black sooty mark off what used to be her favourite pink silk blouse. She smudged it in the process.

The fire officer examined his iPad. 'Well, the bad news is that most of your delivery materials are ruined, and with this being a clear case of arson there will have to be an investigation. But on the positive side, the results should give you supporting evidence for your insurance claim.' He gave a one shouldered shrug. 'Fortunately, the majority of your deliveries were fireproof which prevented the fire from spreading. You were lucky that a house this age didn't have flammable insulation or wall coverings. Awful stuff that was; lit up if you as much as looked at it. There's no structural damage either. All you have are a few scorched walls and floorboards, thanks the prompt actions of yourself and your staff.' He gave PC Bill Nicholson a friendly nod as the policeman stepped in through the front door. A fresh-faced young constable who gave the appearance that he came from farming stock, accompanied him. 'Evening Bill. I'm mobilising a fire investigation team into this lot. Do you need to look around?'

'No, I'm just here to take statements, Alan. Heard about the fire on the car radio so thought I'd pick this one up.' He grimaced as he surveyed the hallway, then patted the bannisters. 'You've a few burn marks on those newels Mrs Hunter, but not to worry, they should sand down okay. I've a lathe at home. If you like I'll replace the missing ones? Hobby of mine, working with wood.' And then he considered her in a kindly manner. 'Although, I dare say a few scorched newels are the last thing on your mind right now. Looks like you need a little care and attention yourself.'

Her lower lip quivered at his thoughtfulness. 'We all do.' She examined her burnt hands then gingerly touched her shoulder from when she was thrown against the stairs. She hadn't realised it was hurting until now.

PC Nicholson watched her before jerking his head towards the kitchen. 'I take it your er ... workers are in there?'

She nodded, and then, for no accountable reason, other than her house had almost burnt down and she ached all over, she suddenly felt ridiculously close to tears. 'They saved my house,' she sniffed.

PC Nicholson pulled a clean white handkerchief from his pocket and handed it to her. She blew her nose fiercely leaving a greasy black smudge before handing it back to him. 'If you must interrogate them, you will be nice, won't you? Don't scare them.'

He examined his handkerchief in disgust. 'I shall be Prince Charming himself, Mrs Hunter, don't you worry.'

Station Officer Alan Holmes gave a snort of amusement.

When Abbie entered the kitchen with PC Nicholson and Fire Officer Holmes, her heart warmed to see the sorry state of her grubby faced workers sitting around the kitchen table. Their clothes were not only black and scorched but drenched from the hosepipe. They looked up worriedly when she walked in with her escorts.

'A few questions folks, that's all,' PC Nicholson reassured them. 'Can any of you give a description of your intruder?'

'I gave chase when he legged it out of the house,' Sid said. He was holding his arm as if he was in pain. 'But I'd be hard pushed to give you a description. He was wearing a black ski mask, army combat jacket, black gloves and heavy boots. I guess he was of medium height, and if he hadn't been in such good shape, I'd have caught him for sure.'

Abbie flopped down on to one of their lumpy settees and curled her legs under her. 'Except you didn't, Sid. He knocked you out. And given the fact you've hurt your arm and have a heart condition I think you ought to go to the hospital for a check-up, don't you?'

The young constable pointed to Sid's arm. 'Shall I call an ambulance for you, sir?'

'No! Definitely not! Thanks, but I intend to drive myself home.'

'With a bad arm? Please Sid. The hospital 'll only keep you in overnight to make sure you're okay, and you do need to have that arm examined. You're a hero after what you did.'

Sid rubbed his hand over his grazed face as he contemplated the matter. 'Aye, okay lass. I suppose it makes sense,' he agreed, but then jerked his head towards her mobile. 'I hate to mention it, but one of us better ring my daughter and your brother. If my adventure doesn't kill me off, Susan and Freddy certainly will if they discover what's been going on at the Blue House via the local news.'

Abbie groaned, then rubbed the heels of her hands into her eyes to clear away the grit. They were all time-consuming activities to avoid the inevitable. 'I suppose you're right. Is that all right?' she asked.'

PC Bill Nicholson simply nodded.

Taking a deep breath, she picked up her mobile phone and pressed Freddy's number. She cleared her throat. 'Freddy?'

'Yes?'

He sounded drowsy, as if he was already in bed, but then glancing at her watch she realised it was almost eleven o'clock. She did her best to keep her voice calm. 'Sorry to bother you Freddy, but I er... have a bit of a problem.'

'Do you know what time it is? We're in bed. Can't it wait till morning?' There was an ominous silence. 'What sort of a problem?'

'There's been an incident.'

There was a slight pause. 'What sort of incident, Abigail.'

'We've ... er we've had an intruder. I was attacked and ...'

'You've been attacked?'

Abbie held the phone away from her ear. 'Yes. There was a fire in the ...

'There's been a fire?'

'Yes. Sid was hurt when he tried to fight off the ...'

'Sid's been fighting?' There was a pause. 'What's Sid doing at your house?'

'He's not seriously hurt, but he ought to go to hospital and ...'

'Not seriously hurt?'

'Yes! I mean no.' Abbie pinched between her eyes. 'Please stop repeating everything I say, Freddy. Can you come over and take Sid to the hospital or not?'

'We're on our way,' her brother said grimly. The phone went dead.

Exhaustion caught up with her after that but then that was nothing new. She was always exhausted after talking to Freddy. She rubbed her aching shoulder from its encounter with the staircase and wondered whether she ought to pop into her caravan to change out of her wet clothes, but as this appeared to be the time for solidarity with her workers, she stayed where she was, nervously listening to the questions and answers and waiting for the arrival of Freddy.

Fifteen minutes later, Freddy stormed into the kitchen with an anxious Susan at his heels. His hair was tousled, and a blue and white striped pyjama collar poked out from under his anorak. Clearly, he had dressed in haste and without his glasses as he wore one brown shoe and one black. Susan was equally untidy but calm; Susan was always calm.

'Right! Tell me what's been going on, Abigail?' Freddy demanded.

'And you are…?' PC Bill Nicholson consulted his notes.

'We've met, constable. I'm Mr Frederick Haines, the brother of the owner of this … er … this establishment. I was the one who asked you to keep an eye on the place. Remember?' His tone was almost accusing. Freddy turned to her. 'What happened?'

Resting her elbows on the table Abbie dropped her wet head into her hands. 'It's a long story, Freddy,' she said wearily.

'And I'm not going anywhere, Abigail.' Sitting purposefully down on a kitchen chair he folded his arms. 'Let's hear it from the beginning.'

PC Nicholson tapped the end of his pen against his notebook. 'Excuse me, Mr Haines. I think the idea is that Station Officer Holmes and I ask the questions.

Freddy raised his hands. 'Fair enough. Susan, take your father to' the hospital.'

'And we say who goes where, Mr Haines. Your father-in-law has insisted on staying to answer further questions. Now Sid, what were you saying?'

It was frustrating having Freddy interrupting all the time. Then Sid, who had found a new lease of life after Joe had spooned honey in his tea, took it into his head to add colour to his original statement. PC Nicholson took further notes with a quizzical expression.

'And have you any idea who could have wanted to set fire to the place, Mrs Hunter?' he asked.

'How on earth would my sister know ...?'

'Mr Haines! Please!'

Abbie glanced uneasily at her workers as Tom's father, Sarah's husband, and Charlie's unsavoury friends came to mind. Charlie was watching her anxiously, Tom appeared terrified and Sarah was holding her breath. She cleared her throat. 'Not really.' The policeman narrowed his eyes and she knew he hadn't missed the exchange with her workers. So, she stared out of the darkened window before adding, 'The only person who really objects to this renovation is my brother, Freddy.'

'Abigail! Honestly!' Freddy glared at her.

PC Nicholson's mouth quivered at the corners and he appeared to take undue delight in writing, 'only ... the ... brother ... objects ... to ...' in his notebook. He clipped his pen into his jacket pocket. 'I think that should about do it for now, Mrs Hunter. We'll let Sid get off to the hospital and the rest of you cleaned up. If you think of anything else that might help our enquiries, you'll let us know, won't you?'

The young fresh faced, apple cheeked constable coughed politely. 'Okay if I ask a question?'

'Go ahead,' PC Nicholson invited.

'Are all the people in this room known to you, Mrs Hunter?'

'Of course. They're my workers. They're helping me renovate my house. But it couldn't have been any of them if that's what you're thinking. They were with me when the fire started.'

Carefully laying his pencil at the side of his notebook the young constable injected a note of importance in his voice. 'Are you aware that Charlie Marr is known to the police?'

Abbie held her breath.

'Charlie has been in and out of jail since he was a kid. As for Joe, he's been on the streets for years.'

'What!' Freddy shot out of his chair.

PC Nicholson glanced briefly at Charlie before leaning forward and addressing his colleague in a low voice. 'I don't think this particular line of questioning is relevant ....'

Charlie, in his scruffy wet clothes and blackened face shuffled his feet uncomfortably.

'Ah yes. Charlie,' Abbie said briskly. 'All I can say is, this is one occasion when he should be given a medal, not a jail sentence. Anyway,' she turned accusingly on both constables. 'You promised you'd be nice to my workers.'

'Constable, are you telling me ....?' Realisation dawned slowly on Freddy, but then it was nearly midnight. 'Don't tell me these are the vagrants ....?'

PC Nicholson glared at his colleague before gesturing Freddy should sit down.

Freddy ignored him. 'That's it!' he stormed. 'This venture of yours has gone far enough, Abigail. Pack your bag. You're coming home with me. We need to talk.'

She shook her head. 'No Freddy. I'm staying with my workers.'

'Your workers? Abigail; they're vagrants, criminals and …'

'Shut up Freddy! Either support me in my venture to renovate the Blue House, or go!' she snapped, and was surprised that despite her tiredness and aching shoulder she had found the courage to stand up to her brother.

Freddy pursed his lips, folded his arms but made no attempt to leave.

'This lovely old house could have gone up in flames if it hadn't been for these gentlemen,' Sid soberly told him.

Freddy glared at him. 'Gentlemen? Gentlemen? Gentlemen is hardly a fitting term for these …. *criminals*. If you want my opinion, constable, they should be cleared off these premises immediately.' He addressed PC Nicholson as if he'd given an order rather than made a comment.

PC Nicholson's patience was clearly wearing thin. 'Mr Haines, the only person to be cleared off these premises tonight will be you if you continue interrupting police procedures. As for these 'criminals' as you call them, according to the Fire Chief here, if it hadn't been for their swift and decisive actions, this whole house would have gone up in flames; your sister included. I've no reason to clear them off the premises, not tonight anyway.'

Duly reprimanded, Freddy sat down again staring ahead of him. This wouldn't be the end of the matter, Abbie knew that.

Chapter 11

No one saw him leave, Charlie was sure of that. It was too dark, and thickening clouds covered what little moon there was. The street was empty and the fish and chip shop, hairdressers, paper shop and grocers were all shuttered up for the night. He walked briskly, head down, the only sound, his boots clunking on the hard pavement or a late-night motorist. He should have known it was too good to last, he brooded thrusting his hands into the pockets of his jean's. They were still damp.

It was being spotted in the nightclub when they were searching for Tom that did it, he decided. Carter and his goons would never have caught up with him otherwise. But a fire? He'd never imagined they'd go as far as arson. What was that? A warning? Revenge? But now they'd shown their hand he could hardly stay. Besides, now that pompous ass Freddy knew he had a prison record he wouldn't rest until he'd got him out of his sister's house, and the last thing he wanted to do was cause trouble for the boss.

He spat a lump of congealed phlegm on to the pavement. Families! Who wanted them anyway? In his experience, fathers weren't worth the breathing space, and if you got a decent mother, you could count yourself lucky. His luck ran out at birth. He'd lost count of the times his silly giggly mother had called up to the room he shared with his three siblings, 'Come and meet your new daddy, Charlie,' as if she was presenting him with a birthday present; not that he got many of those. The trouble was, Charlie ruminated, he was always having a new daddy and they'd all been a waste of space.

"A dysfunctional home, with no parental guidance." That had been the verdict of the juvenile courts after his umpteenth appearance in front of them. Huh! It was all well and good them telling him what was wrong. He knew what was wrong, but there'd been nobody around to help fix it. Was it any wonder he'd been on the move all his life; foster homes, children's homes, juvenile correction facilities, prison? He'd never experienced leaving any place he could even remotely call home until …. The Blue House! In a spate of anger he kicked an empty tin can into the road and wondered why he should even care about leaving that old dump. Why should he have felt such heart-wrenching sadness when he had walked through those tall stone pillars at the end of the driveway? He hadn't expected that. He'd never been sentimental over a *place* before, not even when he and his siblings had been forced out of their home and into care after his flighty mother left them.

He picked up his pace as he headed towards the bright lights of the city. He didn't exactly have a destination in mind other than he wanted somewhere quiet and safe, where he could think, plan, and quench this raging thirst which he guessed was caused by smoke inhalation. Maybe that was why he drifted towards his old haunt, the snooker club, halfway down Abbotts Lane. It was a rough joint, but they were a friendly sort; asked no questions.

Making his way down the stairs into the dimly lit, airless bar he scrutinized the occupants carefully. The last thing he wanted was to come face to face with Carter's goons. But as far as he could make out none of them were around, at least none he recognized. The hardened drinkers stood shoulder to shoulder around the bar, their sweaty bodies mingling with cheap perfume and stale beery smells. Although he had made the effort to wash his face, change his tee-shirt and stick his cap on he was conscious that he still smelt of smoke, his nails were black and his jeans damp and scruffy.

'Hello, Charlie, haven't seen you in a while.' Jack, the bar tender was wiping glasses with a towel turned grey with quick rinses rather than proper washes. 'Here for a game of snooker?'

Jack was a friend, of sorts, although Charlie knew he wouldn't hesitate to tell the right people he had seen him if the price was right. He didn't particularly want to talk to Jack, and he didn't particularly want a game of snooker, he needed time to think.

With a dismissive, 'A pint, that's all, Jack.' he rummaged through the pocket of his jeans and brought out a handful of coins and a few damp and crumpled notes. It wouldn't get him far, but it would buy him a few beers and crisps. Finding a seat in the corner, he sank down on the faded red upholstery and lifted the glass to his lips. The beer was cold against his parched throat and he emptied the glass in less than a minute. Licking the froth from his top lip he placed the glass on a stained coaster, waited for the beer to settle then returned to the bar and ordered another pint.

On reflection, this wasn't the first time he'd experienced this dreadful despondency at leaving a good job, he brooded watching Jack pull his pint. There was a time between prison sentences when he'd washed dishes in the kitchens of a posh hotel. That was where he had met Chef McCormack. The overweight Irish chef with pale blue sleepy eyes, and a smiling face people automatically trusted had, to his surprise, suggested he help him with the basic food preparation, told him he showed potential, and suggested he train as a chef. Charlie couldn't believe his ears. No one had seen potential in him before, certainly not someone as influential as Chef McCormack. It was under his watchful eye he had learnt how to use kitchen equipment, and acquired skills in basic food handling, preparation and cooking while attending one of the local colleges. For the first time in his life Charlie had felt he was heading somewhere other than prison.

'Thanks Jack.' Throwing his coins on the bar, Charlie made his way back to his table, settled back into obscurity, and idly watched two young lads hanging over the snooker table arguing over the rules.

It was Harry Carter what done for him, he decided. Fancy car, fancy luggage, fancy language, but as shrewd a crook you could ever meet. It was the worst day of his life when he'd fallen for Harry Carter's persuasive tongue.

Chef McCormack had shaken his head in dismay when he found out what he was up to. 'You'll get caught, that's for sure, and is in and out of prison how you want to spend the rest of your life Charlie lad? What were you thinking getting mixed up with the likes of him?'

Charlie took another swig of beer. That was the trouble, he brooded. He hadn't been thinking and he'd got caught. If it hadn't been for Chef McCormack's persistent belief in him, and his faithful prison visits he would never have cut his ties with Carter and his corrupt organisation. Although, there had been another reason. Carter's involvement with drugs. Charlie had seen first-hand what drugs could do. Thieving, he could justify. There was a reason behind thieving. But drugs were another matter altogether.

'Another pint, Charlie?' Jack called.

Charlie hesitated, but then, deciding he better not stay in one place too long in case Carter got wind of his whereabouts he stood up. 'No thanks, Jack. Best be on my way.' He headed for the door.

Once outside he found the cool evening air buzzing with night-clubbers. He stepped sharply to one side as four giggling girls in strapless tops, and mini-skirts that looked more like belts to show off their long pimply bare legs, tottered past in high heels. They were slightly the worse for drink and eyeing up a group of macho guys braving the elements in open necked shirts, over-tight trousers and chest hairs bristling with the cold.

Charlie decided to head for 'The Ocean' nightclub where he was less well known. A slightly ridiculous name considering they were miles from the ocean, he'd always thought. Nevertheless, it suited his purpose tonight.

The heavy rhythmic beat of loud music attacked his ears without mercy as he opened the door and as he made his way downstairs a thick heat greeted him; as though someone had forgotten it was summer and put the central heating on. A dim orange light drifted over the pot-bellied drinkers at the bar who, with swinging pints in hand, shirt buttons straining at the seams, were guffawing loudly over some ridiculous joke. Spirit bottles decorated the wall behind the bartender but Charlie opted for a beer. It was better for quenching his thirst.

Finding a high seat at the end of the bar he drank his beer and pondered over his next move. A young girl a few stools down from him caught his attention; not because she was particularly attractive but because she reminded him of .... Jodie! Charlie stared broodily into his pint. His step-sister was the only one in his family that he had genuinely cared for but it was drugs that had got the better of her. He had been worried sick about her until Carter had offered to loan him the money for her rehabilitation. 'The best centre for over two hundred miles and with an after-care programme second to none,' he had assured him. And to repay his loan, Carter suggested he do the odd job for him; nothing much, nothing dangerous. It was blackmail, Charlie knew that but he had done the jobs – for Jodie's sake. He had known his luck wouldn't last, and it hadn't. On his fourth job the law had caught up with him, and it was while he was doing his stretch in prison that Jodie deteriorated.

'The doctor says there's nothing they can do for an addict when their insides have rotted away,' Carter had written him. 'But I personally am seeing she gets the best possible care for her last few months, Charlie, so don't you worry.'

Charlie continued staring into the glass of dark brown liquid, remembering how horrified he had been when Carter had handed him the bill at Jodie's funeral. Then there'd been the interest to pay. Carter hadn't mentioned the interest. That was when he realised Carter had him well and truly stitched up.

Charlie rubbed his bristled chin. 'You'll have to make better plans than this, Charlie,' he muttered before knocking back the dregs at the bottom of his glass. Realising he needed to pee he stood up. The alcohol swam to his head as he zigzagged across to the toilets. The smell of urine in the gents was foul. The floor was littered with toilet paper, the wall with obscenities, and other obscenities were taking place in one of the cubicles from the sounds of it. But then it was that kind of place. Leaving the gents, he staggered out of the club and into the cool night air. It crossed his mind that what he ought to do was head for Glasgow, Manchester, London or one of the bigger cities.

'That's a lousy plan Charlie,' he told himself. 'What's the sense of running from city to city looking over your shoulder all your life?'

Lifting his cap, he ran his fingers through his greasy hair, leant against the wall of the nightclub and tried to work out his options. He could find only one; go back to working for Carter, pay off his debt and risk not getting caught again. His heart sank, and he wished he had JD's clear logical mind. JD would have had a solution to his predicament, but JD wasn't here, was he? Neither was ... Sarah! Charlie furrowed his brow, taken aback by the unexpected sadness when he thought of never seeing Sarah again. The sensation lingered, long enough for it to register before Charlie moved his weight to his other leg. Then there was Joe, he brooded. Who would take that stupid old goat to his drink club now he wasn't there? The old sot would have drunk his bus fare money if he'd thought he could get away with it. Of course, he hadn't got away with it, not while he, Charlie, had been his minder. A slow smile crossed Charlie's lips over his honey rouse. At least it had kept the old sot sober. Aye, come to think of it, he was rather proud of himself for that honey rouse.

His smile faded at the thought of young Tom. He wasn't a bad kid. He might even achieve being a plumber if he kept off the drugs. And Big Ben? The big lad rarely spoke but he grinned at him after every meal to show he appreciated his food. As for the boss; he liked the boss. She amused him. They got on well together. But for an intelligent woman she was a right scatterbrain. Clueless when it came to renovating a house. Perhaps someone should have told her to stick to doing what she was good at, whatever that was.

'What do you know about cookers, Charlie?' she had asked him last week.

He'd shrugged. 'A bit, I reckon.'

'You wouldn't like to come and choose one with me, would you? I know what I'd like the kitchen to look like but I'm not sure about the equipment.'

He had tried not to show his astonishment at having his advice sought, but as it happened, he knew exactly where to take her. While Joe had been at his drink club, he had amused himself in a nearby showroom specialising in kitchen equipment, so he had taken the boss there. They had spent an enjoyable morning discussing cookers, freezers, work-tops and work units. That's what had spurred him into scrubbing down the kitchen, painting it and nagging Joe to show him how to tile. He wanted to imagine the equipment he had chosen going into the kitchen, so that no matter how many chefs followed him into the Blue House, it would always be *his* kitchen.

Loud, course laughter from a late-night bar across the road caught his attention. He shivered, chilled off from standing outside. Lurching across the road he entered the bar.

It was quieter than the last place, but then he guessed the night scene would be quieting down about now. Late night punters lounged over the bar listening to a second-rate pianist imagining he was in Las Vegas. His jacket sparkled, and his spiked blue head bounced in time to a dead-beat ballad no one had ever heard of. Above him a glitter ball circled a half empty dance floor sending speckles of white across the ceiling in a failed attempt to create an atmosphere.

Ordering a beer, Charlie found a seat in the corner next to a couple more wrapped up in each other than him. Closing his eyes, he rested his head against the wall. What time was it, two, three, in the morning? He had spent the entire night trying to plan ahead and he was no further forward. He had nowhere to sleep, and no money to get him to Glasgow, Manchester, London, or anywhere else for that matter. He had no friends and certainly no prospects.

'There you are.' The voice was quiet and cultured. Charlie knew who it was before he opened his eyes. He looked up. JD was standing over him. His face was clean but there was still a smell of smoke around him. It was odd how pleased he was to see him.

'Do you realise I've spent the entire night looking for you?'

Charlie raised an eyebrow. 'You have?'

JD regarded him silently. 'We *all* have,' he corrected himself. 'The others are checking the club across the road.' He studied the pianist tinkling out a familiar jazzy piece, the adaptation of which seemed to please him more than his audience. 'If I'm to listen to that racket I'll need a drink. Excuse me while I get myself one. I'll get you another, shall I?'

Charlie watched him push his way to the counter, order the beers, then return with two glasses. The young couple glared their displeasure at having to shuffle along the seat to make room for him.

'I suppose you have a good reason for walking out?' JD asked after a couple of swigs. He wiped the froth from his upper lip.

'Uh-huh.'

'Mind telling me what it is?'

'It's personal.'

'Oh, I see. Personal, eh? Well, *personally,* I'd rather you stayed.'

'Why?'

'Because if you go the boss might take over the cooking and...,' JD grimaced. 'I think we'd all be forced back on to the streets if that happens, don't you?'

Charlie glanced at his companion, unsure whether he was serious or this was his attempt at humour. He could never quite work the man out.

'Besides which,' JD continued, 'I couldn't handle the likes of Joe and his drink club.' He stretched out his legs in a relaxed manner, his fingers tapping on the beer glass in time to the music. 'We need you,' he added.

For once in his life, Charlie couldn't think of a thing to say. No-one had ever *needed* him before. He focussed on sipping his beer to avoid having to comment. He only looked up when the club door clattered open and to his astonishment, the boss, Joe, Tom and Sarah burst in like a tidal wave.

'Ah! There you are, Charlie!' The boss said in a loud voice, and marched towards him. They then began disrupting nearby drinkers by scrambling for chairs around his small table. Once settled the boss fixed him with a glare which was clearly intended to shrivel but didn't quite come off. 'I've a good mind to dock your wages for causing us all this trouble.'

Charlie examined his employer with some amusement. With her tangled hair, torn jeans, scorch marks on her pink silk blouse and ripped yellow anorak, she reminded him of little orphan Annie. His lips twitched at the corners. 'Dock my wages, boss? You barely pay me as it is, and don't glare at me like that. Remember, who's the hardened criminal around here.'

'Do you realise we've searched every club in this city for you, Charlie?'

'Really? You've been to *every* club in the city, boss? You must be real hung over?'

'Don't try and be smart with me, Charlie. Why did you run away?'

He saw Joe eyeing up JD's glass of beer.

The young couple muttered their disgust at the smoke smelling invasion and left. Charlie downed the rest of his beer and carefully placed his glass on the dark lacquered table.

'Reasons Charlie, give us reasons.' The boss folded her arms authoritatively.

Charlie gave a long sigh. Suddenly, he was tired of fighting, tired of being on the defensive, tired of trying to make his hopeless life work. He pinched between his eyes. 'OK, I'll give you reasons boss,' he said wearily. 'Firstly, the cops. Now they know where I am, they'll never be off the doorstep, hassling me for every crime in the neighbourhood. Secondly, you may have noticed that I'm none too popular with the criminal fraternity these days. Carter's fire fiasco was only a taste of the trouble they'll be throwing my way. And thirdly, I can't see that brother of yours letting me stay on now he knows I've a record. Are those reasons enough for my leaving?'

'No Charlie, they're not,' she said without hesitation.

'OK. How about, I don't want to bring more trouble on the house from Carter.'

Tom gave a derisory snort. 'You think it was Carter what started the fire? It was more likely to have been my old man.'

Sarah shook her head. 'I think you're both wrong. My money's on it being Vince.'

Joe's hand surreptitiously reached over for JD's glass. Without even glancing in his direction Charlie placed a hand firmly over the top. Their roofer glowered at him. 'Who's gonna take me to the drink club if you're not around?' he growled.

'And who's going to finish painting and tiling the kitchen?' Abbie added.

Charlie lifted his cap and ran his fingers through his hair. 'What do you want of me boss? I'm a disaster zone.'

'What I want from you Charlie, is my kitchen finished; the heavy work doing, and for you to oversee where my kitchen equipment should go. But most importantly, I need a chef during this renovation work, and that happens to be you. I need you, Charlie.'

'What about Carter?' He lifted his hand off JD's glass. Joe reached over for it.

'One problem at a time Charlie,' the boss snatched up the distracting glass of beer, gulped down what was left of it and slammed it back down on the table. JD examined his empty glass in disgust. 'We want you back Charlie,' she said. 'Do you want to come back?'

Charlie examined his big hands folded on the table. Did he want to come back? Of course, he did. He nodded. He couldn't trust himself to speak.

'Then let's get out of here.'

They were too exhausted to walk home and too tired to talk so the boss ordered a seven-seater taxi which took them back to the Blue House where Ben and Mutt were anxiously waiting for news. And despite the charred walls, the waterlogged hallway and the overpowering smell of smoke and petrol, Charlie thought the Blue House on the corner had never looked so good, and he had never felt less lonely in his life.

Dawn was breaking with a tinge of red in the sky when Abbie stumbled into her caravan. Dragging off her dirty clothes she crawled naked under her duvet where she fell into an exhausted sleep. It seemed she had barely reached the stage of unconsciousness before Joe was hammering on the door.

'You better wake up, boss. Two delivery vans have arrived.'

She sat up with a start. 'What time is it?'

'Half past eight.'

'Half past eight? We've just got to bed.'

'I know, but you better come. There's a bit of a rumpus. JD's trying to sort it.'

She yawned; then frowned. 'A rumpus Joe, what sort of rumpus?'

'The lorry driver needs to unload the lift equipment close to the front door.'

Throwing back the duvet she grabbed a clean pair of jeans. 'So?'

'He can't 'cos of the burnt materials on the drive and 'cos the other van's already up at the front door.'

'They've sent two vehicles?' She grabbed a fresh tee shirt from the wardrobe.

'No, the other one's a removal van with your furniture in it.'

Pushing her feet into her trainers she opened the door and stared at him. 'But they're not due till August. I haven't finished the painting or got the carpets down yet.'

'That's why you need to sort it, boss.'

Following the sound of revving engines, she discovered that JD must have struck a compromise between the two drivers, because when she arrived in the hallway, both vehicles were manoeuvring around the burnt-out materials on the driveway before reversing up to the front door.

'My furniture wasn't due till the 11th of August.' Her comment was directed to an overweight, sour faced driver with a pair of scruffy cords hanging halfway down his hips and a pot belly hanging over the top. He frowned at his delivery slip. 'Says 11th August here.'

'Exactly! That's what I'm saying. But it's not the 11th August yet, is it?'

The driver shrugged. 'Must've been a mix up. It'll cost you to have it returned.'

'Why should it cost me to have it returned? It's not my mix up.'

'Well, if you want it brought inside, you'll have to shift that lot.' He jerked his head towards the charred building materials in the hallway. 'Looks like you've had a fire.'

'How observant,' she snapped. She hadn't meant to snap but then you do all sorts of things you don't mean to when you're tired. 'Yes, we've had a fire! As for the furniture, you can store that ...' She scratched her head in frustration. 'I don't know ...'

'In the library?' JD suggested quietly from behind.

'Yes, in the library,' she repeated and pointed to the library door.

Her workers, moving at a half their usual pace, which wasn't particularly fast at the best of times, began clearing a pathway from the front door to the library for the furniture removers. The driver for the lift equipment, a skinny middle-aged man with a cigarette dangling from thin lips, watched them. When they had finished, he pulled a disapproving face. 'Shouldn't have moved them radiators over there, mate. You've not left enough space for our stuff.'

Charlie slammed a length of charred pipe against the wall. 'So why didn't you say so earlier, *mate!*'

The lift driver shrugged indifferently and leant against the front door watching them hump the radiators through to the back garden.

'Watch ya backs!' The furniture removers trampled over the reels of yellow hosepipe with a settee.

Abbie ran her hands through her hair in despair. The ends were frizzled where it had been burnt. 'We'll be in the kitchen,' Abbie called after them. 'Shout if you need anything.'

The driver of the lift equipment flicked his ash on the hallway floor. 'Wouldn't mind a cuppa if there's one on the go, luv.'

'A cuppa? 'Abbie felt her nerves stretching like a catapult ready to twang. 'I've been begging your firm for action with my lift for months. Now, when you do arrive, at some ungodly hour of the morning, the first thing you want to do is stop for a cuppa? Then you have the nerve to flick ash all over my floor when it's obvious we've just had a fire.' She could hear her voice rising to screeching point, but there didn't appear to be a thing she could so about it.

'There'll be a mug of tea in twenty minutes, OK?' JD interrupted, and before she realised it, he and Sarah had manoeuvred her into her kitchen.

Flopping down at the table she dropped her head in her hands. 'I know, I know, I should have been nicer.'

A bleary-eyed Charlie pushed a mug of tea in front of her. 'Here boss.'

There was a loud knock on the kitchen door. She spun round, all set to bellow at someone else – anyone – only to find a pleasant little man with a bald head and bright expression. 'Robertson's, the glaziers here to sort out your hallway window, pet.'

She slapped her forehead with the palm of her hand. 'I forgot you were coming.'

By nine o'clock, heavy drills were vibrating through the house as the lift manufacturers installed the hydraulic system, and an unprecedented amount of hammering was taking place in removing the long hallway window halfway up the stairs so the glazier could replace the broken coloured panes. Whatever brief silences did occur were filled with arguments between furniture removers, lift installers and glaziers. By nine thirty she knew her the headache was threatening to become a full-blown migraine.

By mid-day all the vans had left the premises.

JD spent the afternoon dozing fitfully on the garden bench, one arm resting along the back, his head against the brick wall, Mutt was stretched out at his feet. Nobody had been in the mood for work. They were all exhausted after yesterday's fire, a night spent visiting clubs and casinos looking for Charlie, and an early morning start carting their damaged materials from one room to the other. Besides, it was another hot midsummer's day, too hot for work.

He yawned, his gaze wandering over to Abigail Hunter's caravan. She was sitting at her table her windows open wide in the hope of attracting a breeze. There wasn't one. He saw her run her fingers over her brow in a hot, tired manner. They were all like that today. On the spur of the moment, he rose to his feet, made his way into the house, poured two glasses of lemonade from Charlie's jug cooling in a basin of water, and returned to the garden. Stepping in through the open caravan door was like stepping into a hot tin can.

'Lemonade?' he asked. He noticed she had washed her hair. It looked cleaner but the frizz was still there. She looked weary but her face lit up the moment she spotted the drinks.

'Ah! Lovely JD.' She indicated the seat. 'Sit down. I wanted to have a word with you anyway. Where is everyone?'

Clearing a space in the middle a table strewn with bank statements, bills, delivery notes and odd scraps of paper, JD set down the glasses. 'Out,' he said sitting down.

'Out where?'

'Garden centre, college and Charlie's taken Joe to A.A.' JD took a sip of lemonade, surreptitiously scanning the paperwork in front of him. As far he could work out, a chocolate box was acting as an in tray, a Tesco carrier bag as a filing cabinet, and a red exercise book as an account ledger.

She must have seen him inspecting her paperwork. 'I have to inform my Insurance Company about the fire, but I can't seem to find their policy. I can't even remember their name,' she said by way of an explanation, and shuffled the papers around the table as though the exercise would miraculously produce the missing document. 'I can't find the original quote from the firm who stored my furniture either. Trying to keep up to date is a nightmare.' Gulping down the lemonade she placed the half empty glass on the table. It stuck to a bill leaving a round sugary mark in the middle

He watched her shuffling through her bills and was unexpectedly struck by the kindness of the woman. Abigail Hunter could have thrown them out months ago, but she hadn't. Why was that? Regardless of her own personal problems, she had stuck with them. She'd supported Tom through his drug addiction, the beating from his father, and plumbing course. She had employed the alcoholic Joe, and set him up with his drink club; taken in Big Ben with his mental problems; helped Sarah regain her belongings, and was supporting her through her divorce, and had protected Charlie from the police by not mentioning their suspicions over Carter causing the fire. Then she had spent the entire night hunting for her chef. 'What did you want to see me about?' he asked.

Wrapping both hands around the glass of lemonade she sat back. 'Who do you think caused the fire?'

He shrugged. 'Could have been anyone; Tom's father, Sarah's husband, one of Carter's thugs.'

'It could even have been Freddy.'

'You don't really believe that, do you?'

She gave a mischievous grin. 'Not really, but it felt good fighting my own corner last night.' She licked her fingers, sticky from the lemonade. 'Anyway, what I did want to see you about was, I'm expecting the arrival of the kitchen equipment in August, so I'll need the kitchen finished and I'll certainly need to be rid of the old sofas, and mattresses by then. My problem is, where will you all sleep? Then I thought of the rooms in the attic. They're going to be staff quarters anyway. So, I wondered, if you concentrated on the painting and Sarah makes up the curtains, I could order beds, and you could all sleep up there till it's time for you to move on. How do you think the others will feel about that?'

He was surprised, that not only had she had asked his opinion, but that she was even considering how the move would affect her workers. It was after all her house. 'I think they'd like it.'

'I also thought I'd keep the big kitchen table so we can still eat in there, play cards, listen to the archers, read papers and warm ourselves at the old kitchen range at night until I employ my full-time staff. What do you think?'

'An excellent idea.'

'Good! Thank you, JD. Now!' She leant forward and began shuffling the papers around the table again. 'Where did I put that Insurance Policy?'

'You keep your records in a carrier bag, a chocolate box and an exercise book?'

'The caravan's a bit cramped for proper files.'

He hesitated before asking, 'Is there any reason why you're not keeping your accounts on computer?'

She gave an embarrassed laugh. 'I should, shouldn't I? I started using an exercise book because initially we didn't have electricity for a computer. But it's no way to run a business, is it?' She sat back wearily as if the effort of doing anything after the chaos of the last twenty-four hours was too much for her. 'If I'm perfectly honest, JD, although I can use a computer, my secretary used to take care of all my accounts at work, and my husband insisted on doing our finances at home, so I'm not too sure how to keep records on a computer. I had intended to ask Freddy to show me but I'd only be asking for another lecture.'

His eye fell on a scrap of paper with the logo he'd seen on the delivery van earlier that morning. He picked it up. 'This is the furniture storage invoice, isn't it?'

'Ah! Yes!' Snatching it out of his hand she pointed to a figure. 'Ha! I knew I'd been overcharged for the storage of my furniture. Oh!' Her hand flew to her mouth. 'I should have sorted that out while the delivery men were here, shouldn't I?'

'They wouldn't know. You'll need to ring their office.'

The papers shuffled around the table again like cards in 'happy families. 'Their number should be here somewhere.'

JD picked up the same scrap of paper and pointed to their name, address, e-mail and telephone numbers at the top of the page.

'Ah! That's it. Thank you. I'll put that to one side and ring them tomorrow morning. I might be more amenable by then.'

The sun was directly overhead by now making the caravan unbearably hot. He leant back against the open window hoping to catch the faint breeze which had stirred the leaves of a nearby tree. He didn't.

'My priority is finding that Insurance Policy,' she muttered with yet another shuffle of the papers. 'Keeping track of what was going on wasn't so bad at first, but at this stage of the building project, keeping track of anything is a nightmare.'

He didn't miss the fact that this was the second time she had referred to her administration as being a nightmare. He caught a glimpse of her bank statement as it slid by.

'I also need to have to have a word with the benefits people.' She yawned in the manner that suggested tiredness was catching up with her. 'Big Ben and Joe are due to benefits.

I had intended to do that before now but you've no idea how complicated it is.'

He paused a beat before saying, 'Actually, I have.'

She turned to him; curiosity written all over her face. 'You have? How?'

'If you don't mind me asking, have you thought about claiming tax relief on your outgoings?'

Her blank expression was answer in itself. Then she turned away, staring outside towards the log where Tom usually sat to do his course work, as if not looking at the muddle in front of her would make it disappear. He finished the rest of his lemonade, then clearing a space between the papers he placed the empty glass carefully on the table. 'Do you want a hand?' he found himself saying.

She turned and blinked rapidly at him. 'I'd love a hand JD, but what I really need is someone who knows what they're doing.'

He allowed the reticent silence to communicate itself into her sleepy brain, and then a half a smile formed across her face. 'Would you know what you were doing, JD?'

He didn't want to meet her steady gaze so he stared out of the open window wondering why he had offered to help, wondering why he had committed his energies into fighting a fire last night. Why had he done that? And why had he agreed to help Tom with his plumbing course or even search for Charlie? Why? He gave wan smile. 'How do you do it, Mrs Hunter?'

'Do what?'

'How do you draw people out of themselves the way you do?'

'Do I? I wasn't aware I did. Anyway, you haven't answered my question.'

'No, I haven't, have I. But then you haven't answered mine either.' He ran his finger around the glass on the table. 'Do you want a hand?'

'Do you know what you're doing?'

'I wouldn't have agreed to give Tom a hand with his studies if I didn't think I could help him, and I wouldn't be offering to give you a hand now for exactly the same reason.'

'Are you offering to do my accounts?'

He hesitated, unexpectedly nervous. One day at a time JD, he told himself. One day at a time. 'I'm offering to get you started.'

'What do you mean by that?'

Waving his hand over the littered table he said, 'Introduce a filing system; bring your records up to date on your computer, find your insurance policy, pay your bills, and whatever else is needed to bring order to this ... this ....'

'You can do that? I mean, are you qualified to do that?'

'Yes. I'm qualified to do that.' He saw the uncertainty in her face. She was an easy person to read. She was thinking, qualified in what? And why should she trust this man she knew so little about with her private finances? Then the uncertainty cleared and he saw a light of ... what, relief, gratitude? Sliding the disorganised piles of paper and the exercise book across the table she grinned at him. 'You've got yourself a job, JD.'

Chapter 12

July and August glided through without anything eventful happening, which was just as well as it gave Sid and Tom a chance to get on with the plumbing, and Joe and Charlie to decorate and tile the kitchen. At what point it occurred to Abbie that her vision for the house might actually be achieved, it was difficult to say. It might have been the day the carpets were laid in the attic bedrooms, then the bedroom furniture arrived and Sarah hung up the new curtains. Or it could have been the excitement of moving into her spacious new apartment in the attic. At least, she slept and showered there. The cooker, fridge, kitchen units and fitted wardrobes hadn't arrived yet, there were no carpets down, and her furniture and belongings were still in boxes in the library. But she was almost there. At least she lived between solid walls again instead of in a tin box she consoled herself.

There was good news regarding her finances as well. Thanks to JD taking over her administration and transferring her finances to her computer, the letter he suggested she send to Donald's accident insurance company had them paying up in a matter of weeks instead of months. He had also suggested she put an advert in the local paper for their old fireplaces so was absolutely delighted when a builder gave her considerably more than she had expected for them. Although how JD found time to do all that when he was painting and decorating outside when the weather permitted, and restoring the damaged panelling in the library, dining room and hallway when it didn't, she had no idea.

Although, it must be said, not everything ran smoothly. But then she was learning that about the building trade. Sid was held up waiting for radiators to replace the fire damaged ones, and was getting frustrated with Joe because he hadn't finished erecting the stud partitions in the first-floor guest rooms for the bathrooms to allow him to get on with the plumbing. But as Joe and Charlie were fully occupied in tiling and painting the kitchen, larder, laundry and store-room in readiness for the kitchen equipment, Abbie was forced to engage a retired builder Barry Matthew's recommended.

The biggest hold-up was with the lift. 'The construction work's been done. You've installed the hydraulic system but where's the lift?' she demanded.

'Waiting for parts,' the manufacturers blandly told her. But with so many other hold-ups she was getting used to the fact that this was probably normal practice in the building trade.

Perhaps the most upsetting day was at the start of August. It was a grey dismal morning when the lorry arrived to transport her workers battered mattresses, sleeping bags and sofas to the tip. But it was seeing their solemn faces at the front door as they watched their sleeping accommodation bounce along on the back of the lorry and disappear through the stone pillars at the bottom of the driveway that pulled at her heart strings. They might have been delighted at having their own rooms, but had all she done was remind them of the comforts they'd be leaving when she employed professional staff and they found themselves back on the streets again.

Then there was the ongoing police and fire investigation. Frustratingly, they had made no headway with their case whatsoever.

'What do you expect?' PC Bill Nicholson demanded when she challenged him about it. He was fixing the fire damaged newels on to her banisters which he'd been kind enough to restore on his lathe at home. 'According to you, your intruder was just under six foot, wearing a combat jacket, balaclava, gloves, and boots, never spoke and had no identifying marks. With a description like that you haven't given us much to go on.'

Fixing the front door with a strong lock became their top priority.

If anything, Tom, was the one giving the greatest cause for concern. Although he never complained about his visits to the rehabilitation centre, and seemed to enjoy college and doing his homework with JD, and plumbing jobs with Sid, Abbie had noticed that the continual visits from police, solicitors and social workers as they checked, collated and instructed him on the forthcoming court case, was reducing him to a bundle of nerves.

But that was how they drifted into September.

Tom had tried to make sense of the court proceedings, he really had. But the whole process had seemed surreal, as though the individuals under discussion belonged to some other dysfunctional family and none of this had anything to do with him. In his opinion, there were too many long words and complicated sentences. Why? Why use sentences no-one could understand? And why did courtrooms have to be so dark? Dark panelled walls, dark seats, dark grey carpet and dark suits.

He shuffled uncomfortably in his new clothes. Sid and the boss had bought him jeans, trainers and a sweater. He glanced surreptitiously across at his father sitting on the other side of the courtroom with his defence lawyer. There'd been no sense of remorse when his old man had swaggered into court, no sense of shame. Defiance had been written all over his stubborn face and stayed there through the proceedings. His gaze strayed over to his mother, hoping she'd look in his direction. She didn't. But then she hadn't made eye contact with him during the whole nerve-racking procedure. He had wondered if she might have been arrested along with his father but according to the police, she had pleaded ignorance to what had been going on, and there hadn't been sufficient evidence to prove otherwise. How that had come about he had no idea.

The boss, sitting next to him, loosened her jacket; the courtroom was unbearably hot. He felt a pang of guilt knowing that the kitchen equipment and the lift installation were due today and she ought to be back at the Blue House, not sitting here with him, but she had brushed his concerns away.

'You're not going through this on your own, Tom. No arguments; I'm coming!' She had emphasised her decision with a firm nod of the head so he hadn't argued. In fact, he was pleased she was here. JD was the biggest surprise though. His tutor had arrived in the kitchen that morning wearing smart new trousers, shirt, tie and jacket. Sarah had cut his hair, and with a neat stubble in place of his shaggy beard he looked an entirely different person. Charlie had simply stared at him but made no comment. None of them had. JD looked embarrassed enough.

He nudged JD sitting the other side of him. 'What 'll happen if this gets in the papers?' he whispered.

JD spoke in a low voice. 'It won't! You and Ellie are underage.'

Tom chewed his nail while he digested this information.

The worst part had been standing up to give evidence. Even though he had been well prepared by the police liaison officer and his lawyer, it had still been a nerve-racking ordeal. The questions he had been asked had made him squirm, and then just when he'd thought it was all over, Ellie had appeared on video link.

'Can't be long now,' the boss murmured in his ear.

He gave her a wan smile. Maybe when this was over, he could concentrate on his future, he mused. He'd thought of little else but this court case for weeks. Of course, to have a future he had to stay clean, he knew that, and there had been that one tiny slip-up. Charlie had spotted his change of mood first. Hauling him off his kitchen chair he had smacked him across the head.

'I told you what happened to my sister, didn't I? Didn't I? If you think I'm …'

But as Tom soon discovered that wasn't the end of the matter. When the boss found out she was clearly upset and gave him a stern lecture. He hated upsetting the boss. Then he'd had to sit through another lecture from JD, but that was more of a quiet but considered questioning as to why he'd let his standards slip. Then Joe had yelled at him, Sarah had insisted on accompanying him to his next rehabilitation visit, but it was Sid's arrival that really upset him. He never wanted to see anyone looking as disappointed in him again as Sid.

Since then, he had stayed clean. He'd had no option. Not with the Blue House workers watching him like hawks. Instead, whenever he was tempted for a fix, he'd brought up that vision of himself as a plumber, earning a decent wage, and having a decent place to live for himself and Ellie. And he'd imagine himself passing the Blue House in years to come and saying, 'See that grand hotel? I did the plumbing for that.' Dreams! Sid said he should have dreams but he'd never dared dream - until now.

First though, he had to get through this court case.

He waited; his thoughts drifting, his leg spasmodically jiggling nervously up and down, and then, suddenly, the questioning was over, and the judge, a square jawed formidable figure with a long wise nose was addressing his old man. The judge's brow clouded, his bushy eyebrows quivered, and to say he gave his old man a stern reprimand and a lecture on parental responsibilities would be an understatement.

Tom's mind was spinning at this point, and he could only take in half of what the judge was saying because he couldn't take his eyes off his father. There was a mixture of anger, concern, defiance – but not a hint of remorse. Then came the sentence. Tom waited. Afraid; no, terrified there'd be a last-minute hitch and his father would walk free. But then he felt a pat on the back from his lawyer. Prison! His old man was not only going to prison for a good long stretch, but he'd have the shame of being on the Sex Offender's Register for the rest of his life.

Tom let out a shuddering breath of … what, he wasn't sure. Relief probably. Relief that the court case was over. Relief that Ellie was out of that hell-hole. Relief that he'd never have to go back to number 27, Walker Road ever again.

His lawyer, a tall stooping gentleman with severe white eyebrows, patted him on the shoulder. 'So that's it, Tom. It's over.'

Tom gave a wan smile. Over? He couldn't quite believe it. He'd lived with physical and verbal abuse for so long that he found it hard to imagine life without it.

The boss and JD stood up, and as the three of them filed out of the court-room he caught sight of his mother standing in the corridor looking confused over which way she ought to be heading. Baggy kneed trousers, grubby anorak, hair awry, and clinging on to a frayed green shopping bag her downtrodden appearance stood out.

'See what you've done our Tom?' she snapped when she spotted him. 'No consideration of what would happen to your own mother when you and our Ellie started this. Where's the housekeeping money coming from now, that's what I want to know. As for your dad, he's mad, I can tell you.' Pulling a disintegrated tissue out of her pocket she blew into it before wiping the end of her nose on the back of her hand.

Tom stood his ground, his eyes never leaving his mother's face. 'I didn't start nothing, mam. I wasn't responsible for what happened,' he said quietly. He waited, hoping for … what, he wasn't sure. For her to agree with him? Say sorry? Anything would do.

The woman agitated her tissue between her fingers, ignoring the shreds that fell on to the crisp, clean marble floor. 'Troublemakers, both you and your sister.'

'Is that all you've got to say, mam?'

'What more do you want?'

Tom felt a heaviness in his chest as it occurred to him there never would be any words of kindness, no physical embrace, no apology, nothing. This woman who had given birth to him simply didn't have it in her to love him as a mother should. He dropped his head, and was about to move away when he realised there was one question he needed to ask before he walked away – for good. 'Mam, did dad have anything to do with setting fire to the house where I work?'

His mother blinked rapidly. 'You're working? You're bringing in money our Tom? How come you never sent any of it …?'

'Did he?'

The woman frowned at him. 'Fire? Dunno what you're on about.'

JD squeezed his shoulder. 'The arsonist wasn't the same build as your father, Tom.'

Tom stuck his hands into the pockets of his jeans. 'No, he wasn't, was he? And I canna see my old man paying someone to do it for him. Too stingy.'

'Then we'll go, shall we?' the boss said. 'Unless there's something else you want to say to your mother?'

Tom shook his head. 'Bye then, mam.' He turned sharply and walked away, conscious of his new trainers squeaking down the marble floored corridor. He glanced back once, hoping for … what? He had no idea. But his mother was plodding in the opposite direction. There 'd been no interest in his new career. No, 'Good luck with the new job, Tom 'or 'Take care of yourself,' or even, 'I love you, son.' She hadn't even looked back. He thought his heart was going to break it was so heavy.

Reaching the balcony overlooking the hall, he leant dejectedly on the balustrade watching the people in the foyer below bustling around each other like ants in a colony.

The boss laid her hand on his shoulder. 'All right, Tom?'

He couldn't talk – not yet. JD and the boss must have sensed that because they just stood either side of him, not saying anything, just giving him space to think.

Eventually he said, 'You know that church near the underpass? It has a sign up saying, '*Honour your father and mother.*'' He paused. 'How's that possible? You heard the judge. He gave my father a right rollicking over what he'd done to me and Ellie. That's the law's opinion of my parents, but seems to me God's saying something different. He says to honour them.'

'And do you?' JD asked.

'Like hell I do!' Giving voice to his venom felt good. 'Not that I believe in God anyway. At least I don't think I do. But when the two greatest forces in the world, God and the law disagree, what's a bloke to believe?'

There was a long pause before JD said, 'That's a profoundly intelligent question for a lad who only a few months ago claimed to be too ignorant for college.'

'Well?'

'I guess that poster is an instruction of how God wants us to behave,' Abbie said. 'A guideline if you like. God is saying parents have a huge responsibility to raise their children wisely and lovingly, and in return children are to honour their parents. Sadly, that didn't happen in your case, Tom.'

'So that poster's a load of bollocks?'

'I wouldn't say that. No. An abuser like your father doesn't deserve to be honoured because abuse is wrong. Every individual has a right to be treated with respect. You and Ellie weren't. You were forced to endure your father's sadistic actions until you were brave enough to confront him.'

'But I wasn't honouring him, was I?'

Abbie leant on the balustrade. 'Actually, you were, you were honouring his choice. He *chose* to be an abuser, and your mother *chose* to ignore what was happening to her children. So, in a way, you were honouring their choice by saying, "If you want to be abusive then so be it, but me and Ellie can't stick around and be the ones being abused anymore. We're getting out." And you did.' There was a long silence before she said, 'Where do you see yourself in five years' time, Tom?'

'What's that got to do with it?'

'Just answer the question.'

Tom stared down at his chewed nails, thinking before answering. 'In five years?' He paused again. 'Qualified as a plumber, earning a decent wage, in a safe place for me and Ellie and maybe sending her to University – if she wants to go.'

'So, you see your future brighter than your past?'

'Reckon so.'

'Then don't drag the hatred and anger you're feeling now into it?'

'And how the hell am I supposed to forget what happened to me and Ellie?'

'I'm not saying forget it. You're bound to be hurting. You've been through a dreadful ordeal and it'll take time for those wounds to heal. Believe me, I know. All I'm saying is, don't let hatred and bitterness take root and grow bigger than your dream. Hate can destroy, and haven't your parents done enough damage to you and Ellie?' She placed a consoling hand on his shoulder. 'You might never be able to love or respect your parents, but make a determined effort not to hate them otherwise ...' She gave an embarrassed laugh. 'Otherwise, you'll end up bawling on the steps of the church and taking a nose dive into depression like I did.'

'And how am I supposed to not hate, cos I tell 'y boss, wanting to get my own back is eating me up.'

'Of course, it is. And you've every right to be angry, you have. But you've got your revenge, haven't you? The law has done that for you. It's on your side. Can you imagine the life your old man's going to have in prison? I wouldn't want to be in his shoes. And one day, God will judge your parents for what they've done to you and Ellie.'

Tom watched an outsized, gum chewing girl around his own age stomp towards the courtroom with a familiarity to her surroundings that was unnerving. Worried parents followed in her wake.

'I keep thinking of all the things I'd like to say and do to them, 'specially my old man.'

'Do you know what helped me?' Abbie didn't wait for a reply. 'I wrote it all down in the form of a letter? Say what you want to say. No holding back, give it to them straight.'

'And then send it to them?'

'I suppose you could if you want. But what do you normally do with sewage?'

A slow grin spread across his face. 'Flush it down the bog.'

'Exactly! Flush it down the er ....'

Tom's grin widened. This was talk he could relate to. 'Yeh! Flush the crap down the bog,' he said, and then he chortled with amusement, he couldn't stop himself, because the boss had turned quite red with embarrassment and JD had laughed out loud, and he'd never heard JD laugh before.

'Tom really!' the boss reprimanded. 'That wasn't what I ... but I suppose if the image of flushing er ... down the er ... If that works for you then ... Oh dear!'

The worst part of the court proceedings was – well - as far as Abbie was concerned it was all unpleasant. In fact, by the end of the afternoon she felt so wrung out she was relieved when Tom scrambled into Ellie's foster parents' car. It had been agreed by Social Services that a couple of days together for brother and sister would benefit them both.

Only when she had waved their car out of the car park did she allow her emotions to get the better of her. Pulling a tissue out of her pocket she fiercely blew her nose as they made their way towards her car. 'How could Tom's mother treat him like that? There ought to be a law against bad parents. Don't you think so, JD?'

JD didn't answer.

'I'm sorry to be acting like such a wimp, but this whole thing, the court case, the fire, the threats to Charlie, Vince's threats to Sarah, it's awful. 'All I'm trying to do is renovate a house but the work's getting slower and ... and.... the bills are getting higher and ....' She fumbled in her bag for her keys but by the time she had found them she needed to blow her nose again.

They drove back in silence, neither of them in the mood for talking. It was only when she pulled up at the traffic lights that Abbie blurted out what was uppermost on her mind.

'I lost a child,' she stammered, breaking into the silence.

A white mini pulled up alongside her, its engine revving impatiently at the red light.

'His name was Nathan. He was three months old when he died.'

The driver was a teenage girl vigorously nodding her head to the heavy metal music belting out from her stereo.

'I believe a child is the most precious gift we are given,' she continued. 'So, how can a father abuse his children, and a mother ignore what's going on? She must have known. She must have done.'

The lights changed to green. The mini roared ahead with the teenage girl smugly grinning victory, despite the fact she was the only one racing. Abbie swung her BMW on to the dual carriageway. 'And what made Tom's father do those things? Perhaps he was abused as a child and knows no better?'

'Are you making excuses for him?'

'No. Merely wondering what made him into an abusive father. Was he born evil or ... or did something happen to turn him that way?' She pulled up at the second set of traffic lights. 'Do you have children, JD?' The question was out before she could stop it.

JD took his time before answering. 'Losing anyone is ... painful,' he said slowly. 'But losing a child is ... it's devastating. Isn't it?'

There was silence in the car. So, JD had lost a child? She signalled left into Grange Avenue, and then left again into her drive. But all she said was, 'Yes, it is.'

She had an inkling something was wrong the moment she pulled up at the front door. Big Ben was sitting on the doorstep his chin was in his hands, misery written all over his face. Joe was up the ladder fixing a stuck window but he descended with more speed than usual when he saw the car.

'You've not spotted Charlie on your way home, have you?' he shouted from half-way down.

'No. Why?'

'He's gone missing, that's why.'

'What do you mean, gone missing?' Slamming the car door, she hurried into the kitchen. At this time of night there was usually music blasting out on the radio but tonight the kitchen was uncannily quiet. No music, no Charlie. Sarah was stirring something in a pan on the kitchen range that smelled like Spaghetti Bolognese. She looked up worriedly when they entered.

'I thought you might want to eat before we go looking for him.' She indicated the unassembled fridge, freezer, oven and dishwasher with a jerk of the head. 'Your kitchen equipment's arrived.'

Abbie could hardly have missed it. The delivery men had left it where they would be sure to trip over it. Big Ben trailed in with Mutt, and JD took off his new jacket and positioned the shoulders neatly over the back of the chair. 'When did anyone last see him?' he asked.

'Around two o'clock.' Sarah began setting the table. 'He wanted to make lemonade to put in the new fridge, so he asked me to wait in for the lift manufacturers while he popped along to the greengrocers for lemons. It should only have taken him ten minutes.'

'What can possibly happen at two o'clock in the afternoon on a busy High Street?' Abbie glanced at her watch. 'It's after six. The greengrocers will have closed by now. He might have gone to the supermarket?'

'For four hours boss? I doubt it.' Joe sank down on a kitchen chair.

'Vince might have hurt him.' Big Ben had been listening to the conversation and was now rocking agitatedly backwards and forwards in slow rhythmic movements.

Abbie patted his shoulder reassuringly. She didn't like to say so but that thought had occurred to her. 'Vince might not be a nice man, Ben, but he's never been violent. Besides, he's no match for Charlie.'

'Carter?' Sarah offered.

'Perhaps,' Abbie agreed. 'On the other hand, we could be making a fuss about nothing. He could simply have bumped into friends and gone off for the afternoon.'

It was obvious from the shaking of heads that they all firmly dismissed that theory, and they were probably right. Charlie wouldn't walk out on them, not again, not in the middle of Tom's court case, and certainly not when his kitchen equipment was being delivered. Conscious of their depleted numbers they ate their spaghetti Bolognese in silence.

'The lift manufacturers called to say they'd had a hold up.' Sarah volunteered at one point. But no one commented, no-one was interested in the fact that the lift manufacturers had let them down - again. No one suggested listening to the Archers after dinner either. Sid rang to enquire about Tom's court case, and Abbie was amazed how an event she had been so wrapped up in two hours ago had been pushed to the back of her mind.

'Have you tried the pubs and snooker halls?' Sid asked when she told him about their missing chef.

'Not yet, Sid. Besides, none of us think he's wandered off again.'

'Then you've no other option but to ring the hospitals and police.'

'I was about to do that, but if Charlie has simply taken the afternoon off, he'll be furious if I involve the police.'

As it happens there was no need to ring them. Abbie had barely replaced the receiver when there was a knock on the front door. Mutt barked, and Abbie was so concerned over her missing chef that she didn't notice the new front door slide perfectly over the wooden floor as she opened it. A grave PC Bill Nicholson stood on the doorstep.

'Good evening, Mrs Hunter.'

Abbie's mouth went dry. 'It's Charlie, isn't it? What's he done?'

'He hasn't done anything, as far as I'm aware.'

'Is he ... is he okay?'

'No, I'm afraid he's not. Charlie's lying hospital, unconscious. He's been stabbed.'

It was still light when Joe, Sarah and JD headed for the hospital in her BMW leaving a rather anxious Big Ben in charge of the Blue House. Because they weren't relatives, the stiff-faced, buxom matron who guarded her patients with a zeal that gave credit to her profession, was reluctant to allow their visit.

'Charlie has no relatives,' Abbie explained. 'We're all he's got.'

'And you are?'

'His employer, and ...' Abbie gestured to the others. 'His friends.'

There was the slightest hesitation before her face softened. 'A *short* visit,' she said with an emphasis on the 'short', and pointed towards a single room at the end of the ward.

It was odd seeing their big tough chef lying unconscious on a hospital bed. His face was battered and bruised; bandages covered the top of his head and one of his eyes, and a bloody red gash on his chin was held together with white strips. One hand was bandaged, but judging from the bulge in his hospital gown his wounds were not confined solely to those they could see. Yet even more concerning was the life support machine at the side of his bed bleeping and flickering unintelligible numbers and lines at them.

Sarah's face turned white before she gave a shuddering sob. Sliding into the chair at the side of his bed she gently stroked his arm. 'We're all here for you, Charlie, do you hear me?' she whispered.

And even though she knew it was impossible, Abbie found herself waiting for the witty retort, the foxy grin, anything. But there was nothing, not tonight; only the hiss and the bleep of the life support machine. Her chef was fighting for his life and she knew it.

She glanced across at Joe standing solemnly by the door clutching Charlie's cap. Why he had brought it she had no idea. A sober JD was reading Charlie's medical chart at the foot of the bed. Whether he understood it she had no idea about that either.

'Don't let Charlie die! Please don't let Charlie die.' She prayed silently, instinctively, out of sheer necessity, and out of a vague long forgotten belief she used to have in some Divine Being that could intervene. Yet as she stood surveying her hardened criminal lying helplessly in his bed, she had the strangest sense that God was here, somewhere, in this little room, with Charlie.

They didn't stay long, they weren't allowed to stay long, the buxom Night Sister saw to that.

'Any idea what happened to him?' Abbie asked a bleary-eyed young doctor with enormous spectacles as they left the ward.

'The police asked the same question,' he told her. 'A gang of teenagers found him down by the canal early this evening. He'd lost a considerable amount of blood. If he'd been left all night, I doubt he'd have survived.'

'He will be okay, won't he?'

Doctors the world over have a tendency to be cautious when answering that question, and Abbie found this one no different.

'He's strong. I'd say he stands a fighting chance. We'll know more in the morning.'

They made their way despondently down a long empty corridor smelling of antiseptic.

'He only went out for bloody lemons.' Joe grumbled.

The sun had gone down when they stepped outside into the fresh air. An ambulance screeched to a halt outside A&E. A paramedic leapt out of the back, the driver jumped out of the front, and with precision timing they wheeled their charge from the back of the vehicle into the hospital. A second ambulance screamed up to the doors after it. It looked as though the tired young doctor on duty was facing a busy night.

'No-one's to tell Tom what's happened,' Abbie instructed bleeping her key ring around the car park in an attempt to find where she'd parked her car. There was no flickering light of welcome to remind her, but fortunately JD pointed them in the right direction.

They squashed into her BMW and drove back to the Blue House in silence.

Chapter 13

'Charlie?'

The voice and the smell of perfume were familiar. Rolling over in his hospital bed, Charlie opened his one good eye.

'Boss?' His voice was barely above a whisper. The bed creaked as the boss sat on the edge of it. She examined him closely for a while then leaning forward gently wrapped her arms around him. Her warm, soft body penetrated through his thin hospital nightgown. Closing his eye Charlie did what he had never permitted himself to do with anyone, relax into her embrace. For instinctively, Charlie knew this show of deep affection should be taken for what it was; a friend who merely wanted to give love but asked for nothing in return. He'd never experienced that before. A tear ran down his cheek and on to his split lip, and for the first time in his life he dared allow himself the luxury of being loved.

'I couldn't pay them,' he whispered.

Her voice was warm in his ear. 'I know, but we'll find a way Charlie. Don't worry. We'll find a way when you get home.'

'Home?'

The boss gently released him back on to his pillows. 'Yes Charlie. You're coming home on Friday.'

'I didn't like cutting our visit short but I was anxious about leaving Big Ben in the house alone with the lift manufacturers.' Abbie said to JD as they waited to pull out of the hospital grounds. She bit her lip worriedly. 'I didn't like Sarah going to her solicitors by herself either, or letting Joe make his own way to his drink club. I only hope he doesn't spend his money in a pub. Christmas? Fat chance of me being open for ...'

She reckoned later that she pulled out of the hospital grounds without looking because her thoughts were elsewhere. A horn blared, her foot slammed on the brake, tyres screeched, and JD shot forward, his hands banging against the dashboard. A large white van with an equally white-faced driver glared at her before mouthing some obscenity in her direction; at least judging from the two raised fingers it was obscene. Then with a shake of the head and a change of gear he edged away from the bonnet of her car and roared down the road.

Guiltily she released her grip on the steering wheel. 'Sorry.'

JD let his breath out slowly.

Shaken, this time she looked cautiously both ways before edging out of the hospital grounds. 'JD, do you have a driving licence?'

He cleared his throat and scratched his beard before responding. 'Not with me.'

'Because if you want to start using it again you can drive my car. Might be handy for ... something. Having two drivers, I mean.' The offer was met with a stony silence. 'Anyway, it's up to you,' she concluded lamely.

There was a long pause before he said, 'Right!'

Big Ben was waiting anxiously for them when they pulled up at the front door. He didn't even wait for the car to stop before thrusting a scrap of paper through the open window. 'The lift manufacturers have left you a note.'

'Really?' Following her gardener, Mutt and JD into the hallway she sat on the bottom stair and opened the single sheet of paper.

"Dear Mrs Hunter,'

We would like to offer you our sincere apologies for the delay in installing your lift. This was due to a number of unforeseen problems with our suppliers. However, we would like to assure you that our workers will be with you 9.00am Monday morning, and we expect the work to be completed by the end of the week. I hope we can conclude our business together in an amicable manner; without you feeling you need to take this matter further.

I remain, yours sincerely

Robert Dixon: Area Manager.

Puzzled, she handed the letter over to JD. 'What do you make of that?'

He read it through. 'Did they say anything to you, Ben?'

Ben was pulling grass cuttings off Mutt's shaggy coat. 'Yes.' He continued pulling at the grass cuttings.

'And would you like to tell us what it was?' Abbie prompted.

Ben examined the rose on the hallway ceiling, his frown deepening in his attempt to recall the conversation. 'First, they wanted to know where you were, so I told them you were going to see your lawyer then on to visit Charlie.'

'And?'

'I said you were angry.'

'Angry?'

'Yes, I heard you slam down the phone this morning and say …' He took a deep breath … "You were pig sick of the whole damned business and you were going to your lawyer to get action one way or another!" he repeated parrot fashion.

JD raised an eyebrow. 'You were consulting lawyers about the lift manufacturers?'

'No; I was consulting my lawyer about the length of time Donald's firm were taking in paying out his final share of the business,' she said puzzled, but as understanding dawned she smiled at Big Ben. 'So you repeated that conversation to the lift manufacturers Ben?'

Big Ben nodded.

'They must have thought I'd been referring to them.' She patted Ben's hand as she stood up. 'Excellent work, Ben.'

Big Ben's cheeks reddened in delight. 'And Sarah rang,' he added.

'Did she leave a message?'

'Yes.'

She sat down again. 'And would you like to tell us what it was?'

Ben gazed up at the ceiling-rose again. Abbie glanced at her watch before making a mental note to ask Ben to write messages down in future. If he could write.

'She says how about a take-away because no-one's had time to cook anything.'

'Fine!' Abbie stood up.

'And a lady rang.'

'A lady?' She sat down again. 'What lady? What did she say?'

'She said she'd heard you'd be opening at Christmas and would like to make a booking over the Christmas holidays because she's on her own.'

Abbie stared at him aghast. 'What!'

'A lady rang....'

'Yes! Yes! I heard that part. What did you say?'

'I said I was your gardener and didn't take bookings, so she said if she left her phone number would you ring her back?'

'And do you have the phone number?'

Watching Ben rummaging through his pockets for the scrap of paper was almost as tense as the judge's summing up in Tom's court case. But eventually a scrap of paper was unearthed, along with a filthy handkerchief, a Mars wrapper, a dog biscuit and a few coins. Abbie took the crumpled piece of paper out of his hand. The numbers were large and round and sat neatly on the lined paper.

'How did she get our phone number? I haven't advertised yet. So how on earth did she hear about us?' She didn't wait for anyone to answer as, like a sudden awakening, it dawned on her that it was actually going to happen. The Blue House on the corner was going to become a hotel. She felt a flutter of nervous anticipation. 'Christmas? We'll never be ready for Christmas! Never!'

'And that's the trouble,' Abbie moaned to the Reverend Paddy on one of her diversionary visits to escape the chaos. 'I'm supposed to be renovating a house not running a Social Services department. Half my workers are incapacitated; funds are low till Donald's business partners pay up; I still haven't fitted my kitchen, or the guest rooms, and I haven't even thought about decorating the dining room or library. I'll never be open for Christmas!'

Paddy scratched his bald head, made tutting noises with his tongue which suggested he was about to offer a suggestion, when Abbie burst out with another concern.

'It's Charlie that worries me. Other than a scarred face, a swollen eye, three cracked ribs, being stabbed and barely being able to walk, his wounds aren't too bad.'

Paddy raised his eyebrows.

'What does concern me are his morose silences. He's clammed up completely since coming out of hospital. I'm at a loss to know what to do with him.'

'Perhaps. ...'

'He's even lost interest in cooking, and while the rest of us are working flat out he sits around doing nothing. Sid's working at half the pace given his injured arm, and between college, studying, rehabilitation, helping Sid and supporting Ellie, Tom's worn out. It's a nightmare! She took a breath. 'On top of that ...

Abbie gazed up at the early morning sun streaming through the hallway windows leaving a floating rainbow of colours around the walls. To her delight the glazier had managed to replace the coloured glass shapes, and although it had been costly, she was more than happy with the finished result.

'Imagine what this entrance hall is going to look like when it's painted,' she enthused.

'Imagine it with curtains, carpets, a reception desk and plants.' Sarah said dreamily.

'And with radiators,' Tom added. He sat on the bottom stair, chin in cupped hand and followed the shimmering prisms across the walls.

Joe surveyed dreamers apprehensively. 'Aye, well we'll need more than imagination if you wanna be open for Christmas, boss,' he said gruffly. He ran his calloused hand over the banister. 'What we need is Charlie back on the job that's for sure. Canna get 'im off that darn kitchen seat though. He won't even take me to my drink club.'

Abbie spread her hands. 'I'm open to suggestions if anyone's got any.'

Clearly no-one had, as they all gloomily meandered off into various parts of the house shaking their heads.

'Joe not back from his drink club yet?' Sarah asked. She was stirring the gravy as they congregated for their evening meal. Normally, that would have been Charlie's job, but he remained glumly at the kitchen table twirling the salt cellar.

'Haven't seen him.' JD dumped his blue paint pot on to the new stainless-steel unit, and began cleaning his paintbrushes with turpentine. A rancid smell drifted through the kitchen. By unanimous consent they'd decided they didn't want to cause a riot in the neighbourhood by painting the new front door of 'The Blue House," any other colour but blue.

'I hope he hasn't stopped off at a pub.' Abbie aired her concerns out loud but nobody answered. They were all thinking the same thing.

The first hint of Joe's arrival was three hours later when the front door burst open with a raucous rendition of, *'Home, home on the range.'* By the time he had reached, *'...a discouraging word'* their roofer was propping up the kitchen door, and his alcoholic fumes were almost as overpowering as the turpentine.

Sid was with him. 'Saw him in town, Abbie love. Decided I better bring him back.'

Abbie glowered at her roofer. 'Joe! You're drunk!'

'Yup ma'am. As drunk as a skunk. Would've been drunker if my friend Sid here hadn't found me. Good old Sid.' He slapped their plumber across the back before staggering over to the table. Bending over Charlie, he affectionately patted the ugly red scar on his head. 'How are you today, Charlie boy?'

Charlie's face slowly soured. Slamming his fist on the table he eased himself slowly to his feet. Everyone held their breath as their chef stabbed their self-appointed site foreman in the chest with the knuckles of his good hand. 'Y' *stupid* old goat,' he bellowed. 'How many hours have I pounded the streets waiting for you to come out of your drink club so that you can get cured of the drink? What a waste of time that was!' He gave the old man a shove. Joe staggered back against the half-tiled wall. 'Why? Why'd you get drunk?'

'Wouldn't have got drunk if you'd been with me, Charlie. Asides, I was depressed.'

'Depressed? What've you got to be depressed about you disgusting old sot? I'm the one what's depressed. I'm the one with problems.'

'But you're not doing nothin' to solve them, are you Charlie? You're just sitting there looking miserable.'

Charlie cuffed the old man over the head with his good hand.

'He's right, Charlie,' Tom intervened. 'You're not doing nothin'. In fact, it looks to me ... to us ... like you've given up.'

Charlie turned angrily on their plumber's mate. 'Shut it! Just shut it!'

'Tom's right, Charlie,' Sarah added. 'At least if you talked to us about the problem we might be able to help.'

Charlie glowered at the faces around the table, and then, almost as if the effort was too much he limped back to his chair, flopped down and spread his hands. 'All right! You wanna help? So tell me how? I owe Carter money and I can't pay.'

'How much?' Abbie asked.

Charlie dragged a crumpled piece of paper out of his pocket and pushed it across the table towards her. 'The ultimatum is, I either pay them or work for them.'

Abbie unfolded the paper and frowned. 'But this is a bill from St. Oswald's Rehabilitation Centre. It says you owe ...' she stared up at him horrified. '£35,000?'

There was silence around the table.

JD took the invoice out of her hands and studied it.

'The deal was, Carter would pay for my sister Jodie to go to the best rehabilitation centre, and I'd pay him back by doing jobs for him.'

'What have you paid so far?' Abbie asked.

Charlie shrugged. 'The job before the one I got nicked for brought in a sizeable sum. But while I was inside Jodie got worse. St. Oswald's transferred her to their private hospital, and that's what made it costly. That was where she died.'

Sarah leant across the table. 'I could lend you the money when my house is sold Charlie, but it's not even on the market yet.'

Charlie's expression softened. Reaching over he squeezed Sarah's hand. 'I wouldn't take your money, Sarah luv. I could never pay you back. Besides, Carter won't wait but ... thanks for the offer.' Abbie noticed he took his time withdrawing his hand. 'As I see it,' Charlie said. 'I've two choices. I go on the run, or pay off the debt by working for Carter again.'

'And risk prison?'

'Which is why I've more or less decided to head off. What?' he asked when he saw the alarmed faces around the table.

Abbie chewed her lip. 'I suppose I could go to the bank manager for a loan.'

JD laid the invoice on the table. 'And say what; that your chef was recently released from prison and needs the money to pay off a criminal?' Leaning his elbows on the table he twirled his thumbs around each other. 'How long have you got before you need pay up, Charlie?'

Charlie snorted through his nose. 'Bastard brought me in a bag of grapes when I was in hospital and told me he'd give me till the end of the month.'

'So; a couple of weeks?'

'Reckon so.'

JD puffed up his cheeks, and then ran the air thoughtfully through his lips with a concentrated expression on his face. Abbie watched him, sensing there was a glimmer of an idea lurking. Eventually, he turned to her. 'Any chance of a few days off?'

Abbie hadn't expected that. 'I suppose ... yes, of course.'

JD picked up the invoice and stood up. 'Can I take this, Charlie?'

Charlie narrowed his eyes. 'What are you up to 'y sneaky sod?'

But all he received was a reassuring pat on his shoulder as JD left the kitchen.

Righting the saltcellar, Charlie examined his new kitchen units. 'And stop leaving paint pots on my new units!' he bellowed after the receding figure. And although the bellow didn't have its usual unnerving ring to it, Abbie found it to be the sweetest sound she had heard in weeks.

JD walked swiftly through the underpass. He was in plenty time for the eight-fifteen train but he was anxious to be on his way.

'Train? You're going ... a distance then?' Abigail Hunter had asked.

If he hadn't been so concerned over this visit, he would have found her inquisitiveness amusing. 'Yes, I'm going a distance.'

'And you expect to be away for how long? Not that you're under any obligation to be back by a certain date,' she had added hastily.

'I'm not sure. Four, maybe five days'

'And your trip will help Charlie, will it?'

He'd hesitated before he'd said, 'I think so. In a roundabout way.'

The railway station was cold and draughty as most railway stations are. Commuters glanced impatiently at their watches as though that would make the train arrive sooner; bleary eyed, ragged jeaned students lugging canvas holdalls, lounged untidily against the pillars on the platform as they awaited transportation back to university; smart suited business men and women with leather briefcases multi-tasked with a mobile phone to one ear and an eye on the electronic timetable on the station wall. He might have enjoyed the familiarity of civilization again if he hadn't been so anxious over the reception he would get when he reached his destination.

When the train did arrive, he settled himself at a window seat. It was slow gathering momentum, but when it did it rattled over the tracks with a rhythmic beat that could have been pleasantly soothing if he'd been in the mood. He stared of the window. Cattle and sheep grazed peacefully in the fields, and trees, tired and heavy after a long hot summer, were showing a hint of autumn approaching. Autumn! Was it only last autumn he'd ended up on the streets? He'd been drowning then, he reflected. But come to think of it, he had been drowning long before that. He hadn't needed a doctor to tell him he'd had a nervous breakdown. He knew that. When he was eventually released from hospital he couldn't face going back to his old life– so he didn't. From then on, one day on the streets had blurred into the next, one week into the next – until he had met Charlie. Charlie!

The train clattered over an intersection of rails, momentarily distracting him. Only when it had settled down to its gentle rhythmic movement again did he allow himself to pick up his thoughts. This time he picked up the day he had found oak panelling in the library. Seeing such splendour shut away behind unsightly green gloss paint had motivated him to remove it from its hardboard prison; and it had been a long time since he had been motivated to do anything. But as he had gently pulled away the hardboard, and then applied the micro porous finish to restore the wood to its natural grain, he had discovered that he enjoyed working with wood. It was calming, therapeutic. Perhaps that was because wood-work had once been a hobby, long before he'd got too busy to have hobbies.

Then there'd been Abigail Hunter's persuasive suggestion he help Tom with his studies. Why he had agreed to that he had no idea. Yet he had, and surprisingly, he had enjoyed helping this messed up young lad, and found the effort of using his brain again stimulating. But even more stimulating had been offering to help her with her accounts. He was still puzzled why he had done that. Perhaps because he was astounded how anyone thought they could keep their records in an exercise book, their invoices in a chocolate box and the rest of their administration in a carrier bag. Besides, this was work he knew. At least he used to. And now there was Charlie. Charlie! Without Charlie he would never have survived on the streets.

As usual, King's Cross Station was busy, and the London underground crowded, so it took him a while to reach the leafy suburbs of Orchard Crescent, which was just as well as it gave him time to figure out what he would say. Even so, his body tensed as he rang the bell of number fifteen, then tensed again when he heard her footsteps echoing on the tiled floor. The door opened. Her eyes widened when she saw him. With shock? With pleasure? He couldn't tell, but he noticed there were more lines on her face and grey in her hair that hadn't been there before, but that was only to be expected after what she'd been through.

'Hello Hilary.'

He was unsure what her reaction would be at seeing him so he waited. But then he saw tears gathering in her eyes, and with a sob she fell towards him. He wrapped his arms around her, holding her gently, feeling the familiar softness of her skin, the silkiness of her hair and the warmth of her body. Then he kissed the top of her head and rested his cheek against hers.

'I missed you,' he whispered, but it was only when he felt her body shaking with sobs that he allowed his own tears to fall. 'I missed you so much!'

Opening one eye, JD squinted out of the window to a dull grey sky, then over to the alarm clock. It was six-thirty. Plenty time to get across London for the train home. Home! He smiled to himself. Never in his wildest dreams would he have imagined calling The Blue House, home.

The door creaked as Hilary poked her head around it. 'Ah! You're awake.' Tying the belt of her dressing gown she came and sat on the edge of his bed. 'I got up early assuming you'd want breakfast before you left?'

Reaching out he grasped her hand. 'That would be nice.'

'Did you get it sorted?'

'Mostly; it took longer than imagined. But at least I've done what I set out to do.'

She squeezed his hand. 'I'll make breakfast, shall I?'

He waited until he heard the pans clattering in the kitchen before heading for the shower. The water was hot and the jet forceful enough to wash away the last dregs of sleep. Flattening his hands against the tiled walls it was easy to recall the last time he had stood here. It felt like a lifetime away but in reality, it was less than 3 years. Yet simply standing in the same spot seemed to give his memory permission to wander back.

'The children and I never see you. You're always working,' his wife had complained, and guiltily he realised she was right. Determined to resolve the situation, he had taken his family on a sailing holiday around the Greek Islands in an attempt to re-establish his failing relationship with them. He had no qualms about leaving his older brother Digby, to handle any problems in the firm; they had worked like that for years. And Digby would have managed in his usual admirable fashion, if he hadn't been fighting a losing battle with cancer. JD hadn't known that. He hadn't known their brother-in-law had been embezzling from their lucrative accountancy firm either. Well, he'd had his suspicions, but hadn't expected the whole nasty business to blow up while he was on holiday. He knew nothing about the police enquiries or the splurge of newspaper headlines because he had been sailing idly around the Greek Islands trying to re-connect with his wife and their two teenage children – *with his mobile phone switched off*. On hindsight, he shouldn't have done that. But in hindsight there was a lot of things he shouldn't have done. The pressure had been too much for Digby. A sudden deterioration in his already failing health, the media intrusion, and with no-one around to ease the load, he had taken his own life.

JD gripped the shower head with both hands, and as the jet of hot water ran down his naked body, for the first time in three years he wept; for the death of his brother, Digby; for his own total lack of responsibility in not knowing what was going on; for ... He took a deep breath, knowing that the rest he couldn't look at yet - not yet. Switching off the jet of water he stepped out of the shower.

Chapter 14

As JD opened the front door, he found himself greeted by poles of scaffolding stretching from the hall to the top of the stairs; dust sheets, pots of paint, brushes and work benches, and standing in the middle of it all was Abigail Hunter, hair awry, blue overalls daubed in paint and carrying a crate of beers. Her face lit up when she saw him.

'Nice to see you, JD. Did you have a good journey?'

'I did.' They gazed at each other steadily for a moment before he averted his eyes. 'I'm afraid I was away longer than anticipated.'

'You said you'd be back so I knew you would be.' She jerked her head towards the kitchen. 'There's food if you're hungry. Charlie and Chef McCormack have done us proud.'

He frowned. 'Chef McCormack?'

'Charlie's old mentor. Charlie spoke so highly of him I thought I'd ask if he would help with our party. It took me four days to track him down.' She lowered her voice. 'When I found out he was retired I asked him to stay a while hoping he'll lift Charlie's spirits.'

A loud cheer echoed down the stairs. He raised his eyebrows.

'It's a football match,' she said by way of explanation. 'They're watching TV in my apartment. Manchester and ...' she waved her hand dismissively. '... some other team.'

'They?'

A voice shouted down from the top floor. 'Need a hand with those beers, Abbie?'

'Coming Barry! That's Barry Matthews.' She gave an embarrassed grin. 'The thing is, I was grumbling to Paddy, the local vicar, or whatever he is, about not getting finished for Christmas and the next thing I know, he's knocking on my door and helping me organise a wallpaper party. All I had to do was make a list of jobs, which Joe did; plan food and drink, Charlie and Chef McCormack did that, and send out invitations; Sarah made a really good job of the cards. So, we have Barry Matthews, Mick the delivery driver, Fire Officer Alan Holmes, Ellie and her foster parents, Doreen the hairdresser, Paddy and his organist, PC Bill Nicholson, the milkman and Big Ben's friend from the garden centre. Even Freddy and Susan have come - at Sid's invitation I hasten to add - not mine. You'd be amazed at the amount of decorating, sewing and assembling of furniture they've got through in one morning.' She beamed at him, clearly pleased with the progress. 'Anyway, did you have a good journey?'

'You've already asked me that.'

'Oh! Yes, I did, didn't I. And you did what you had to do for Charlie?'

She was fishing for information he knew that. 'I think you're really wanting to know what I've been up to.'

'So, I should mind my own business?'

'No, I didn't say that. Your concern for Charlie is … touching.''

A second shout came from the top of the stairs. 'Are you sure I can't give you a hand with those beers Abbie?'

She gave him a lopsided grin. 'They're after their beers I think.'

Picking up his luggage he was about to head for the kitchen when she rested her hand on his arm. 'Interesting!' she said with a twinkle in her eye. 'You left here without luggage but you've returned with a fancy suitcase and briefcase, both with the initials EJ on the front.'

Early the following morning, Abbie trailed downstairs in her dressing gown, slightly hung-over after an over-indulgence of food and drink. Assuming her workers would be in the same condition, she was surprised to find them stationed on various parts of the scaffolding.

'Gotta finish this painting 'afore Barry comes to take his scaffolding back Monday morning boss,' Joe shouted from the top platform. She examined the area of ceiling he was working on. It had originally shown patches of damp and signs of crumbling, and Freddy had been quite adamant she'd need to replace the whole ceiling. That would have meant losing the decorative mouldings that gave the hallway its distinguishing features. But at the wallpaper party, Joe and Barry had tackled the problem by lifting the floorboards above, replacing the affected areas and saving the decorative mouldings. Abbie couldn't resist a sneaking sense of satisfaction at having proved Freddy wrong.

'So, we've got eight weeks before we open,' she loudly informed her staff, then winced as the sound of her own voice pounded through her head. 'Are we all busy?'

'We're slogging our guts out here, boss,' Joe yelled. 'What are you doing?'

She was standing in the middle of the hallway, her hands on her hips. 'I'm thinking.'

'Aye boss, that'll get the work done.'

In actual fact, she was ruminating on what JD had been doing on his trip away, as the closer they got to the end of the month, the closer they got to another visit from Carter. She only hoped Charlie wouldn't take it into his head to disappear before that. She'd miss him. In fact, she'd miss them all when she employed professional staff. She'd miss the way she and JD sorted the post every morning, paid the bills, and poured over the computer together. Then there were all those little memos he wrote to remind her what to order and who to ring before he lost himself in his painting and ….

'It's working! It's working!'

All working, thinking and otherwise stopped as Tom thundered down the stairs, a wide beam across his face. 'It's done! Me and Sid have got the central heating working!'

By Tuesday, JD still hadn't mentioned his trip away, but that might have been because the carpet fitters arrived to carpet her apartment and the attic rooms. Then the guest room furniture arrived and as it needed assembling, they were all kept busy. The only frustration came when the lift engineer signed the lift off as operational – *after* she and her workforce had trailed her furniture and countless boxes up two flights of stairs to her apartment.

It was Wednesday. They were sitting around the kitchen table after their evening meal when JD asked, 'Abigail, do you mind if Charlie and I have tomorrow off?'

'Eh?' Surprised, Charlie looked up from his newspaper.

'Of course,' Abbie replied easily and JD couldn't quite tell from her expression whether she had realised he had called her Abigail for the first time or not. 'Can I ask what you're up to?'

'Yes, I'd like to know as well,' Charlie said lowering his paper.

'And could I take you up on your offer to borrow your car? If not, I'll hire one.'

'Of course.'

He gave a brief nod. He could tell she was burning with curiosity, but he needed to speak to Charlie before he enlightened her. Unfortunately, it wasn't until everyone had gone to bed, that JD had the chance to talk to him. The two men sat quietly by the kitchen fire.

'So, what's all this about?' Charlie asked.

JD stretched out his long legs and stared into the flames. Knowing their proudly independent chef he knew he would have to handle this carefully. 'Remember that beating I took when we first met?'

'Yeh.'

'Why did you come to my rescue, Charlie?'

Charlie shrugged. 'Why not?'

'And why did you give me a roof over my head and food? I never paid you a penny or said thanks for letting me tag along, did I?'

Charlie shuffled his feet. 'Okay, thanks duly noted. Now unless there's a point to ...'

'There is.'

'So?'

'I'd get to my point quicker if you'd answer my question. Why did you do it?'

The chair creaked as Charlie pushed it back on two legs and put his feet up on the range. 'I suppose, 'cos I don't like seeing a bloke being kicked when he's down. As for you tagging along, I could hardly leave you behind, could I? You're not exactly street wise.'

'So, being a street-wise guy, you saw I was in trouble so took me under your wing because you were on familiar turf and you could see I wasn't? Right?'

'Aye, I suppose.'

JD gave a nod of satisfaction. 'Well, I think you may be on my turf now, Charlie.'

'Eh?'

'The world of fraudulent finances is my turf, and this …' he pulled Charlie's invoice out of the back pocket of his jeans, 'smells suspiciously fraudulent to me.'

The legs of Charlie's chair righted themselves. 'Go on.'

'This invoice from St Oswald's Rehabilitation Centre shows Jodie's fees for the rehabilitation Centre and the private hospital. Except St. Oswald's doesn't have a private hospital, I checked. So, where did Carter send Jodie?' He waited for Charlie to digest this news before saying, 'Of course, there could be a perfectly simple explanation. Perhaps they have an agreement with a private hospital but if they have, why is it not named or their fees shown on this or a separate invoice? Something doesn't add up.'

A slow grin spread across Charlie's face. 'Your turf, eh?'

The two men made an early start the following morning, mainly to fit Charlie up with new clothes to give him an air of respectability. Then they drove north for an hour until the satnav directed them on to a narrow country road. Ten minutes later they were driving through St. Oswald's gates and staring at an elegant modern building of glass, steel and brick set in spacious leafy grounds.

Charlie gave a whistle of admiration as they pulled up in the car park. 'Wow! This is not the sort of place I imagined a street addict like Jodie would stay.' Stepping out of the car he slammed the door.

'And there are no signs pointing to a hospital either,' JD added looking around.

Taking the steps of the building two at a time they found themselves in a lightly, airy, marble floored reception hall. A lofty, white haired, white coated gentleman came towards them. He had kindly face, faded blue eyes and a high forehead which gave him the appearance of intelligence. Having been out of the work scene for some time JD momentarily hesitated as nerves got the better of him. But then, taking a deep breath, he strode forward, his hand outstretched, hoping he portrayed more confidence than he felt. 'Good morning. Dr Halle? My name is Edward Jefferson.' It felt odd using his own name again, and he was aware of the sharp glance from Charlie. 'We spoke on the phone earlier. This is Charles Marr, Jodie Marr's brother.'

'Ah, yes, Mr Jefferson.' Dr Halle gestured towards an office overlooking a garden with a hint of autumn colours. Bending his head to avoid the lintel he indicated two red leather seats. 'Please sit down.' Easing himself into a black swivel chair behind a desk he pressed a couple of buttons on the computer. It responded with a ping. 'Yes, here we are, Jodie Marr.' His eyes zigzagged across the screen. 'On the phone you mentioned the invoice, Mr Jefferson. I see that as Mr Marr was away at the time of Jodie's admittance the invoice was sent to a Mr Carter who ... yes, he paid us in full.'

JD opened his briefcase. 'Would it be possible for me to have a copy of that invoice and the receipt?'

'Of course.' The words were barely out of the doctor's mouth before the hum of the printer delivered the required documents. He handed them to JD.

Dr Halle turned to Charlie. 'My condolences on the passing of your sister, Mr Marr.'

'Thank you.'

There was silence while JD scanned through the invoice, his index finger running down the page. 'I see there's no date for when Jodie was transferred to the private wing of your hospital, Dr Halle.'

'Private wing?' Dr Halle blinked foggily at him. 'We have no private wing. If I remember rightly, when we released Jodie, it was to the local NHS hospital.'

JD slid Charlie's crumpled invoice across the desk. 'This invoice was sent to my client from Mr Carter.'

There was silence as Dr Halle examined Charlie's dog-eared invoice. It was a while before he spoke. 'I don't understand. Your invoice has the St. Oswald heading, it bears the same number as the one on my computer, yet your figures show the cost of a private hospital. As I said, we have no private hospital, Mr Jefferson. We're a rehabilitation centre.' He pressed a button on his telephone. 'Miss Wells, can you bring me Jodie Marr's file, please?'

A crackled, 'Of course, Dr Halle,' responded and a moment later the shapely Miss Wells, who looked as though she'd be more at ease in saucy films than a rehabilitation centre, clicked into the office with heels, high and spiked.

Charlie leant towards him. 'Carter's lass,' he whispered.

'Thank you, Miss Wells.' Dr Halle opened Jodie's file.

Mona Wells eyed the two visitors guardedly, although JD noticed it lingered longer on Charlie, as though trying to place where she had seen him before, but after a brief smile, she clicked back across the floor and closed the door behind her.

They waited while Dr Halle examined the file, his face clouding over as he did so. 'I er ... I'm afraid I don't know what to say, Mr Jefferson. Other than er ... 'he cleared his throat. 'There's obviously been a serious ... error. Jodie Marr was with us for *two* months, not *four* months as *your* invoice states. And as for this exorbitant amount for a private hospital on the bottom of your invoice, I have no idea what that is. When, at the end of two months, Jodie's health deteriorated with respiratory problems, we transferred her to the local NHS hospital.'

JD leant forward and lowering his voice so that it wouldn't carry through into the next office said, 'How long has Miss Wells been with you, Dr Halle?'

'Two years.'

'And did you know she was Mr Carter's girl-friend, the man who is demanding payment from my client on these falsified figures?'

Dr Halle's face paled. 'No, I didn't. But that would explain a lot, wouldn't it?' He was about to press the button on his phone when JD raised a hand to stop him.

'I wonder if you would be good enough to give us a few hours grace, Dr Halle?' JD pointed to Charlie's invoice. 'You might want to make a copy of that, and perhaps I could have a copy of Jodie Marr's transfer documents to the NHS hospital.'

'Yes, of course.' There was a hum from the photocopier as copies were made. 'All I can say Mr Marr is that you have my deepest apologies for what has happened,' Dr Halle's lips narrowed. 'As if losing a sister is not bad enough, having to deal with fraud is beyond belief. Please be reassured that I will meet urgently with my board members to make sure there have been no other discrepancies, then we will have Miss Wells dealt with.'

JD slid the papers into his briefcase. 'Thank you, Dr Halle.' He stood up.

'No private hospital!' Charlie stormed as they made their way back to the car. 'And no doubt all letters that were sent to Jodie would be diverted by Mona Wells. That lying ...' He let rip with a stream of profanities that were worse than when one of his meals didn't meet up to his expectations. But as he flung open the car door he calmed down. Throwing a foxy grin over the top of the vehicle he said, *'Edward Jefferson, eh?'*

JD switched on the engine of the BMW. Although he was relieved this visit had gone without a hitch he was not looking forward to this next step. 'Now, how do I find Carter?'

An hour later, the broken-nosed boxer led them into Carter's office. Carter himself was lounging in a high-backed, brass studded, green leather chair, a giant unlit cigar jammed between his teeth, a vulgar marble desk in front of him. The spikey red-headed gum chewer with the bad breath stood behind him. Carter rose as they entered.

JD stretched out his hand. 'Mr Carter? Good afternoon. My name is Edward Jefferson. Charlie Marr, I believe you know. Thank you for agreeing to see us at such short notice. I'm with Jefferson's Accountancy. My card.' JD handed over one of his old cards hoping that Carter wouldn't recognise him from his earlier visit to The Blue House. He doubted it. At Carter's invitation he and Charlie sat down.

Carter removed the cigar from his mouth, his gaze moving warily from JD to Charlie and back again. 'So, what can I help you with Mr er …' his lids lowered as he examined the card '… Mr Jefferson. What brings you north of the Thames?'

'My client, Charlie Marr.'

Carter looked dubiously at Charlie. 'You can afford a London based firm, Charlie?'

'None of your business, Carter.'

Opening his briefcase, JD brought out a file, hoping it would look as though Charlie was one of many clients, instead of the only one. Sliding the two invoices across the desk to Carter he said, 'Can you explain how two invoices from St. Oswald's Rehabilitation Centre have the same numbers and dates, yet reflect so differently in pricing?'

Carter picked them up, examined them, then flicked both invoices back across the desk at him. 'How should I know? Why don't you ask them?'

'I have.'

'And?' Carter rammed the cigar back in his mouth.

'They too were puzzled how the original invoice from St. Oswald's didn't tally with the one you're asking my client to pay.'

Carter pointed at Charlie. 'My only connection with them was to pay for the treatment of that junkie sister of his.'

'And your other connection of course is Mona Wells?'

'What Mona does is her business,' Carter snapped.

'But her presence there might explain how we have two invoices.' JD paused. 'My understanding of the arrangement you had with Charlie Marr, is that he was to pay what he owed you by doing …shall we say … a few private jobs which would cover his sister's stay at St. Oswald's. The invoice you sent him shows she stayed four months. St. Oswald's records show she stayed only two. Your invoice shows she was then transferred to their private hospital. How is that possible, Mr Carter? They don't have a private hospital. They transferred her to an NHS hospital where, sadly, she died.'

Carter took his time lighting his cigar. 'As I said, what Mona does at St Oswald's is her business.'

'But I do wonder whose instructions Mona is acting under, because what would she have to gain from this fraudulent transaction? Although, I've no doubt the police will be asking her those very questions when Dr Halle rings them.' JD made a steeple with his fingers, feeling he had the upper hand but wondering how far he dared push his luck. Deciding to take a gamble he added, 'And the police aren't stupid. They might link this fraudulent invoice to the fire your ...boy... here started in The Blue House.' He made a point of not looking at the red headed gum chewer with the bad breath or the goon with the nose that appeared to have lost a fight with a heavyweight boxer. 'I've no doubt if we decide to pass our suspicions on to the police, they will link that to the pretty accurate description the plumber gave them.'

The red-headed gum chewer's eyes widened in alarm. 'There's no way ...!'

Carter raised his hand sharply, like a policeman attempting to stop a speeding car. 'What do you want, Mr Jefferson?'

Reaching across the desk, JD picked up both invoices and slid them into a plastic folder. 'I think my client has more than paid you back for Jodie's fees, Mr Carter, don't you? But now he wants a line drawn under this whole sordid affair. What St. Oswald's do, or do not do, is none of our business but I wish you luck in sorting that one out.' JD closed his briefcase with a snap. 'As for the arson attack?' He lifted his briefcase off the table. 'If Mr Marr finds himself harassed, we will of course air our suspicions to the police. Otherwise, as far as we are concerned, the matter is closed.' He pursed his lips. 'Unfortunately, the Fire Service are still investigating, and l have no idea what they've come up with. That too is out of our hands.'

Both he and Charlie knew exactly what the Fire Service Investigation Team had come up with. Absolutely nothing! No descriptions, no fingerprints; nothing!

JD made no attempt to stretch out his hand when he stood up. 'Thank you for your time, Mr Carter. You won't be hearing from us again unless ...' he looked pointedly at Charlie.

Chapter 15

The wallpaper party had been a tremendous success. The painting and wallpapering were finished – other than a bit of touching up here and there; the guest rooms were ready - other than the hanging of curtains, a faulty mattress and a late delivery of furniture; and the carpets downstairs were laid – almost – the carpet fitters had mis-measured so there were a few complications. Seeing the transformation taking place, made Abbie realise that opening day was only weeks away, so she frantically poured over books on management, worried that she had been so pre-occupied with other things she hadn't yet worked out her primary market or how her hotel would stand out from others in the town. Suddenly, this whole aspect of opening a new business seemed a mammoth task, until she discovered Chef McCormack had worked in some of the top hotels in the UK.

Chef McCormack was a big shouldered Irishman with apple red cheeks and a hearty laugh. Originally, he had only planned to stay a few days to help the incapacitated Charlie with the wallpaper party, but when he saw their chaotic lifestyle and how worried Abbie was over the prospect of opening, he offered to stay a while longer. And although she had a sneaking suspicion that his ulterior motive was that he had been finding retirement lonely, she was nevertheless grateful for his advice.

Perching on a high stool in front of the kitchen range, she watched him dice onions for their evening meal with the rapid chopping movements of a professional chef. He glanced across at her, and seeing her chewing her lip, left his onions, ran his hands under the kitchen tap, dried them, then rummaging through his jacket pocket produced a brochure. 'Take a look at this.'

Abbie flicked through a glossy brochure showing a well-established hotel by the sea with fifteen elegant rooms and a mouth-watering cuisine. She gave a wistful sigh. 'I could never get The Blue House anywhere near this standard.'

'Of course, you could.'

Unconvinced, she flicked over a page.

'I worked there for over fifteen years. They started small, like you. Now look at them.' The chef went back to chopping onions, but it was a while before he said, 'I hope you don't mind but I took the liberty of telling the manager about you, and he wondered if you'd like to visit them for a crash course in hotel management. It would have to be the end of November as that's their quiet period.'

Abbie glanced up in surprise. 'That's extremely kind of him but why would he do that?'

Chef McCormack threw the onions into a pan of hot oil. 'Because, like Charlie, he came to us as a homeless rebellious teenager in trouble with the law, and now he actually manages the place.'

'He does? How did that come about?'

Chef McCormack stirred the sizzling onions. 'He started off washing dishes, but I suspected he had potential, so I persuaded the owner to keep him on. He worked hard, and over the years he was trained up in various aspects of the job.' Chef McCormack shook the pan. 'Think about it. It's a good offer.'

Abbie stared thoughtfully into the fire. 'November, eh?

'You're sure I haven't pushed you into this, Barry?'

Barry Matthew stretched his stumpy legs under the kitchen table. 'Positive Mrs Hunter. Just make sure it's not looking like charity. Joe hates charity.'

Abbie twiddled her thumbs nervously. 'They should be arriving for lunch any time now.' She nodded towards the ham, tomatoes and pickles. 'Help yourself, Barry. Lunch is a pretty casual affair around here.'

The builder didn't need a second bidding and was buttering a roll when Sarah drifted in from the hallway, then the door slammed as Joe came in from the back garden. As Barry was a frequent visitor it was no surprise to see him sitting at their kitchen table. A moment later, Charlie emerged from the cellar with a crate of beers.

'That's our first delivery from the brewery stacked away, boss,' he said dumping the crate by the fridge. 'I'll store this lot in the drinks fridge, eh?' He opened the fridge door.

Abbie made a conscious effort to stop twiddling her thumbs to give the impression she was relaxed. 'Fine! And as we're nearly all here ... er ... where's JD and Big Ben?

'Big Ben's gone to the garden centre to get spring bulbs,' Jo said. 'Told him he wouldn't be here by spring but ...' he shrugged his shoulders.

'JD said he had business to attend to,' Sarah said. 'Didn't say what it was.'

Abbie bit her lip. This was one occasion she would have liked them all to be present. 'The thing is,' she hesitantly began. 'I'm now in a position to hire permanent staff.'

There was an ominous silence. Charlie began stacking bottles in the fridge, his face hidden by the open door, but she didn't miss the tightness in his voice when he said, 'Makes sense, boss. Can't do all the work yourself, can you?'

'No, I can't.'

He slammed the fridge door. 'So, this is it then, is it?'

'It is.' Leaning forward she rested her arms on the table. 'I've spent the last few weeks churning over what I would need to build up my business, and came to the decision that my priority is having loyal, trustworthy staff who are skilled at what they do, yet willing to multi-task and be trained further in the business. So,' she made a steeple with her fingers. 'Charlie! If you agree to those conditions, would you be willing to stay on as Chef to The Blue House?'

There was a long silence. Charlie blinked rapidly. 'Eh?'

'What I'm looking for is a top-quality chef. We know you can cook Charlie, but Chef McCormack believes that if you agree to continue with your training you will make an excellent chef. He has agreed to stay on - for a few weeks anyway - to advise me, train you, and help to launch The Blue House. What do you say?'

Charlie blew softly through his lips and there was another long silence before he said, 'Aren't you forgetting something, boss?'

'What's that?'

'I've been inside.'

'Yes Charlie, I know, but I'm hardly likely to advertise that on my brochure, am I? The fact is, you've stuck loyally with me – all of us through our ups and downs, and I think we've worked pretty well together this last year, don't you? I trust you. You have potential. That's why I'd like you on my team.'

'You would?' A slow grin spread across her chef's face. 'You trust me?'

'I do – as long as I have your assurance you've given up your former profession.'

'My former ...? Ah! Yes! You've got that, boss. I'm a reformed man already.'

'Excellent! And stop calling me, boss.'

'Congratulations, Charlie,' Barry raised his teacup as a salute.

'Good for you,' Joe said quietly but Abbie didn't miss the anxious look on his face.

She turned to Sarah. Judging from the girl's worried expression she was clearly expecting the worst. 'Unless you have plans to return to hairdressing, will you stay on as well, Sarah?'

A wan smile appeared. 'I'd love to but ... I've no skills or experience at all.'

'You're used to dealing with people, aren't you? You'll be dealing with our guests at reception, checking them in and out and dealing with their problems. As for experience; you've been managing our housekeeping since last Christmas. You have the ability to see what needs doing and getting on and doing it. You would be managing cleaners, ordering what we need and working alongside me. I need that. I need someone with better organisational skills than I have to keep the place running smoothly. As for gaining experience, Chef McCormack has organised a four-day training course in a Yorkshire hotel that will help us; that includes you, Charlie.'

'Right boss,'

'And don't call me boss.'

Sarah slumped back in her chair like a limp rag doll. 'Fancy you noticing I had skills. I didn't know I had any ... yes, I'd

love to stay on.' A slow smile emerged and her eyes glazed over as if she was visualising her future.
'What about Big Ben?' Charlie asked.
Abbie gave a sigh. 'Ah! Big Ben. You have to admit he's transformed the gardens. But I can't afford to house and feed anyone who doesn't work and there's very little garden work in the winter. So, I've asked JD to sort out his benefits; that's probably what he's doing now, and I thought, if I could keep him on as gardener in the summer, he could see to the fires in winter and we could find him tidying or cleaning jobs; things like that.'
Charlie nodded his approval. 'We'll think of something, boss. And Tom?'
Abbie clasped her hands. 'He won't be staying. Because …,' she added hastily when she saw their crest-fallen faces, 'I've spoken to Sid, and he's agreed to take him on as a plumber's apprentice. He's also agreed to rent him a room in his house till he qualifies.'
She noticed Sarah's gaze had drifted anxiously over to Joe, and as if sensing where the conversation was heading, he cleared his throat. 'Actually,' he began.
'You haven't made plans have you, Joe,' Barry interrupted.
'No, no, not exactly but …'
'Good!' Barry said. 'Because I was hoping you'd help an old mate out.'
'What old mate?'
'Me. That's why I popped in. Percy, my regular bloke, has retired and moved away and I'm desperate for part time help down at the yard, especially someone who knows the building industry. I thought, as you've nearly finished here, and if you've no other plans …'

'No, no, no,' Joe said hastily. 'I've no other plans, and if you need me …'

'I was hoping you would stay on here as my handyman, Joe?' Abbie interrupted. 'You know more about this house than anyone. In fact, we'd never have got this far without you.'

'I suppose,' Barry said turning to Abbie, 'If you're agreeable, Joe could fit any work you may have for him with his work at the builder's yard?'

Joe looked from one to the other. 'And do I get a say in this?' he asked gruffly.

Abbie did her best to look shamefaced. 'Sorry, Joe. What do you think?'

Joe shrugged his shoulders in an embarrassed fashion. 'Aye, you're right. I know this old place inside out, but at the same time I canna let an old mate down.' He rubbed his chin thoughtfully. 'So, I'll stay on here so you've no need to worry on that score boss, and I'll fit it in with the times Barry wants me. Will that do the pair of you?'

Barry reached out his hand to Joe. 'Absolutely! Thanks mate.' They shook on it.

Abbie rubbed her roofer's arm affectionately. 'Thank you, Joe. I really appreciate it.'

'Aye! Right!' Shrugging her off, Joe grabbed a lump of cheese and sticking it inside a bun, shoved his chair back with his legs and marched out of the kitchen into the hallway. But his parting shot sounded choked when he bellowed back, 'But this place 'll never get finished on time if you lot sit round yacking all day.'

Abbie never did manage to have a quiet word with JD about his plans. At the back of her mind, she was hoping she could retain him as her accountant, but she didn't hold out much hope given he appeared to come from somewhere down south and no doubt he would want to return to his family, friends and work. Wouldn't he? That was why she was surprised when, after hearing about their trip to Yorkshire, he asked if he could tag along.

'But I insist on paying my own way,' he added. 'And I expect I shall still be here when you open at Christmas so you might need an experienced bar hand.'

'You've had bar experience?' she asked curiously.

'Years ago, when I was at university. It helped pay the bills.' He avoided eye contact when he added, 'Besides, a complete break in Yorkshire might help me decide.'

Abbie tried not to get her hopes up but simply said, 'Glad to have you along, JD.'

When mid-November arrived, it was only Charlie, JD, Sarah and Abbie who left for Yorkshire. Training was obviously of no use to Big Ben or Tom, and Joe was quite adamant he wasn't going.

'I'm too busy to go gadding away on holidays, boss. Still jobs to be done. Besides, someone has to be around to finish off the work, take in deliveries and show Chef McCormack the ropes.'

Their journey took longer than expected due to road works and heavy traffic heading for a rock concert but none of these hold-ups could dampen Abbie's spirits. As JD sped down the motorway at the wheel of her car, she felt excited by the whole prospect of learning the hotel business – as well as having time to herself.

'Have you got a clean driving licence, Charlie?' she asked at one point on the journey. Charlie's long legs dictated he sit in the front with JD but she could see his face through the mirror.

There was a pause before he answered. 'Couldn't really say boss. If I remember rightly, I've been suspended.'

'Suspended? What for?'

'A little matter of parking on a double yellow line.'

'They don't suspend you for that.'

'They do when you're parked outside a bank and there's a robbery taking place.'

She let out an exasperated sigh. 'Why do I get the feeling you're winding me up, Charlie?'

'Not me, boss?'

'Well, I don't want to know. Stop calling me boss and sort out your licence so you can use my car for business.'

'I can?' Charlie peered at her through the mirror. 'How about for social purposes?'

'Yes, *if* I don't need it, *if* you've got a clean licence, and *if* it's not for robbing banks.'

Abbie found the Harriot Hotel to be even more charming than its brochure had portrayed. It was an old Victorian building snuggled between the cliffs of a quaint Yorkshire fishing village. Thick carpeted floors, cosy nooks, beautifully set tables and quiet lounges with roaring fires, and a library of books and magazines gave it the ambiance she was hoping to give her own hotel. The six-foot four manager, Brian Conrad, was a man in his mid-forties, immaculate in dress and speech. He welcomed them warmly and showed them personally to their rooms. It was hard to imagine him being the scraggy rebellious teenager in trouble with the law that Chef McCormack had described.

Abbie found her room comfortably warm with heavy drapes and a panoramic view overlooking the sea - at least, it would have been a panoramic view if there hadn't been a thick blanket of fog. Throwing her case on the bed she stared out of the window at the swirling mist and mulled over Chef McCormack's parting advice. 'Learn, but rest. The last thing your guests will want is to be greeted by a baggy eyed, exhausted manager.' Good advice, she decided. So, when they had finished their evening meal, she retired for the night with a novel she'd been promising herself to read all year.

She awoke eight hours later to a watery sun pushing its way through the crack in the curtains. Stretching lazily, she luxuriated in the pleasures of a day with no responsibilities. But eventually, deciding she ought to check on her staff, she slid out of bed, opened the curtains and found to her delight that the fog had lifted. Pulling on her dressing gown she brewed herself a cup of coffee, then curling up on the wicker chair watched the fishing boats unloading their catch in the harbour.

When she emerged downstairs an hour later, she discovered Brian Conrad had already involved Charlie and Sarah in the breakfast routine alongside the staff of the Harriot, and JD was talking to the barman. The rest of the morning, she and Sarah spent with a plump friendly housekeeper who showed them around, gave them copies of her daily routine, and answered the mountain of questions they had prepared for her. Then Abbie had an informative working lunch with Brian Conrad, the manager. They discussed advertising and brochures, being aware of local events, ordering, finances, and how she could best play to the strengths of her staff.

They were finishing off their coffee when Abbie ventured to say, 'I hope you will forgive me for asking but ...' she bit her lip. 'It's hard to believe Chef McCormack's story of you being a rebellious teenager, living on the streets and in trouble with the law.'

Brian gave a short laugh. 'It's not something I'm proud of. But if it hadn't been for Chef McCormack giving me a break and persuading the owner to let me go to college, I dread to think where I would have ended up. There's not a day goes by where I'm not grateful that he saw potential in me. That's why, when he told me how you'd taken in Charlie and the others, I was keen to help.' He shook his head. 'I know what it's like to be a hopeless case, and I tell you Mrs Hunter, the world would be a far better place if there were more folk like you helping folk like me get a foot on the ladder.'

Abbie had no idea how to answer a compliment like that so she simply blushed.

Lunch over, she was pleased to find she had the afternoon to herself. So, wrapping up warmly against the cold November breeze from the sea she walked briskly into the village. Discovering it was market day, she deliberately closed her mind to anything to do with hotels and took pleasure in joining gossiping women with wicker baskets, farmers in green wellingtons, backpackers and bargain hunters and browsed around the covered stalls. There was a smell of fish and chips in the air alongside seaweed left by the outgoing tide, and for a while she revelled in the fact that, for once, she didn't have to focus on some major purchase for the house. Instead, she spent time choosing an easy-to-read gardening book for Ben, gloves for Joe, a tee-shirt for Tom, and a scarf for Chef McCormack. Come mid-afternoon she stopped off at a small teashop and lingered over a currant scone and a pot of tea. It was a delightfully lazy afternoon. She couldn't remember when she'd last had a lazy afternoon – or in fact, when she'd last had a holiday. Then meandering through the cobbled streets to the harbour she found a sunny seat out of the wind, pulled the collar of her leather coat around her ears, and sat watching the activities in the harbour.

'I wondered where you'd disappeared to.'

Shading her eyes against the glaring sun she squinted up.

'Hi, JD. I've been shopping.'

'I can see that.' He pushed the parcels along the seat and sat down beside her, but he didn't ask what she had bought, he just stared out to sea looking uncomfortable. 'Actually,' he said after a pause. 'I don't know if Charlie's told you but the name's Edward Jefferson.'

Charlie hadn't told her; he was loyal like that. And although it hadn't been hard to guess JD wasn't his real name, she felt pleased that he'd felt able to tell her. But glancing across at him she saw his discomfort over revealing the truth, so she extended a gloved hand. 'I'm pleased to meet you, Edward Jefferson, I'm Abigail Hunter,' she said lightly.

If he was surprised by her response, he didn't show it but playing along with the charade solemnly shook her hand.

'And what are you doing in this lovely fishing village in the middle of November?' she asked in a manner that suggested they had just met, 'Holiday or business?'

'A bit of both. I … I needed time to think; make decisions.'

Pulling at the fingers of her glove she removed it from her hand, conscious that she needed to be careful with what she asked him. 'And how is the thinking going so far?'

JD sat forward, his elbows on his knees. She followed his line of vision. A small fishing boat, surrounded by squawking gulls, was rolling towards the shelter of the harbour leaving a wash of white in its wake.

'Not too badly.'

'Good!' She waited.

Eventually he said, 'Circumstances drew me into a new business. But now I find I'm reluctant to leave it.'

'Drew you?'

'I tagged along with a ... with Charlie ... because I ... I needed time to recover.'

'Recover? You'd been ill?'

'You could say that,' he said quietly. 'I had a nervous break-down after my wife and children were killed in a car crash.'

Abbie controlled her sharp intake of breath, allowing the revelation to sink in before saying, 'I'm so, so terribly sorry, JD. Do you want to tell me what happened?'

At first, she thought he didn't because he continued staring out to sea where the fishermen in their fluorescent orange overalls busied themselves on deck, positioning the boat for entry into the harbour.

'There were three of us running our accountancy firm; me, my brother, Digby, and my brother-in-law, Trent. Business was booming but we were working such long hours my wife and children complained they never saw me. So, I took them on a sailing holiday around the Greek Islands. Stupidly ...' JD closed his eyes, shook his head. '*Stupidly*, I switched off my mobile phone.' It was a while before he opened his eyes again, and when he did they were filled with pain. 'When I did switch my phone on again, I knew something was terribly wrong by the long list of calls. The first was from my sister, Hilary, telling me that Trent had been arrested for embezzlement. I'd suspected financial discrepancies in the firm for a while but to my shame, I'd done nothing about it. I'd been so busy I had hoped the whole thing would sort itself out. There were also calls from the police, the press, and from my brother Digby urging me to return immediately.'

He stopped talking as a handful of sightseers paused in front of them to watch the fishing boat docking. It was only when they got bored with the process and had moved on that he continued. 'Amy, my wife, flung a few clothes into a suitcase so we could catch the first flight out. It ... it was the early hours of the morning, I was driving, the Greek country roads were dark and wet, I was tired, preoccupied, and I'd been drinking the night before.' He stared across the harbour. 'I'm not making excuses I'm merely telling it the way it was. I don't remember the ... accident. What I do remember is my son shouting a warning; seeing my daughter's terrified face through the rear-view mirror, and my wife screaming. I ... I still hear her ...' He cleared his throat. 'I woke up in a Greek hospital two days later. They told me my family hadn't .... I had a few broken bones, nothing that wouldn't mend, but mentally ...' He dropped his head. 'The Greek authorities called it a tragic accident but there's no getting away from the fact that I had acted irresponsibly. I was still in hospital when Digby ...' He paused and his voice shook when he said, '...What none of us knew was that my brother Digby had been diagnosed with an aggressive form of cancer. I should have noticed, but I didn't. I was too wrapped up in my own affairs. I think the tragic loss of my family and the business and the court case against Trent ... it was too much for him. He took his own life.' JD ran his hands slowly down his face and there was a tremor in his voice when he said, 'Other than the doctors, I've never told anyone that before.'

She waited for him to compose himself before rubbing his arm affectionately. 'Then I'm privileged. Thank you for telling me, JD,' she said softly.

He rested his hand over hers and she found the closeness between them pleasant. They sat like that for a while, watching the fishermen, until she felt his body relax. 'So, do you want to tell me your thoughts on this new business?' she asked.

There was a slight hesitation. 'I believe The Blue House has potential,' he said. 'In fact, I wouldn't mind helping out behind the bar from time to time and continuing to do the accounts but...' he shrugged his shoulders.

'But what?'

Seagulls hovered around their feet waiting for the catch to be unloaded. He turned to her, his gaze searching. 'My employer might not be so keen to have me around now she knows how irresponsible I was.'

She released his hand, and pulling her gloves over her cold hands smiled at him. 'JD, for an intelligent man, that's a very silly remark. Of course, I'd like you to stay. I'd have been totally lost without you this last year. Didn't you know that?'

He gave a wan smile. 'Perhaps.' The seat wobbled when he sat back, and she was conscious of his warm arm against hers. 'There's a lot to think about, so no commitments, not yet,' he said, and reaching out grasped her gloved hand and gently squeezed her fingers, and it felt comfortable and rather nice. So, they sat like that until the crates were unloaded from the fishing boat, the gulls had flown away, and the sun had disappeared behind the horizon. It was only when the late afternoon mist rolled in from the sea that they made a move. Silent, but at ease with each other, they made their way up the hill towards the Harriot Hotel.

Chapter 16

Abbie readjusted the bulky box of silver baubles under her arm to make the heavy shopping bags easier on her fingers, then blew softly through her lips. Her breath came out visible in the cold frosty afternoon sunshine. Glancing down at her shopping list to make sure she'd bought all the last-minute items for tonight's party, it dawned on her that it was exactly a year today since she had moved into The Blue House. A year! She stopped abruptly in the middle of the High Street. There was a 'tut' from behind when a woman laden with Christmas shopping tripped over her. As she blurted out an apology and followed it up with a 'Merry Christmas', her eye fell on the Christmas tree outside the old church. On the spur of the moment, she cut across the busy High Street.

As the church door slammed behind her the roar of the traffic on the dual carriageway was replaced by the soft piped tones of the organ. The organist was playing Bach's, 'Jesu Joy of Man's Desiring'. Quietly making her way to the nearest pew, to listen as much as to relieve herself of heavy shopping bags, she sat down.

Other than a glimmer of light from the organ music stand, the church was cool and dim. A bushy Christmas tree overflowing with colourful decorations commandeered the dais. Below it stood the Nativity scene with a cardboard Mary and Joseph, presumably made by the Sunday School or Messy Church. She stared at the baby doll in the manger, remembering how last Christmas she'd been dreading her first Christmas alone.

'How can I celebrate the birth of Your Son when You've so cruelly taken mine?' That was what she'd screamed at God. The problem was, she brooded, through her grief she thought she could hold God to account for the death of her husband and baby. She had even believed her pain would be easier to cope with if she didn't bring God into the equation. Why had she done that? God had never promised her life would always be safe and happy if she believed in Him. All He had promised was that He would never leave her but would always be with her and guide her through the awful mess life could throw at you. But she hadn't been able to cope with that so had shut Him out. In fact, it had been easier to deny His existence altogether. But this Christmas...?

It was then, in the vast, cool emptiness of the church, that she brought what scraps of faith that still remained to the surface. Sheepishly clasping her hands, she began her whispered prayers. It didn't seem to matter that they weren't flowery or carefully thought through. She simply spoke from her heart, and all the while the organist played, 'Jesu Joy of Man's Desiring,' softly in the background.

And then it came; that warm familiar Presence. It crept up on her to surprise and please her. Tears rolled uncontrollably down her cheeks, but she made no attempt to wipe them away because they were tears of knowing you were still loved by Him; tears that He had understood your pain.

Time passed. Bach moved on to Handel's, 'Messiah', and as the tears dried up her mind opened up to the enormity of the past year and how He had brought so many people into her life. Friends, helpers, encouragers, and strugglers – like herself. Yes, He had been with her, hadn't He?

It was only when, for some ridiculous reason, the organist decided to play, 'O I do like to be beside the seaside', that it occurred to her that she had guests arriving that evening and she still hadn't finished decorating the tree. Hastily leaving the church, she stepped out into the cold winter sunshine and trotted back home.

'So, we're on schedule, Sarah?' she asked.

Sarah was arranging flowers on the dining room tables. 'That's the third time you've asked me that. Yes, we're on schedule. Joe and Ben are laying fires, Charlie and Chef McCormack are preparing food in the kitchen and Tom's bringing up more wine and beers from the cellar. Why don't you relax in a hot bath before you get ready?'

'Right! If you're sure you don't need me.'

'Yes! I'm sure I don't need you!'

Ten minutes later she was in her apartment, piling her hair on top of her head, sinking into a hot foamy bath with a glass of white wine, and brooding over the forthcoming party. The initial idea of having it a week before they officially opened was so they could thank the friends who had helped them decorate in October, and to give her staff a trial run at having guests. It had all seemed such a good idea at the time - until she invited Freddy.

'Those tramps won't be there, will they?' had been his reluctant response.

That had annoyed her. Pulling fiercely at the tap with her toe she sent a fresh flow of hot water drifting up her body, and wondered why her relationship with Freddy was always so fraught. Reaching for her glass of wine to help calm her nerves she came to the conclusion that fretting over how

Freddy would behave tonight was a complete waste of time. This was *her* party. She had achieved what she had set out to achieve and she was darn well going to celebrate!

Half an hour later, attired in a new silky green dress, she did a twirl in front of a mirror and decided it was rather nice to feel like a woman again instead of a labourer. Answering the sharp rap on her apartment door she found an equally smart JD in a crisp white shirt and bow tie standing on the threshold with a bottle of champagne. A flicker of amusement crossed his face when he saw the wine glass in her hand.

'You look very nice.'

She blushed with pleasure. It seemed a long time since anyone had complimented her on her appearance. 'Thank you.'

'I was about to suggest a celebratory drink before we went down but I see you're one step ahead.'

'Dutch courage. Freddy's coming.'

'Ah!' He held out his bottle. 'I wanted to give you my news before your guests arrived.'

'News?' She waved him in and pointed him to the cupboard where she stored her glasses. There was a loud 'plop' as he opened the bottle followed by a 'glug' as he poured the champagne. He handed her a glass. 'Cheers.'

'News?' she repeated perching on the arm of her settee.

'I'm returning to work.'

She hadn't expected her heart to plummet the way it did. 'You're moving back south?'

JD sank into the chair by the window. 'No. My sister, Hilary, will continue running the London side of the business.' He didn't look at her when he said, 'I wonder whether you'd be prepared to let me rent my room until I establish a branch of my firm in this area?'

She tried not to show her pleasure when she said, 'Of course.'

'Which brings me to my next point. In my official capacity as your accountant; incidentally, you're my only client and a non-paying one at that; I have to tell you that despite your insurances and Donald's firm paying up, you're not far off being broke so you'll need to boost the advertising. But,' he hastily added when he saw her alarmed expression. 'We can solve that problem easily if you'd consider an investor.'

'I don't know any investors.'

'Yes, you do. Me.'

'You have money to invest?'

'I have a considerable amount of money to invest thanks to my sister paying my wages while I was out of the loop, so to speak, and I would like to invest it in this place.' He studied the fizz in his glass for a moment before draining it. Standing up he placed the glass on her kitchen sink. 'Anyway, I don't need an answer tonight. Think about it.'

'I don't need to think about it.' The fizz shot up her nose as she tossed down the remains of her champagne. Placing her glass on the coffee table she stood up. 'I could think of nothing better than having you as an investor, JD.'

'That's good of you to say so.' He opened her apartment door. 'And seeing as how I'm going to be around for a while, I don't suppose you could get used to calling me Edward, could you?'

They made their way downstairs.

Abbie's vision for this place had been to create a homely and comfortable atmosphere for her guests, and to do that she had been determined to keep the magnificent fireplaces in the dining room, lounge and library. Tonight, as she surveyed what the Wheatsheaf family had used as their dining room, she felt a sense of satisfaction at having created the atmosphere she had been after. Fires crackled in the hearth, Christmas lights flickered on the mantelpiece, and soft music echoed around the house. Their friends and helpers from the wallpaper party were already sipping champagne as they laughed and enthused over the part they'd played in the transformation of the house. And Charlie, looking every part a chef in his tall hat and pristine white overall, was standing at a long table carving a variety of cooked meats.

Seizing an opportunity when the queue for Charlie's meats had gone down and she wasn't being commandeered as hostess, she made her way over to him, champagne glass in hand. 'How's it going, Charlie?' She stifled a hiccup.

'How's what going, boss?'

'How's work in the kitchen going? Is everything under control? And don't call me boss in public,' she hissed.

He nodded down to her glass. 'More under control than you by the looks of it.'

She glared at him indignantly but there was no chance of a retort as Freddy arrived by her side. 'Have you a moment, Abigail?'

Abigail? She knocked back the rest of the champagne in her glass. 'Be with you in a moment, Freddy. I'll just get myself another drink.'

Charlie waited until Freddy had moved away before shaking his head. Laying a selection of meats on a plate he handed it to her. 'Eat boss. Mop up some of that alcohol.

That's an order. Can't have you sozzled in front of Freddy and our guests.'

'Good idea, Charlie.' He added a spoonful of vegetables to her plate as she refilled her champagne glass. Then picking up her plate she made her way over to Freddy and Susan's table. 'What do you want, Freddy?' She sat down.

Splaying his knife and fork on his plate, Freddy made a steeple with his fingers. 'I know we've had our differences of late, Abigail, but looking around this place has left me rather concerned over the amount of money you've spent. You will come to me if you get into difficulties, won't you?'

She focussed on cutting a slice of pork on her plate. 'That's kind of you Freddy, but as it happens, I've managed to secure a reliable investor.'

Freddy looked surprised. 'You have? Why didn't you tell me? Someone with money and standing is exactly what you need. I was under the assumption the only people you mixed with these days were vagrants, losers and criminals.' His gaze drifted around the room. 'Where are they by the way? Hidden them away from your investor, I hope. Is he here by the way? I'd like to meet him.'

She saw Freddy's gaze drift over her head and didn't need to look up to know who was standing behind her.

'Vagrants, losers and criminals?' JD repeated levelly.

'Excuse me? You are…?'

'Edward Jefferson; formally one of the vagrants, losers and criminals.'

There was an awkward silence.

'Although, I wouldn't necessarily have called myself a criminal or a loser,' JD continued pleasantly. 'My problem was having a mental breakdown after my wife and children were killed in a car crash while I was driving, and my brother took his own life before cancer could.'

Freddy's mouth opened then closed again, like a fish out of water. JD pulled out a chair, sat down and jerked his head towards Tom. 'I wouldn't have called Tom a loser either, poor kid. He just didn't stand a chance; drugs and an abusive father were too much for him. Thankfully, your sister took him under her wing. He's now a plumber's apprentice and doing well. As for the rest of the staff you impertinently call 'losers, vagrants and criminals;' life threw some hard knocks in their direction. If it hadn't been for your sister, none of us would have survived. Not only did she have a vision of what a derelict old house could become, but what *we* – as people - could become, if we were given a chance. She gave us that chance. ' There was an awkward silence as JD poured himself a glass of red wine from the bottle on their table. 'As it happens, I'm also the investor she was talking about. My family has a lucrative accountancy firm in London. I wanted to invest in the person and place that brought me through the worst nightmare of my life.'

Freddy's face flushed up with embarrassment. 'I ... didn't mean to imply ...'

'Didn't you? I hope not. It's bad policy to assume that everyone who finds themselves on the streets is either a criminal, a loser, or had voluntarily become a homeless vagrant. Granted, there are some rogues out there, but we're not all like that.'

'No, no, no,' Freddy forced a laugh and pushed his glasses up his nose.

JD stood up. 'Now, if you'll excuse me.'

A breath of relief whistled through Freddy's nose as JD left their table.

Abbie stared at the receding back of her accountant. 'That's the longest speech I've ever heard him make.'

Susan wiped the corners of her mouth and chuckled. 'Serves you right, Freddy.'

Freddy glowered at his wife. 'There's no need to make an issue of it, Susan.' He ran his finger around his collar. 'As it happens, all wanted to say was that I have to admire the way you've transformed this old ruin, Abs.' He pushed his spectacles up his nose. 'Although I don't know whether I would have kept those old fireplaces. They're ….'

Abbie placed a finger over her brother's lips. 'Shut up, Freddy. Don't spoil a wonderful complement. I've had so few of them from you lately, so let me wallow in it before you have another go at me.'

'Go at you?' Freddy looked at her steadily for a moment before his face softened. 'What? And break the habit of a lifetime?'

'Yes Freddy,' she said quietly. 'Please, *please* break the habit of a lifetime.'

Later in the evening, Abbie invited her staff and guests to move into the lounge. In this room too, the fire was crackling in the hearth, there were soft lights around the bar, an assortment of books and ornaments in the dark oak shelving, coffee brewing and a gentle ballad playing softly in the background. Tom threw another log on the fire.

Taking the gin and tonic Sarah handed her, Abbie raised her voice. 'Ladies and gentlemen, drinks will be served at the bar, but if you prefer tea, coffee or some other beverage, please have a word with a member of my staff.'

After sherry, champagne, red wine, white wine and a gin and tonic – or two, Abbie wasn't too sure what time the party ended. Sometime after midnight she guessed. It was only when the door slammed behind their last guest that she was able to fling off her shoes, pour herself a liqueur and flop on to the settee.

'Oh boy! I'm sozzled. Freddy actually complimented me. Can you believe it? I think that's why I'm sozzled.' She frowned. 'Joe? What are you doing behind the bar?'

'Tidying up, boss. What do you think?'

'Huh-huh! As long as that's all you're doing behind the bar.'

'Asides, Sarah's keeping an eye on me.'

'No, she's not, she's in the kitchen with Big Ben helping clear up.'

'Then I suppose it's you what's keeping an eye on me, boss.'

'Huh-huh.' She yawned, and with semi-closed lids listened to the flames hiss as they licked around a log in the fire, and the glasses clink as Joe tidied up behind the bar. Then she heard JD walk across the room.

'You look tired,' he said.

'I was thinking.'

'Oh dear! That sounds ominous.'

She smiled contentedly at him. 'I was thinking, I've spent a whole year worrying about you all. Do you think I can stop now?'

He came around the settee, sat down and slipped his arm around her shoulders. 'Not a chance! You're a born mother hen.'

Mother?

His arm tightened around her and she quivered with pleasure as he kissed the top of her head. That was when she instinctively knew that whatever happened to her wayward staff, JD would always be here, in The Blue House on the corner, with her.

Printed in Great Britain
by Amazon